WARP OF CHAOS

A DRAGONHEIR NOVEL

BY

SARAH EDGERTON

ELIZABETH HAWK
PUBLISHING

LAKE CHARLES, LA

TO MY MOTHER,
THE STRONGEST WARRIOR I KNOW

The Order of Dragons

Chaos Dragons - Chaos Dragons are the most powerful Dragons to exist. They created the unnamed world and the Elemental Dragons. Their scales are colored in exquisite shades of purple from the deepest violet to the richest amethyst. Their eyes are an intense violet. They can wield all magic.

Chaos Dragongoddess: Nimerah
Chaos Dragongods: Ragnar and Amram

Fire Dragons - Fire Dragons command the flames, breathing forth infernos from within. Their scales are colored in shades of crimson, orange, and gold. Their eyes are like the flames with red and specks of gold intertwined. Their secondary power is shapeshifting.

Fire Dragongod: Vukan

Water Dragons - Water Dragons embody the mysterious waters, conjuring torrents that can both cleanse the senses and engulf their victims. They can manipulate water in any form. Their scales are colored in shades of cerulean, turquoise, and sapphire. Their eyes are dazzlingly blue. Their secondary power is telepathy.

Water Dragongoddess: Anahita

Earth Dragons - Earth Dragons are one with nature. They can connect to the earth itself, shaping mountains, summoning tremors, and upheaving the landscape. Their scales are colored in shades of greens and mossy hues. Their eyes are green like the forest trees. Their secondary power is strength.

Earth Dragongoddess: Dhara

Air Dragons - Air Dragons are ethereal and intelligent. They can harness the power of the wind, creating gusts and whirlwinds that sweep through the air. Their scales are colored in shades of gray and silver. Their eyes are sparkling silver. Their secondary power is empathy.

Air Dragongoddess: Ilmari

Light Dragons - Light Dragons hold power over the light of the world. They can illuminate any space at any moment. Their scales are colored in shades of iridescent white that reflects the sun. Their eyes are bright white. Their secondary power is healing.

Light Dragongod: Endrit

Darkness Dragons - Darkness Dragons embody the essence of night, harnessing shadows and plunging the brightest day into absolute darkness. Their scales are colored in shades of gray and black, making it easy to disappear into the veil of night. Their eyes are an unsettling onyx. Their secondary power is teleportation.

Darkness Dragongoddess: Tamasvi

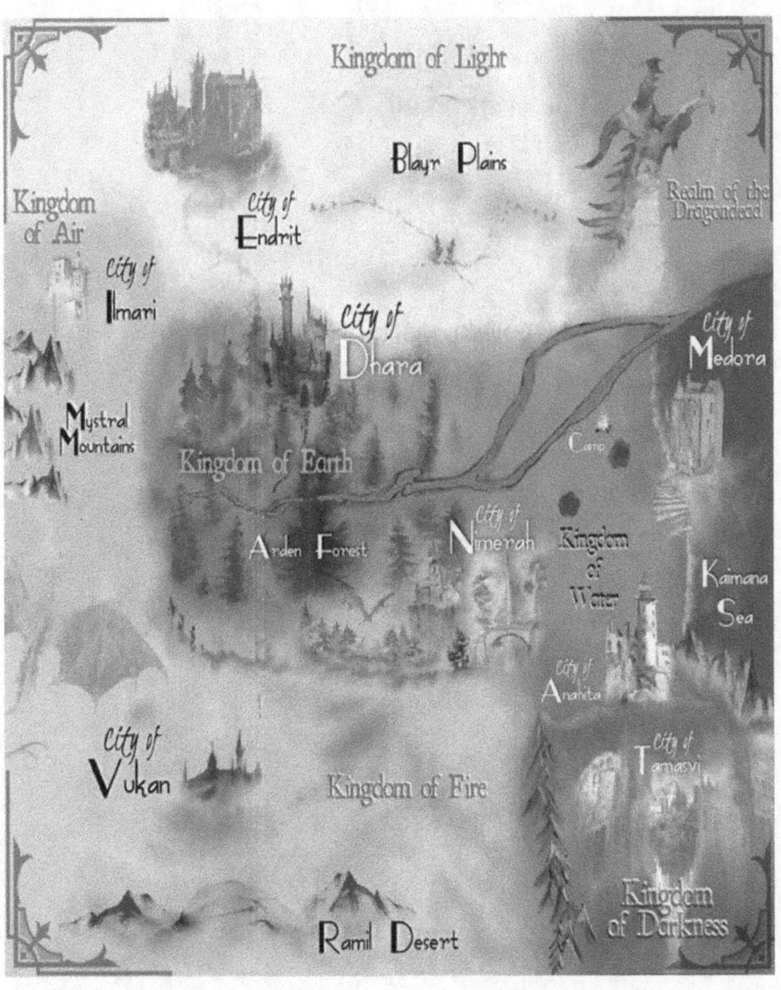

Kingdom of Light
Blayr Plains
Realm of the Dragondead
Kingdom of Air
City of Endrit
City of Ilmari
City of Dhara
City of Medora
Mystral Mountains
Kingdom of Earth
Camp
Arden Forest
City of Ninerah
Kingdom of Water
Kaimana Sea
City of Ananta
City of Vukan
City of Tamasvi
Kingdom of Fire
Kingdom of Darkness
Ramil Desert

Pronunciation Guide

Dragonborns and Humans	Dragons, Including Gods
Emera: Eh-mair-uh	Nimerah: Ni-mair-uh
Dwyn: Dwin	Ragnar: Rag-nar
Benigno: Beh-neeg-noh	Amram: Am-ruhm
Struan: Stroo-uhn	Anahita: Ann-uh-hee-tuh
Cordelia: Cor-deel-ee-uh	Tamasvi: Tuh-mahz-vee
Calian: Cal-ee-uhn	Vukan: Voo-kuhn
Dhruv: Droov	Ilmari: Ill-mar-ee
Fin: Fin	Endrit: Ehn-drit
Morwen: Mor-wen	Dhara: Dar-uh
Rehema: Reh-hee-muh	Hadeon: Hey-dee-ohn
Zari: Zar-ee	Gawen: Gah-wen
Erjon: Air-yon	Bud: Buhd
Senna: Sen-nuh	Risna: Riz-nuh
Avani: Uh-von-ee	
Anwir: Ann-wur	
Jimmu: Jim-moo	
Valda: Val-duh	
Kedron: Ked-ruhn	
Elio: Ee-lee-yoh	
Hestia: Heh-stee-yuh	
Tellus: Tell-uhs	
Calder: Cahl-der	
Eteri: Eh-tair-ee	
Leora: Lee-or-uh	
Orpheus: Or-fee-uhs	
Zepherin: Zef-er-in	
Tuuli: Too-lee	
Nyx: Nix	

SUMMARY OF BOOK ONE

When Emera Edevane's hand is accidentally cut on a ceremonial dagger, her dormant Dragonblood activates. Emera learns soon after that she is the Dragonheir of Nimerah, one of the three Chaos Dragons.

Captain Calian Westbow, Emera's Deliverer and the Dragonheir of Vukan, helps Emera escape from murderous Cultists in her town. While traveling, Calian tells Emera that she must pass the Dragontrials. The trials are how Emera will receive blessings from the Dragongods to fully wield her magic. She needs magic to fulfill the prophecy of restoring peace to the six kingdoms.

Emera trains at a secret camp alongside Fin, a human, and Morwen, the Dragonheir of Anahita. She learns more about her destiny by a Dragonpriestess named Rehema. During her time at the camp, Emera is almost poisoned by a Cultist. Calian heals her in secrecy.

Calian decides to initiate Emera's Water Trial. Emera is successful and now has the full blessing of Anahita. The camp, including the Dragonpriestess Rehema, is ecstatic with Emera's progress. Later, Dragonheir Erjon, the Dragonheir of Ilmari, takes Emera to the Obsidian Mountains to initiate her Air Trial. Emera succeeds and is blessed by Ilmari, the Dragongoddess of Air.

Following her Air Trial, Calian and Emera go to the City of Dhara to find the Dragonheir of Dhara. While at an inn, Emera meets a stranger who says the Cultists are not Emera's enemies, but the Dragoncouncil is. The stranger tells Emera the true history of "The War of Three" and that the Dragoncouncil has a plan to resurrect the Dragongod Amram to eliminate all humans. They need the blood of the daughter of a Chaos Dragon to do it.

The next day, the Dragonheir of Dhara is revealed during the Partition. A dragon appears, and Emera fights the dragon with fire. In doing so, she obtains the blessing of Vukan, the Dragongod of Fire. To get the Dragonheir to safety, Emera calls to her earth

Dragonmagic. She obtains the blessing of the Dhara, the Dragongoddess of Earth. Calian, Emera, and the new Dragonheir named Avani escape through underground tunnels.

The three arrive at camp safely and discover it has been destroyed in flames by the Dragon in Dhara. Emera sees Dwyn emerge from the flames. Dwyn is actually Valda, the daughter of the Chaos Dragongod Amram. Valda taunts Emera, whispers in Calian's ear, and then morphs into her Dragon form and leaves. Calian reveals that Morwen is missing and Rehema is dead.

Emera blames herself for the destruction of the camp, Morwen's kidnapping, and Rehema's death. She ventures out and sees the hurt soldiers. Pulling from the Dragonmagic deep within her, she pleads with the Dragongods to take all of her Dragonmagic to save them. She heals the soldiers, thus obtaining the blessing of Endrit, the Dragongod of Light.

Emera falls asleep and awakens to find her mother sitting before her. It turns out that it is Nimerah in disguise, and they are on the Dragonsoul Plane of Existence. Nimerah is alive, but her body is in a deep sleep. Nimerah introduces Emera to Tamasvi, the Dragongoddess of Darkness. Tamasvi convinces Emera to use the darkness as her refuge. Emera breaks through her darkness and has the blessing of Tamasvi.

The remaining soldiers of the camp split into two groups to travel to the City of Nimerah so that Emera can finally meet the Dragoncouncil. Emera leaves with Fin in the second group. Fin is suddenly needed ahead, so he takes off, and Emera follows him. Emera can't keep up, so she arrives alone. The city is empty, and Emera is suspicious.

Two guards take Emera to the Temple of the Dragoncouncil. Emera comes face-to-face with Dragonmaster Anwir, Valda, and Calian. But it's not the Calian she knows. The real Calian was taken prisoner in Dhara. This Calian is a shapeshifter named Elio and the true Dragonheir of Vukan. The real Calian is gone.

Anwir wants Emera to join them, but she gets away and escapes below the Temple where she finds prisoner cells and one of the two guards who led her to the Temple. His name is Kedron, and he's the Dragonheir of Tamasvi. Kedron is tasked with getting the real Calian out of the cells. Kedron tells Emera that she can teleport out like he can. The three escape that way.

The three make it to a cave where they find the other Dragonheirs, including Morwen, the remaining citizens of the City of Nimerah, and the Cultists. The Cultists are a group of rebels that snuck the citizens out. Senna tells Emera that they never tried to assassinate Emera with the Stormshade. Calian had been their target because he was working for the Dragoncouncil. Calian wonders what he is since he's not the Dragonheir of Vukan.

Elio shows up and warns Emera and Calian that Valda is on her way, but Valda is already inside the cave. Valda comes out and tries to kill Calian, but Emera jumps in front of the blast. Instead of dying, Emera is lifted into the air. Nimerah gives Emera her final blessing. Emera wields pure chaos magic and blasts Valda into the cave. Valda dies by being impaled.

Safely in the Kingdom of Air, Calian comes to Emera and tells her that Dragonmaster Anwir resurrected Amram. They must find Nimerah, and Emera knows exactly where to look.

CHAPTER ONE
EMERA

The stench of burning flesh stung my nostrils as I scanned the smoke-filled sky. The Dragon was still hidden, so I continued my ascent until my foot bumped into an unmoving obstacle. Another lifeless, charred body was sprawled on the broken palace staircase. Bile scorched my tongue, and I seized my throat with my hand. It took all my might to swallow the vomit down. I stood for a moment; my feet remained rooted to the palace steps while I acknowledged the pain of another loss to the unnamed world. It cut deep in my heart. One might think a powerful Chaos Dragongoddess such as myself would be unaffected by death, but that wasn't the case. I felt everything excruciatingly deep. Every mind.

Every body. Every soul. They were a part of me. And with their deaths, there was a void in my soul.

I opened my eyes slowly and blinked away tears. Looking down behind me, I studied the body I'd failed to save. Its blackened, flaky skin made its features unrecognizable, but the size indicated the person was small. My breath hitched in my throat.

War was cruel and unjust.

I closed my eyes and silently prayed to my Dragonmother, hoping Nimerah would hear my plea to guide every soul—Dragonborn and human—to peace.

"My Mother. Please hear my prayer. These souls did not deserve such brutal deaths. Regardless of who they were—human or Dragonborn—they are yours. Welcome them into the afterlife." I brought my hand to my heart and held it there. No words were spoken back, but she heard me. My heart knew it.

When I finished praying, I returned my attention to the dark sky.

The Dragongod Amram had wasted no time in finding us—mainly me—after being resurrected by Dragonmaster Anwir, once head of the dismantled Dragoncouncil. In just a few days following our arrival in the Kingdom of Air, flames devoured the City of Ilmari. Most of the majestic city, once distinguished with its tall towers and dwellings carved into the side of the Mystral Mountains, was now all rubble and flames. The palace was the only structure that remained somewhat intact. A statue of the Dragongod Ilmari lay in pieces on the palace steps, having fallen from the northern tower. The crystal-clear waterfalls that cascaded from the highest peaks flowed with the blood of the fallen. Bodies were strewn about the city streets.

I loosened my grip on the white bow that I clutched tightly in my hands and fastened it to my back. With a hint of air magic, I lifted myself from the palace steps to a nearby balcony. I needed a higher vantage point if I couldn't catch a glimpse of Amram from the ground. My chaos magic was still new and untamed, so I didn't know if I'd match up against him. But I'd try. Erjon would say it was a fool's hope. I shook my head to rid myself of the image of his smirking face.

I squinted my eyes, attempting to focus my vision. "Where are you, you scaly monster?" I mumbled to the sky. Amram remained hidden, so I lowered my gaze and searched for Calian, my prophesied General and the man who held my heart. I didn't see him either. My pulse quickened. Was he alive, or was he dead and cold on the ground? Where was he? No, I wouldn't think like that. I couldn't. I took a long breath to steady myself so that my fears wouldn't control me. Calian was alive. My heart would know if he wasn't.

My eyes darted back and forth, scanning the palace courtyard for the faces of the other Dragonheirs when a ground-shaking roar erupted from within the clouds.

The palace rumbled beneath my feet. I whipped my head around in time to see Amram appear from behind a thick cloud of smoke. He was a giant, intimidating beast with dark purple scales that were almost black. The castle almost paled in comparison to his monstrous size. I couldn't imagine a more terrifying creature. My breath caught in my throat as he flew overhead. He angled his head downward, and our eyes met. Did he just smile? Violet chaos swirled from my lifted palms. I just needed the right moment. Holding both hands outward, I lifted them to the sky while twisting my wrists. A rotating funnel formed from the clouds and connected to the ground just as Amram dove downward. The Dragongod flew into the chaotic tornado, his body twisting and turning within the tornado's powerful winds. Once I had him, I thrust my arms outward, and the tornado threw the Dragon into the side of the mountain. A large cloud of dust exploded from his impact. Wasting no time, I used my air magic to propel myself from where I stood to the ground below. Once my feet connected with the blood-stained concrete, I turned my palms over and called to my earth magic. The ground beneath Amram split, and large columns made of rock and clay rose toward the sky. One of the columns pinned Amram's wing to the mountainside. I continued my attack, blasting Amram with a mighty torrent of water to hold him against the side of the mountain. He thrashed about wildly and slashed the mountainside with his sharp claws, trying to free himself from the rock while fighting against the water. He growled and roared so furiously that the ground shook beneath my feet.

I released the freezing water, and when Amram stood on his shaking legs, I blasted a bright, unwavering beam of light directly into his eyes. He reared back, and his wings wrapped around his head, shielding his eyes as a piercing shrill escaped his snout.

"Time to kill a Dragon," I purred. My eyes burned but not from pain. From the darkest depths of my Dragonsoul, my chaos magic sprouted. It took root in my core and then blossomed throughout my body. The magic coiled down my arms and exploded from my palms.

I felt exhilarated. I felt powerful. I was a Dragongoddess.

"You've caused enough death and destruction," I said, loud and steady. I called to my water magic and let it wash over me, providing a sense of calm and peace to subdue my chaos magic.

Fire blazed in the Dragon's eyes. He blinked slowly, and I swore he smirked at me. My knees buckled slightly, but I held onto the tranquility of my water magic to keep from falling. I refused to fail.

Heh, heh, heh, the Dragon chuckled. Yes. The Dragon chuckled. The sound made my toes curl and my pulse quicken. His voice invaded my mind. *So, you think you have beaten me, child?*

"It sure does appear that way."

Amram clicked his tongue three times, and he plastered on a wolf-like grin. *On the contrary. You have done no such thing.*

My eyebrow raised involuntarily at his peculiar demeanor. I pushed away the suspicions that tugged at my mind, planted my feet, and pulled my hand back. But before I could release my chaos upon him again, my vision blurred, and a dull pressure plagued my head. What was going on? My legs gave out, and my knees hit the ground. I pressed my fingers tightly against the sides of my head, hoping to alleviate some of the pressure. But I couldn't. I forced open one eye and then the other and blinked furiously until everything became clear and focused. My mouth gaped open in horror. The side of the mountain no longer caged Amram. The world around me became quiet, still, and empty of…*everything*. There was no mountain…no city…no light. Only a void of darkness.

Out of the nothingness, a large pair of menacing violet eyes blinked. The eyes drifted toward me slowly then disappeared. A breeze suddenly infiltrated the air, blowing fallen hair strands away from my face. I lifted my chin, and clenched my mouth to keep it from trembling. Amram stood before me now in human form. His eyes, once large and commanding, were now small and lethal with a violet gleam. He had a fair complexion that seemed to glow—thanks in part to his lavender hair which was so light, it almost appeared white. His pale skin made his violet scales more prominent, unlike the average Dragonborn. Although the only thing human about him was his form, he looked like a handsome prince in a fairy tale. His long dark purple coat swayed in the breeze as he walked toward me. Gold buttons fastened at his chest accentuated a slightly muscular form, yet his overall physique hinted at a lean build.

The Dragongod walked closer and closer to me until he towered over my small frame. I smothered the fear that clenched my heart and made my knees tremble.

You will not show fear, Em, I thought to myself. *You are not weak.*

I clenched my teeth together and balled my hands into fists so tight that my fingernails cut my skin. Blood broke through the surface, but I didn't care. I needed to feel. I needed to stay focused. Everyone would die if I didn't.

Amram gazed down upon me. "So, young. So naive," he taunted with nothing but a whisper. His breath was surprisingly cool, like a breeze rolling off the ocean waves. I'm not sure what I expected? Something foul. Like rotten eggs.

"So old. So arrogant," I retorted.

The god ignored me. "Undisciplined," he added, his voice louder.

"Where are they?" I demanded.

The god cocked his head to one side, and his lips spread into a foul smile once again. His eyes twinkled with delight. He loved this game. "You mean them?" he asked excitedly. He looked over his shoulder, and I followed his line of sight. Light filled the air around us, and we were back on the mountain. But this time, my friends were behind Amram.

And they were all dead.

The bodies of Morwen, Fin, Senna, Avani, Kedron…and *Calian*…lay piled on top of each other like garbage. Their eyes were open, devoid of vitality, and their limbs hung loosely. I didn't move. I didn't speak. I was paralyzed from the horror of it all.

A hint of a smile tugged at his lips. "This will happen should you and your so-called Dragonheirs attempt to stop me. You will fail."

I didn't answer him but focused on my breathing instead. *In through the nose. Out through the mouth. This isn't real.* I was losing my inner battle. My gaze remained on Calian. Tears welled in my eyes as I continued to breathe.

"Ah, yes. Calian Westbow. He certainly is *interesting*. Well, his past is."

"Leave. Him. Alone," I growled.

The god laughed. Then, with a snap of his fingers, a woman stood beside Amram, her eyes glowing purple and her lips contorted into a cruel grin.

I gasped. "Valda?" I took a shaky step forward.

She waved, her fingers fluttering in a taunting fashion.

The tears I harbored dried instantly. Rage spread throughout my body, and I ached with a desire to unleash my fury. I conjured a ball of pure chaos magic and threw it at her head. With a quick wave of his hand, Valda disappeared, and the ball of chaos diverted to the side, hitting the mountain instead. The crack of the mountainside echoed around us. The sound of falling rocks made me flinch.

Amram clasped his strong hands together. "Your power is raw and filled with potential. Don't let it go to waste. Join me, Emera. Together, we can rid the world of humanity and rule as we should. As true gods." His voice was manipulative. I knew what he was trying to do.

"Humanity brings balance to this world. Only a tyrant would want to destroy that."

"Hmm," he hummed, his sly eyes wandering. He focused them back onto me. "Where did you hear that? Did the lousy Dragonpriests teach you that? Their indoctrination of tolerating those inferior to us has ruined the world. There was once peace here. Now that peace is dead. I'm here to revive it."

"By killing everyone? You have no right."

"It is my right!" he thundered.

My spine straightened, and my breathing stilled. *Don't show weakness. Don't show weakness.*

"I helped create this world! Then your *Dragonmother…*" he huffed, clearly disgusted. "She created her precious humans. Everything we built together was destroyed in an instant! Why? Because she wanted our children, their children, and their children's children to have pets. The humans are filthy, disgraceful beings that do not deserve to breathe in our presence." He prowled up to me. The air between us became hot and thick, almost suffocating me. I tried to step back, but my feet wouldn't move. Amram had me in his complete control. Not only had he infiltrated my mind, but he now had me paralyzed. Both were testaments to how powerful he was. He leaned in and whispered into my ear. "If you fight back, you will lose. And all those you love and hold dear...*will burn.*"

Flames instantaneously engulfed the bodies of my friends. My eyes widened in horror as a scream escaped my mouth. The Dragongod backed away with a smile plastered onto his evil face and snapped his fingers, releasing his hold on me.

My knees hit the ground as my mind slipped into unconsciousness. When I opened my eyes, the familiar setting of my bed chamber within the City of Ilmari's palace took shape. My chest rose up and down rapidly as I willed the beating of my heart to slow down. I hopped out of my bed quickly, raced to the window, and threw back the curtains. The sun shone brightly in the sky, illuminating the pristine city below it.

"It was just a dream," I said to no one. "Wasn't it?"

CHAPTER TWO
EMERA

"Well, that didn't work."

I raised my head from the ground and angled my neck toward the condescending voice that plagued my ears. I glared while Calian held up his red-scaled hands, spread his ten fingers wide, and wiggled them. I'd just failed my tenth attempt at shifting into my Dragon form.

"It's harder than you think," I spat. I slowly dragged myself from the ground and brushed off my pants. Heavy dust peppered the cool mountain air. Embarrassment warmed my cheeks.

So did anger.

With a flick of my wrist, I conjured my magic and used my air element to push the lingering dust into Calian's chiseled face.

"Calm down, Em," he said while coughing—and with a hint of laughter. "And stop flashing those fire eyes of yours. I'd prefer not to have to locate another change of clothes." He looked down and inspected the fresh pair of black trousers and the white shirt he'd just changed into.

A smile tugged at the corners of my mouth. In the days following the attack at the cave where I'd gained my final blessing from Nimerah, I'd spent my afternoons in the City of Ilmari training my Chaos Dragonmagic. Calian trained with me every day. He was there for every success and every victory with a congratulatory nod. He was also there for every failure and every setback with a snide remark. Those remarks were met with brutal elements such as fire, wind, and rain–and okay, sometimes the occasional lightning bolt. Erjon scoffed at my *lack of emotional regulation,* as he called it.

We were now back in the training ring of Ilmari's illustrious Arian Winged Warriors–who were training higher in the mountains for the next couple weeks thanks to Amram's arrival–and I was feeling particularly testy. Amram's warning and the image of my dead friends immersed in flames haunted me day and night. Five days had passed, and no matter how hard I tried, I couldn't shake the terror of what Amram had shown me. Even now, I climbed to my feet but remained hunched over. Sweat trailed from the scales at my forehead down my nose and dripped onto the dirt of the ring. My heart raced wildly. Closing my eyes, I called on my water magic and let it wash over me.

"You're back there, aren't you?" Calian asked softly.

"It was all so real," I whispered. "The flames. I was paralyzed where I stood. I couldn't get to you." Calian lifted my hand to his chest, resting it on his heart.

"I'm here. Alive and well," he said.

"For now."

"I'm not going anywhere."

"You say that now, but you don't know, Calian. At any moment, Amram could attack. He's more powerful than Valda. He'd level this city. All these people would die, and I couldn't stop him. Some powerful Dragongoddess I am," I mumbled, hanging my head in defeat.

Calian cocked his head to the side. "You are powerful. You just haven't reached your full potential yet. Besides, we're a team. Just because you're some goddess, doesn't mean you have to face him alone."

I closed my eyes and sighed. He was right.

"Besides, Amram isn't going to attack just yet. He's planning something. Like I've been planning this." He brought his lips to mine. I thought about pulling back, but his warmth revived my failing heart. I leaned in and savored the moment. It was a gentle kiss, but the electric feeling behind it was still there. A feeling I learned was the indication that we were mates. Well, that we should be mates.

Calian finally pulled back. "Let's stop for the day. I think you need a break."

"I can't take a break. The six kingdoms depend on me."

His eyes flashed. "The six kingdoms should depend on no one," he huffed. "They have their armies."

Well, that was different.

"How can you say that? After all we've been through?"

He ran his hand through his hair and rubbed the back of his neck. "I haven't forgotten."

The cities don't have forces strong enough to slay a Dragon, let alone a Chaos Dragongod. The cities will burn."

He threw up his hands. "Then let them."

I sighed. "You don't mean that."

"And what if I do, Emera?"

"Innocent people are living throughout the kingdoms. Innocent *humans*. We owe it to them."

Calian turned his back on me. "We don't owe them anything. You don't. I don't."

Before I could respond, an arrow flew by Calian's ear, just missing his head. Fin stood at the entrance to the training ring, grinning like a fool.

"Was that necessary?" I asked.

"It was the only thing I could think of to get your attention." Liar. He cleared his throat, straightened his back, and announced, "You've been summoned."

Calian pushed past me, clearly refusing to answer my question. Lately, he had odd mood swings. One minute, he was ready to adorn battle armor and fight to the death. The next minute, he talked of us leaving it all behind and finding a remote island where nothing nor no one would bother us. His mood swings gave me a headache.

I sighed. We could table the discussion for later. "Summoned for what?" I asked Fin.

"Queen Eteri requests we all join her for the evening meal. Her spies have given word that Amram is busy resurrecting his Dragons from the war. She wants a plan of attack in case any Dragon infiltrates the city."

I glanced at Calian to gauge his reaction. His eyes flickered to mine before speaking.

"We'll be there momentarily," he said.

Fin nodded and left. My clothes were dirty, and my hair was messy, so I was in no shape to meet with the queen. I needed a hot bath and fresh clothes. I followed Fin, but Calian's hand shot out and grabbed mine.

"Wait," he said. "I know humans need our aid. I know that we are their only hope of survival. But I wish we weren't. I know too well what it's like to be a pawn, and I don't want that for you." He gestured toward the palace. "For them." My eyes followed his hand. Behind those walls, Morwen, Senna, and Avani were probably gushing over the numerous gowns Queen Eteri sent us.

"They understand what—who—we're fighting for," I said, shaking my head. I caressed Calian's cheek with my palm. "You don't need to worry about us. We, women, are tough."

Calian chuckled. "I know that."

"You're tough, too. You're a powerful Dragonheir," I said.

He took a step back and shook his head. "I don't know what I am."

I took his hand in mine and led him out of the ring toward the palace. "We'll find out," I promised him.

*　　*　　*

I found Morwen standing at her window, staring out into the Mystral Mountains. Her dark blue gown—the color of the night sky just before the sun vanished—was exquisite. Its sheer sleeves, adorned with black jewels, started just below the shoulders and extended past her wrists. The bodice, also covered with black jewels, stopped at her hips. From there, the skirt flowed to the floor. She wore a silver tiara to signify her position as Princess of the Kingdom of Water. Against her dark skin and blue scales, she looked more like a princess of midnight instead of water.

My eyes scanned her bed chamber. Dresses were flung over the gray velvet furnishings and scattered across the intricate rugs of Morwen's room. Morwen was tidy and organized, but her room was not—it was more reminiscent of Avani's room, to be honest. The disarray of the clothes meant her thoughts and feelings were also in disarray. The weight of our grave situation weighed heavily on her heart. Morwen had confessed to me her longing to return home, but I knew she'd never leave without my permission. She took being a Dragonheir seriously, claiming it was her duty to stay with me. In my heart, I knew she was waiting for me to tell her it was okay for her to leave.

But I couldn't, and I was selfish about it. We needed to

go home; that was true. I knew in my heart that my Dragonmother was there somewhere. But I wasn't ready. I'd already lost Rehema. I couldn't bear to lose Morwen, too. What if there was a Dragon attack in the City of Anahita, and I wasn't there to protect her?

"You do not need to protect me, Em," Morwen murmured. I rolled my eyes for forgetting about the secondary gift from the Dragongoddess Anahita. Morwen was becoming an assassin of the mind. She easily slipped into someone's thoughts without any indication she was there. Morwen and Calian insisted I should practice since I had the same ability, but I found sneaking into one's thoughts intrusive. Morwen found it useful to construct diplomatic responses if she knew what her opponent was thinking.

"Enough with the mind-reading, Morwen," I retorted.

Morwen chuckled. "I didn't. I don't have to read your mind to know your thoughts."

She had me there. "I have to protect all of you," I said. I heaved a heavy sigh and threw myself on her bed. Morwen wrinkled her nose with irritation. I was a filthy mess, and I'd just made myself comfortable on her pristine silk sheets.

"You can't protect everyone. You must accept that."

I sat up abruptly. "I won't."

"The wisest kings and queens know that regardless of the outcome of any war, many lives will be lost."

"I know that."

Her eyebrow raised slightly. "Do you? Because you seem to think you'll be able to protect everyone which is impractical. You're only seventeen. You must let the guidance of your elders help you."

"Technically, you are all my elders," I pointed out. Which was true. Calian, Fin, and Erjon were at the ripe age of twenty while Morwen, Senna, Avani, and Kedron were all eighteen.

"You know what I mean."

Morwen was speaking of the kings and queens that ruled the six kingdoms. Anwir had done a great job of keeping the prophecy a secret. But once we'd gotten word that Amram was alive and well, we knew it was time to notify everyone. Calian started by locating the remaining Dragoncouncil members. Anwir had murdered most of them when they tried to flee from the City of Nimerah, but a few managed to escape into the Kingdom of Air. They were given titles as ambassadors to Queen Eteri and sent to warn the kings and queens of the six kingdoms about the impending war. At this moment, each kingdom was preparing their armies as we made plans to locate Nimerah.

A light knocking came at the door. "Come," Morwen answered.

The door creaked ajar, and Avani poked her head in. "Am I interrupting?" she asked.

"No," I managed with a hint of a smile.

"Good!" The door crashed open, and she rushed into the room, pulling Senna along with her. "Because I have to show off how amazing Senna looks!" Senna blushed—which I didn't think possible—and glided across the room. Her white gown sparkled in the light. The dress was plain underneath, with a soft shimmering fabric sewn over it. It reminded me of the snow that illuminated the Mystral Mountains. The neckline of the gown was asymmetrical with one arm covered. The billowy sleeve had a slit from her shoulder to her wrist, causing my eyes to linger on the glimmer of her scales. The fabric clung to her chest and down her sides before flaring slightly at her waist, flowing down into a train at her feet. She was breathtaking, especially with her hair pulled back into a simple knot, exposing her glowing face.

Morwen bounded from the bed and took Senna's hands. "You look exquisite, Senna."

"Quite the vision," I added, with what I hoped was a light and airy tone. I couldn't spoil their mood.

"I don't know about that, but I agree that the gown is very

pretty," Senna said. "I'm not used to such lovely clothing. I'm the daughter of a schoolmaster."

"Well, it suits you," Morwen stated matter-of-factly. "And you," she said, facing Avani. "Let's not forget to mention how stunning you look."

Morwen was correct. Avani was stunning. Her luscious curls were braided on each side of her head while the top rose upward and back, falling past her shoulders. The gown she wore was deep emerald and matched her green scales. The fabric was plain and smooth, embroidered with black sequins in the shapes of leaves. It hugged her beige skin in all the right places, outlining her powerful physique. Thin straps crisscrossed over her shoulders, revealing a tattoo of the Dragongoddess.

While they admired their gowns, the image of their dead bodies flashed in my head. I bit my lip.

It wasn't real. It wasn't real, I thought. The drumming of my pulse quickened beneath my skin, and the temperature in the room rose, getting hotter and hotter. The image of my dead friends dissolved and was replaced by Amram's creepy grin.

"Emera?"

Amram's stare vanished at Morwen's voice. "Yes?" I squeaked.

Morwen placed her hand on my forehead. A wave of cooling tranquility washed over me. "Where were you?" she asked.

I cleared my throat and plastered a fake smile on my face. "I don't know what you mean."

Senna's eyes flashed with warning. "Don't play games." "You look pale," Avani pointed out. "And you've been off for the past few days. What is going on?"

I couldn't tell them what I saw. I couldn't worry them like that. I glanced quickly at Morwen, who angled her head to the side and raised an eyebrow.

"If you're seeing visions, you need to tell us. Something you see could be useful," Senna added.

My knees shook as I stood and crossed to the window. The Mystral Mountains were an enchanting sight to see. Their steep slopes rose into pointed, snow-capped peaks that pierced the sky. Trees covered their sharply chiseled edges, looking like paintings on nature's walls. The mountains granted peace to any on-looker.

I sighed profoundly and rested my head on the glass window. What I wouldn't give to make the world as it was before I became a Dragongoddess. To see Mother and Father working diligently into the night, mixing and grinding powders in our apothecary shop. To wake the next morning and hear the waves of the Kaimana Sea and the smell of saltwater. To take a stroll down to the docks and talk to Dwyn…

My eyes snapped shut at the thought of her. Dwyn—er, Valda—was dead. And I was responsible for her death. Just like I'd be responsible for the deaths of everyone in the room if I didn't defeat Amram.

Morwen's voice broke the still silence between us. "Your mind is restless," she observed.

Before I could gather the courage to tell them what happened, a sharp rapping came at the door.

"Come," Morwen commanded gently.

A small servant girl entered wearing a dark gray robe with a cowl attached. The bottom half of her face was covered with a silk mask, but her blue eyes were wide and bright. Her hands were smooth, showing no signs of age—and no scales. So, she was young, and she was human. A mixture of shock and irritability stirred in my chest and rose to my cheeks. Why was Queen Eteri employing a ten-year-old human? There better be a rational explanation for it.

"The evening meal will be served just after sundown. Queen Eteri has asked that you all make your way to the great hall within the hour." When she spoke, a dense trepidation released from her soul, and it saturated the room.

My knees buckled from the weight of her anxiety, and I grabbed the edge of Morwen's bed frame to hold myself up.

Em?

Morwen cleared her throat. Our eyes met briefly, and hers were infused with worry. I nodded slightly. I closed my eyes and let my calming magic permeate throughout my body to soothe me. When I opened my eyes, I noticed Morwen's shoulders sagging a little. She turned back to the girl.

"We don't bite, girl," Avani added. "Except her." She threw her thumb in my direction. "Beneath that pretty exterior is a full-fledged Dragon. Sharp teeth. Sharp claws. Fire. Don't look too closely into her violet eyes. She'll steal your Dragonsoul."

The girl's eyes met mine, and she immediately fell to her knees.

"Your Majesty."

I snorted. "Ignore Avani. She thinks she's funny." Avani pressed her hand to her chest, pretending I'd just shot an arrow into her heart. "And...I am not a queen. You don't need to address me as 'Your Majesty.' Emera will do just fine. If you should bow to anyone, it should be Princess Morwen." I held out my hand for her to take, but the girl remained in place.

"Of course, I apologize, Princess Morwen. I am a

Dragonpriestess in training, so I have wanted to meet the prophesied savior ever since your arrival at the palace."

Avani snickered, and Senna rolled her eyes. But they both wore an endearing smile.

"Please get up," I said. She looked at me through thick, wet eyelashes, making me feel uneasy. I still wasn't good at these types of encounters. I always felt suffocated. "I should probably be presentable for the queen. I am going to go back to my chambers and clean up." If was at least presentable to the queen, maybe she'd provide an explanation for this young girl's situation.

"Our conversation is not yet over, Em," Senna insisted as I strode to the door. I lifted my hand, waved in acknowledgment, and headed for my own chambers.

A bathtub was calling my name, so I hurried down the long hallway past the chambers of the other Dragonheirs. I paused momentarily at Calian's door and placed my palm against its cool surface. It reminded me of my family's apothecary back in Medora, a small port city in the Kingdom of Water. If I closed my eyes and focused hard enough, the smell of saltwater and the caress of a sea breeze flowing in with the tide filled my senses. As did the piercing ache from missing my parents.

Footsteps sounded down the hallway, so I backed away

from the door and hurried to my own chambers. I didn't have much time, so I gritted my teeth and quickly washed myself using the—now cold instead of hot—water in the tub. No matter how much pressure I used, I failed to scrub off the dreadful feeling that ached beneath my skin. How did one face a queen of a powerful kingdom and say, *Gee, Queen Eteri. I'm sorry I've been so moody lately. It seems I've had a bad dream, and I just can't shake it.* It sounded silly just thinking about it. I'd only run into Queen Eteri a handful of times, and they were increasingly brief. It seemed the only Dragonheir allowed to stay in her presence was Erjon. I couldn't for the life of me figure out why she chose Erjon. Why not Morwen? She was a princess, for gods' sake.

I glanced out my window at the dimming evening sky. Stars already started to shine above the mountaintops, a reminder that I needed to be in the Great Hall quickly. Standing in front of a golden-framed full-length mirror, I did my best to replicate the intricate hairstyle my mother often wore when visitors from King Calder docked at Medora. I braided, twisted, twirled, and fastened my hair on top of my head into what I hoped was an effortless-looking updo.

"Good enough," I said to my reflection.

My eyes scanned the room and instantly landed on their target: a deep purple gown draped over a large velvet chair by the fireplace. I held the dress up and stared at its perfection. A pressure of unease formed in my throat. The dress Queen Eteri chose for me was simple yet luxurious. I hastily lifted the gown over my head and tugged gently. Once in place, I stood and contemplated the reflection in the mirror.

The gown was a dark purple satin. Its neckline sat just below my collarbone and extended to my shoulder, exposing some of my scales. The long slender sleeves clung to my arms, traveling over the top of my hands into points. I turned in the mirror and admired the gown's backless design. The fabric clung to the small of back then flared slightly from my hips. It was the dress of a goddess.

And I felt like an impostor wearing it.

The scent of an autumn fire brought me back to the present. I glanced over my shoulder to find Calian leaning against the door frame. Handsome wasn't an accurate term to describe him. Suave? Debonair? Nothing worked.

His long black coat covered an all-black vest. A crisp red shirt peeked out from his cuffs and neckline. The shirt remained open just below his throat. He ran his bronzed hand through his dark, disheveled hair and then rubbed the back of his neck. I couldn't read his expression with his face tilted toward the floor, so I tapped into my magic to get a feel for his emotions. A mixture of awe, shock, and admiration greeted me. He peeked up through his lashes, and his dark eyes flashed red with heat.

"You…look…"

I cut off his train of thought. "Like an imposter." I turned back to the mirror and blushed. Gods, kill me now.

"No. I was going to say beautiful, but that word is inadequate."

"I can't wear this. This isn't me."

"It's very much you, Emera," Calian whispered. I'd been so focused on my reflection in the mirror that I hadn't noticed him stalk directly behind me, standing with only a small space lingering between us. The drumming in my chest quickened, forming a bright and fervent cadence. Did he hear it? Did he hear how my heart played for his?

The electric energy I'd grown to love sparked to life and hummed beneath my skin. His hands tenderly climbed up my exposed back. The small hairs on the back of my neck rose from the warmth of Calian's breath. A small bead of sweat trickled down my spine from the heat that resonated in my core. He was close, but my heart wanted him closer. This was a feeling I'd never encountered. It was strong and carnal. What was it?

"You are every bit the Dragongoddess you were born to

be," he said, his voice low and gruff. I struggled to maintain my composure but stayed rooted to the floor. Did we have to go? Did we have to meet with the queen? My mind finally won the battle between itself and my heart. I shimmied away from his reach.

"I think we should go to the Great Hall," I said breathlessly and walked out the door of my chambers.

CHAPTER THREE
EMERA

Calian offered his hand once we were in the hallway, and I took it, reveling in the energy that had yet to dissipate. Our hands remained locked together even after we pushed open the doors to the Great Hall. A few of the queen's advisors were present, along with servants and a few other Dragonborns who probably held royal titles. Two long gray and white stone tables sat on opposite sides of the hall. They were covered with gray silk table runners, candelabras, and simple yet elegant plates and utensils. Tapestries adorning the northern and southern walls depicted the history of the Kingdom of Air and were separated by the kingdom's banners. The eastern wall was purposefully different. An enormous mural of the Mystral Mountains etched in stone with silver lining embellished the wall behind the queen's table. The mural was divided into three time periods: The War of Three, the formation of the Kingdom, and the present. Queen Eteri's table—which was a smaller stone table covered in dark gray silk—stood on a slightly raised platform with her lavish throne-like chair behind it. On each side of her chair were three other chairs. I wondered if I had met the trusted few who sat at her side.

The large doors to the hall opened suddenly. Avani's familiar laughter filled the room as she and Senna entered, talking and laughing. Kedron followed behind them, looking boyishly handsome in all black. His black scales and clothes which consisted of pants, a vest, a shirt, and a simple overcoat, contrasted against his pale skin and golden hair. Our eyes met, and although his were black as night, they twinkled when he saw me. I let go of Calian's hand and threw my arms around Kedron.

"I thought you wouldn't be back for a couple of days!"

An almost inaudible chuckle vibrated Kedron's chest. "I got back just a few hours ago."

"Is the Kingdom of Fire willing to stand beside us?" Fin stepped out from behind Kedron. I hadn't noticed him entering the hall. One day I'd get him to tell me about his past. How did he manage to traipse through the shadows, unseen?

Kedron addressed our small group now that Fin's question had grabbed the attention of everyone in the hall. "Queen Hestia did not hesitate," Kedron answered. A collective sigh echoed around us, and I could feel the relief that flowed throughout the bodies standing around me.

"That's great news," Senna said.

"I'm sure it didn't take Hestia much convincing." In a synchronized movement, everyone's heads turned toward the entrance of the hall. Queen Eteri stood in all her splendor. She was a young queen, not much older than me. Her golden hair twisted into several braids and lay piled on top of each other at the base of her neck with jewels weaved into them. She wore a tiara of gold so dark it could be mistaken for bronze. Embedded within the gold metal were jagged diamond-shaped gems of opaque white and gray. It matched her gown perfectly. The fabric's color depended on the position of the light. At one angle, it was dark gray with a shiny overtone. At another angle, it was black with gray peeking out. Rock-shaped crystals were sewn into the bodice, mimicking mountain tops. Her ensemble, along with her sparkling gray scales, made her resemble gusts of wind blowing through the Mystral Mountains. She was an absolute vision of beauty.

Jealousy grabbed me with its tantalizing fingers so much that I bit my lower lip to distract myself from its choking feeling. How did a queen so young carry her own power with such ease? The weight of the kingdom was on her shoulders, but her fierce confidence never wavered. According to Erjon—yes, he actually engaged in pleasant conversation with me one evening—her parents died from a paralyzing disease several winters ago. Eteri Vayu was just a child when she ascended the throne, but her family had wasted no time training her in diplomatic affairs and hand-to-hand combat when she was young, so she took over with ease. She excelled in diplomacy and could defeat almost any foe on the battlefield. Despite these attributes, she focused her attention on her kingdom and not her personal life. Looking around, I didn't see anyone in the hall that I would identify as a potential suitor.

Kedron smiled. "Queen Hestia did not," he answered. It had been agreed by our circle that Kedron would teleport to the kingdoms he'd been to before. He had offered to teleport as close as he could to the others, but since he needed to envision his location with precise detail, we wouldn't allow it. Kedron was invaluable. We couldn't have him teleporting into a tree.

Kedron had been to the Kingdom of Fire before, so he could clearly picture his jump in his mind. Next, he would travel to the Kingdom of Darkness, although the point was probably moot. The Kingdom of Darkness kept to itself.

"Hestia has always been vocal regarding her distaste for the Dragoncouncil and Dragonmaster Anwir," Erjon stated. His hands were clasped behind the hooded robe of faded gray he wore. Beneath it was his usual gray silk attire. He looked more like a Dragonpriest than a Dragonheir. For some reason, it made me giggle. No one seemed to notice my amusement but him. He didn't say anything, but his eyebrow raised slightly. "There was no doubt she'd eagerly take up arms against him," Erjon continued. He was correct as usual, which was no surprise because, from what Calian told me, Queen Hestia loathed the Dragoncouncil, specifically Dragonmaster Anwir. But what did catch me by surprise was the lightness of Erjon's voice. His tone seemed…nicer if that even made sense. I studied him a moment longer and noticed him stealing quick side glances at Queen Eteri.

"True. Hestia is not one to shy away from her feelings. She refused to reconsider her Priests and Priestesses sitting on the council, bowing down to that Dragonmonster," Queen

Eteri spat.

I snorted at the word Dragonmonster being used to describe Anwir because he truly was a monster. I always loved a play on words.

"It astonishes me that my parents never thought to do the same. Now, look at what Anwir's done. All in the name of the Dragonborns. It's truly despicable." She waved her hand dismissively. "No matter. Let's hope that our other ambassadors can convince the remaining monarchs to join our cause."

I noticed that Erjon looked unusual. No, that wasn't the word for it. Was he…mesmerized? He didn't just look at Queen Eteri; he admired her. His eyes, usually characterized by a piercing gaze under furrowed brows, were soft and tender. The slight twinkle of his eyes—no matter how much he tried to conceal them by looking away sparingly—revealed what I could only describe as *longing*. I closed my eyes and recalled the meetings from the past few days. Whenever I met with Queen Eteri, he was always in her presence whether it was at her side or lurking in a corner. Whenever she spoke, his demeanor changed. He became less rigid and hung on to her every word. He even—dare I say—smiled.

He wasn't just smitten with her. He loved her.

"Ahem."

I jumped slightly, startled by Fin clearing his throat. I tossed him a sheepish smile and pretended to focus on their conversation about Hestia's army. But once again, my gaze wandered, and eventually, my eyes locked onto Erjon's. With his head cocked to the side, he looked at me curiously. A sly grin tugged at the corners of my mouth. His eyes widened in response, clearly startled. He knew that I knew.

But it wasn't enough. I wanted—no, needed—to learn more. Were they friends? Lovers? Before I could stop myself, my magic created wispy threads of gleaming violet from my fingertips. The thin violet threads snaked—visible to no one else but me—toward Erjon's feet, slithered up his legs, and wrapped around him. They continued to entwine his stomach, arms, and neck before penetrating the temples of his head.

In an instant, I stood fortified in Erjon's mind. Looking left, then right, images of every part of his life flew by. In those images, I knew him. I knew his thoughts and feelings. I knew his memories and potential futures. This experience was euphoric.

One of the images stopped and expanded. Before I knew it, I was living his memory.

In the soft glow of a bedside candle, a young woman sat

on the edge of a plush bed with gray covers. The candle cast a faint light into the room, and the open window welcomed in the soothing sounds of crickets and gentle hush of a night breeze. Erjon, looking to be about ten, lay beneath his blanket, his eyes filled with tears and his face etched with worry.

The young woman, maybe sixteen years of age, placed her hands gently on Erjon's trembling shoulder. His eyes were filled with fear and sadness. My heart ached for him.

"Everything is going to be okay," she whispered, her voice soft and comforting, like a child's lullaby. "I'm here. I'm not going anywhere, Erjon."

Erjon hoisted himself up on his elbows, his eyes yearning for more reassurance. "I'm scared, Tuuli," he admitted in a quivering voice. "What if something happens to Mother now that Father is gone?"

Tuuli smiled warmly, brushing a strand of fallen hair out of Erjon's eyes. "I know, Erjon. Sometimes, we all get scared of the unknown. But just because Father isn't with us, doesn't mean Mother is going to lose all sense of herself. She has her children to keep her living. Me...Zeph...and you. We're going to be strong for her. We're going to help her get through this."

Tears welled up in Erjon's eyes, and he threw his arms

around Tuuli, seeking solace in his sister's embrace. She held him close, her arms a safe haven for her younger brother.

"Everyone is feeling so much. I am feeling so much. Too much. I can't bear the emotions. It's suffocating me."

"Remember," Tuuli replied, "you are strong. Ilmari wouldn't give you so much emotion if she didn't think you could handle it. Trust in her."

"Can't I just turn the emotions off?"

Tuuli laughed, and it filled the room with a reprieve of joy and warmth. "You can try, Erjon, but in the end, it would be of no use. You have to feel in order to live."

Tuuli remained at Erjon's side as the memory blurred, and I was alone yet again. The memories flew by again, and another materialized before me.

This time I was out in the open expanse of a meadow filled with lush green grass swaying back and forth in the summer breeze. Erjon, now a Dragonheir with his gleaming gray scales, sat on a log eating an apple. As he sat there, his lips curved into a blissful smile. He threw the apple to the ground and laughed when a blue bird snatched it up immediately. He then raised his face to the sun, allowing its warm rays to caress his skin. He radiated happiness which seemed to make the world around him brighter and more *beautiful.*

The shock of seeing him so happy and full of life almost knocked me over.

In the skies above, figures flew overhead. They weren't birds, and they certainly weren't Dragons. They were the Winged Warriors. And Tuuli was one of them.

She had silvery-white wings—a contraption of some sort—that shimmered like moonlight. She smiled joyfully as she glided through the sky at an accelerated speed. Following her, was a young man with black wings. They dipped and swerved in harmonious synchrony.

Together, they streaked through the endless sky, weaving in and out of fluffy clouds. They practiced intricate maneuvers and combat techniques while they used their air magic to stay suspended in the air. They nodded at each other and began a sparring session, releasing blades that were strapped behind their backs. It took great effort and skill to fight each other while keeping their air magic flowing. They exchanged lightning-fast strikes, but they obviously fought each other a lot because they each anticipated the other's moves.

As the two fought above in the air, Erjon stood below on the ground as darkness fell upon the meadow. We both looked up to see a dark, fast-approaching cloud in the distance, bringing with it lightning and thunder. Tuuli and the young man didn't seem to notice. They were too busy trying to overpower one another with their strength and sword skills. Erjon flailed his arms wildly, trying to get their attention. He created two gusts of wind to propel himself into the air. He lacked the maturity to handle his magic properly, telling me that he'd just gone through his Partition. Panicked, he yelled to gain their attention.

"Tuuli! Zeph! A storm is approaching! Tuuli! Zeph!"

Finally, the young man named Zeph caught sight of Erjon. He turned behind him, catching sight of the storm. Tuuli saw the cloud, too, and started to put away her blade. But Zeph didn't want to stop. He said something to Tuuli—of course, I couldn't hear it from the ground. Instead of putting her blade away, she smiled, and raised it over his head. They were going to continue fighting? Lightning and swords were not a good mix!

I opened my mouth to scream at them, but nothing came out. So, I tried propelling myself upward, but I couldn't form any magic. The only thing I could do was stand there as the wind picked up and the rain started to fall.

Erjon was distressed. He shouted their names over and over as the thunder shook the mountains, but they either couldn't hear him, or they ignored him. Just when he was *about to give up, Tuuli looked down at Erjon and her demeanor changed. She fastened her blade to her back and motioned at Zeph to land. I exhaled the breath I'd been holding.*

Zeph dove suddenly and Tuuli followed. Lightning cracked around them as they made their way back to the ground. They were a mere twenty feet from landing when a strong gust of wind caught their winged contraptions. Zeph was thrown into the mountainside, but Tuuli was propelled upward. She somersaulted through the air, unable to gain control with her magic.

Erjon watched in horror as Zeph's body slumped to the ground, his eyes closed and body motionless. Erjon ran to Zeph's side and ensured that he was breathing. Erjon placed his palm on Zeph's chest. It lifted and lowered with Zeph's breathing, indicating he was alive. Relief coursed through my body.

Erjon whipped his head back to the sky. He scanned the skies for Tuuli, but the pouring rain made it difficult to see anything. Lightning flashed, and we finally spotted her. She was no longer careening out of control but instead was making her way back to safety.

Suddenly, in a blinding spectacle of energy, a bolt of lightning materialized from the sky. Its jagged path crackled with white brilliance. It arched downward, and then, with a deafening pop, the bolt struck Tuuli. Sparks flew in all directions and a plume of smoke trailed from her wings. Her body went limp as it fell to the ground.

Erjon let out a blood-curdling scream. He raced to where she landed, scooped her up in his arms, and held her tight. Tears fell in large droplets down his cheeks.

I needed to get out. I was not meant to see this memory. It was too personal. But how did I get out? I looked frantically for an exit from where I stood, but the connection joining my magic, and his mind held strong.

"Let me out, Erjon! Let me out!" I screamed.

Erjon's magic retaliated. His magic, in the form of a dark swirling wind, wrapped around my ankles.

I clawed at the wind with all my might, but it was useless. My heart hammered beneath my chest, driven by pure panic. Sweat trickled down my scales. No matter how much force I used, the wind wouldn't let up. A scream tore from my throat.

"This is it. I'm going to die here," I said, my voice shaking. Suddenly, darkness fell over me, blanketing my already limited view.

"You will not," a familiar voice whispered. It was ethereal and comforting, yet powerful.

"I don't know how to get out," I replied. I reached out

my hand to grab hold of whoever spoke. At least, I thought I was reaching out my hand. I couldn't see anything.

"Follow me," the voice instructed.

"I don't know where you are," I cried. My eyes darted back and forth, searching for a figure in the darkness.

"Calm your mind and still your beating heart, Emera. You know me. Trust your instincts, my daughter. Trust your Dragonheart. It will lead you to me."

Daughter?

"Nimerah? Mother?" I pleaded. "Why do you sound so distant?"

"Come to me, Emera."

I closed my eyes and breathed deeply, letting my taut shoulders relax, and my arms fall slack to my sides. Channeling what strength I had left, I summoned the element of air. I coaxed the swirling wind to loosen, and it listened. I stepped forward once and then twice until a light appeared before me, slicing through the void.

"I think I've found you." Relief swept through me, brushing away any remnants of anxiety, and I let out a sigh. Placing one foot gingerly in front of the other so as to not disturb Erjon's magic again, I tip-toed toward the light that pierced through the darkness like sunlight coming in through a stained-glass window. It was so bright I shielded my eyes

from being blinded. Looking ahead, I saw her: the Chaos Dragongoddess Nimerah, my Dragonmother. She was radiant in her flowing, multi-colored gown. She was the morning sky the moment the sun greeted the world after a long slumber.

"What have I done?" I asked in a hushed tone. My guilt weighed within my chest.

"You've committed your first Dragonmeld, my daughter."

"Dragonmeld?"

"When a Dragonheir connects with the mind of another, be it Dragonborn or Dragonheir, they can meld their Dragonmagic. Most initiate a Dragonmeld when both Dragonborns need additional Dragonmagic to complete a mutual task. The purpose of that meld is the siphoning of power. Now, a Dragonmeld is difficult to achieve. The Dragonheirs must be deeply connected on a personal level. Most melds only work between Dragonmates because of that."

"Please, no," I blurted.

Nimerah laughed; the sound was rich and joyful. I realized how much I missed her. "No, my daughter. Erjon is already spoken for." Her wink confirmed my suspicions. Erjon and Queen Eteri were together. I sighed with relief.

"Then how did I do it?"

Nimerah laughed again as if the answer were obvious. "You're a Chaos Dragon, Emera. Your chaos power surpasses all elemental power. You were able to conquer Erjon's quite easily."

Yeah, it didn't seem that easy to me.

"You just need to work on your control," Nimerah added. "You must take care when entering the mind of another. For you, a Chaos Dragon, a Dragonmeld has the potential to be more than just siphoning another's Dragonmagic to your advantage. You have the ability to strip down all their mental and physical defenses. You can burrow yourself deep in their mind. You can learn who they were, who they are, and who they will be. Without control, you could paralyze them."

"Like what Amram did to me," I murmured.

"Yes," she said. "Until you have more control over your chaos magic, I do not recommend Dragonmelds unless you are connecting with someone who has the ability to fight back."

"Like Erjon just did," I suggested.

"Exactly. Other Dragonborns and Dragonheirs cannot overpower you, but if they possess great power of their own, they can alert your magic of its hold by fighting back. If not,

as you just discovered, you can lose your way easily."

"Which could permanently damage the mind of whomever I've connected with," I gathered.

Nimerah nodded her head to confirm. "And yours." I shuddered from a chill that rushed down my spine.

A sudden tug of my magic pulled me forward slightly. Nimerah smiled and lifted her palm to my cheek. I leaned into it. The connection between our minds was the only opportunity to see her. I felt the familiar prick in my heart. This was goodbye again.

"Until we see each other again," she whispered.

I looked into her wondrous violet eyes. "And when will that be?"

Her eyes dropped. "I cannot say. Amram grows stronger each day, and I don't know how. It is risky for me to enter your mind. He can easily join us here."

"How do I stop him from doing that?"

"You will figure it out." She leaned in and kissed my cheek.

I closed my eyes, savoring the moment. When I opened them, I was back in the Great Hall.

And Erjon wasn't happy.

CHAPTER FOUR
EMERA

"Let us eat!" Queen Eteri declared. She clapped twice in rapid succession to signal the commencement of the evening meal. Servants clad in refined dark gray coats made haste to bring in several platters of food and wine bottles.

The queen cleared her throat then smiled. "Once we're seated, we can interrogate Emera about invading Erjon's mind. That was quite the Dragonmeld if I've ever seen one." She turned to Erjon, who continued to stare at me. If looks could kill, I would already be in the ground, rotting.

Calian's hand warmed the small of my back. He guided me to a seat, pulled out the chair, and scooted me toward the table after I sat down. "He'll calm down," he assured me as he lowered into a chair beside me.

"Doubtful," I mumbled.

Fin passed behind us at that moment but stopped. "He's not even mad that you broke into his head. He's more upset that he couldn't keep you out," he said.

Fin pulled out a seat on my other side and sat abruptly.

"Oh yeah? Did he tell you that?" I asked.

"Nah. He didn't have to. I can read it on his face." A servant stole his attention by pouring wine into Fin's goblet.

I scoffed at Fin's words. Could tell by Erjon's face? No one could tell what Erjon was thinking. He placed a strong emphasis on suppressing his emotions. Like he viewed emotional expression as a source of vulnerability. Maybe it was his way of dealing with his sister's death?

I felt the slightest touch as Calian's lips brushed my ear. "He can't be mad forever," he replied, his voice low and husky. I felt a jolt in my stomach.

"Everyone, please sit," Queen Eteri said, her voice louder to grab the attention of everyone in the room. "And, please, try to relax." She threw a sideways glance at Erjon, who grumbled something to himself as he sat down across from Calian and me.

The centerpiece of the queen's lavish meal was a whole pig on an elegant silver tray with an apple stuck in its mouth. It lay atop fresh greens and vegetables. Alongside the pig were other meats including boar, venison, and poultry. My eye caught on the fish that was set by Morwen. We both glanced at each other with knowing eyes. Growing up in the Kingdom of Water meant that fish was an everyday occurrence during dinner.

Other dishes decorated the long table including pies, pastries, fruits, and cheeses. Wine and mead were plentiful; whenever anyone needed another drink, a servant was there to refill their glasses.

No one mentioned my Dragonmeld during our meal. The sounds of utensils clattering and wine pouring into goblets, along with playful banter and laughter, reminded me that good times were still possible despite the impending arrival of war. And death.

When everything was cleared away, Queen Eteri nodded at Erjon. He twisted his body toward me, his eyes sharp and lethal. "How did you do it?" he demanded. I couldn't tell if he was genuinely curious or upset because he always spoke in a monotonous tone.

"It was an accident," I told him and shrugged.

He paused, contemplating his next question. "How did

you get out?" That's what he was going with? Erjon was more concerned with his ego than discussing tactical advantages. His narrow-mindedness woke my magic, and it hummed beneath my skin.

I shifted in my seat so that my entire body faced Erjon. "Nimerah guided me out."

"That does make sense," he replied curtly, as if my Dragonmother helping me was the only way I could ever have figured it out. Not everyone would have taken his words as an insult, but I did. Heat flared in my cheeks. He may be able to keep his emotions under control, but he was certainly gifted at provoking those of others.

"To perform a Dragonmeld, Emera, is irresponsible," he said. "You could have been trapped. Time and time again you prove that you are young and…"

I rose to my feet and rested my hands on the table as I leaned over it. "Don't say it," I warned him.

He ignored me; his face remained neutral. "And undisciplined."

A few audible gasps from the servants echoed through the room. Everyone and everything went still.

"You," I pointed a finger at Erjon's smug face, "are just an overconfident, overbearing, soul-sucking Dragonass." Shock flashed in his eyes for a brief moment. He opened his mouth to retaliate, but Queen Eteri raised her slender hand and shook her head, signaling him to remain silent. He closed his mouth, and his lips pressed into a fine line. He wanted to say more, but he wasn't going to disobey his queen.

"Em…" Calian drawled.

My chest heaved a forceful exhale. "What?" I seethed between clenched teeth.

"Just breathe. You could demolish the palace if you really wanted to. Getting a rise out of Erjon isn't worth it."

I slowly tore my gaze away from Erjon, who still sat motionless and silent. He wasn't going to say anything, so I met Calian's eyes. "I would never destroy a palace just to prove a point," I said.

"I know that." He threw his chin toward the strangers in the room. "But they don't." I looked at the faces of those I wasn't acquainted with, mostly the staff. They were frightened. In their eyes, I was an all-powerful Dragongoddess with no care for their well-being. I couldn't have them thinking that. I didn't want them to.

With deep breaths, I willed my heart to slow. "That's exactly what Amram said in my nightmare several nights ago. I am young. I am naive. I am undisciplined." I glared at Erjon. His eyes softened just a little.

"I saw you. All of you. Your bodies piled one on top of the other. Your eyes were open but empty. Your faces were ashen. There was no life…Only death." I swallowed the scorching lump in my throat. No. Absolutely not. I wouldn't cry. I was a pillar of strength. "The nightmare was so real. Too real. Amram stood before you in his human form, the embodiment of death with a handsome face. He told me that what I saw would come to pass should I try to stop him."

Senna stood and began pacing the room, her furrowed brows indicative of her deep thinking. She was once the leader of a group sworn to protect the kingdoms from the prophecy—she'd given up her position after we arrived in Ilmari. If she had a plan, I was all ears.

The room was eerily silent. It seemed they were waiting for me. I breathed deeply and released, relaxing with each exhale. I didn't know when my shoulders had gotten so tense. I rolled them back, stretching them out.

"Ever since that night, I've been on edge. To make matters worse, I accidentally started a Dragonmeld that I didn't even know was something I could do. And! No matter how hard I try, I can't shift into my Dragon form. You're all counting on me to be a powerful Dragongoddess, yet lately I can't seem to recreate any of the power I unleashed at the cave. I feel as hopeless as I had before my mother's blessing." I slumped back into my chair and let my head fall back.

"Is that all?" Queen Eteri asked, breaking the tension.

"Amram asked Emera to join him," Calian added.

Erjon's eyebrows raised, and he leaned forward on his elbows. "So, you knew about Amram's intrusion," he said. It came out as more of a statement than a question.

"I'd hardly call a nightmare an intrusion," Senna quipped.

Erjon narrowed his eyes like he was talking to a child. "It wasn't a nightmare. He invaded Emera's mind, just as she just did to mine."

Avani's eyes widened. "He's that powerful?"

"Allegedly," Erjon answered before turning back to Calian. "We have yet to see his power, and he's been raised from the dead for several days."

"Maybe the process took some of his power?" Morwen offered.

Erjon contemplated Morwen's words. "Maybe." Then he spoke directly to Calian, "You shouldn't withhold anything pertaining to Amram."

Fin laughed. "He's her General, remember? Or…Y'know…something else." He wiggled his eyebrows at me. Calian still hadn't mentioned to Fin that he'd received purple Dragonmate wings. Wings that I didn't have.

Erjon's jaw tightened with frustration, but he didn't change his neutral expression. "You and Calian should have confided in all of us. At any moment, Amram could hold your mind hostage, and we wouldn't know. It is unwise to keep things of this magnitude to yourselves. Especially after…" his voice trailed off, and he didn't finish his final thought.

Calian's eyes flashed red. "Especially after what?"

"Especially after you let down your guard and got yourself captured by Valda. I'd think you'd know better at this point." Erjon's voice didn't even rise a little. He was in complete control of his emotions even though I could tell he was furious.

"I should know better. Like you. You know better?" Calian asked, his voice tense.

"Perhaps."

It only took Erjon's one word to poke the bear. Gusts of wind started to circulate in the room. The tapestries flapped against the walls, and the chandelier swayed. Both men shot to their feet. Fire erupted from Calian's palms. The flames of the candles responded, lifting higher and higher.

Queen Eteri stood abruptly, "That is enough!" she yelled, her voice booming above our heads. "I will not have your arrogance destroy my palace. Stop acting like children, and let's get on with our plans."

Fin started to raise his hand, probably to make some asinine joke that he, Calian, and Erjon were over twenty years of age, so they weren't children. But Morwen shot him a look that said, "Don't you dare," so he lowered his hand.

The queen didn't seem to notice. She sat down and smoothed her dress with her hands, then took a sip of wine. Calian and Erjon also sat down but continued to glare at one another.

"The queen is right," Morwen said. "You both need to be level-headed, or we're doomed to fail. Besides, if Amram is indeed invading Emera's mind, then we need to formulate a plan to stop that."

"Morwen's right. If Amram makes anymore visits, we need to teach you how to successfully push him from your mind," Calian contended.

"He's right," Erjon replied coolly.

Fin slapped both of his cheeks. "You two agree? Is Amram here? Will the world end today?"

"Funny," Calian grumbled.

"Calian and I can train you," Erjon said. "We'll need Morwen's help, of course."

"You were almost at each other's throats, and now you want to work together?" Avani asked incredulously. The men glanced at each other and shrugged. Well, Calian shrugged. Erjon just lifted a brow like he was bored again. Fin laughed.

"Men," Queen Eteri said and rolled her eyes. Morwen, Avani, Senna, and I all nodded in agreement.

"Let's hold off on any formal training until tomorrow," Morwen said, standing. "You need to rest, and tonight's events have made me fatigued." Morwen headed for the door. Fin bolted out of his seat and ran to her side. My heart fell when he took her hand and kissed the top of it. I wanted that. The love and the adoration. The stolen glances and pecks on the cheeks. But maybe being a goddess meant that I couldn't. It seemed silly for a goddess to have a fated mate. Nimerah didn't.

I looked at Calian, who was deep in conversation with Erjon. Their relationship gave me a headache. One minute they were at each other's throats, and the next minute, they were like old friends. But maybe that's what true camaraderie was, and I just didn't know it.

"I'm going to bed as well," I said. "I'm more frazzled than anything. Maybe a good night's rest will help."

"So, we're not going to talk about Ilmari's defenses?" Fin asked. "That's why we were called here." No one, not even the queen, responded. I threw him a lighthearted smile. I just wasn't in the mood to talk about defense strategies.

Calian stood abruptly, stopping his conversation mid sentences, and pulled out my chair. My heart skipped a beat in my chest.

With his hand placed on the small of my back, he guided me out. It took no time for us to reach my bed chamber. We both stood there silently, somewhat awkwardly. I didn't know what to say, and it was clear that he didn't either. We had this connection, but the gods didn't see us as Dragonmates? Was it as heartbreaking for him as it was for me?

"Well, goodnight," I whispered, finally taking the courage to break the silence.

"Goodnight," he murmured.

I reached for the handle, but before I could open the door, Calian grabbed my arm and spun me toward him. He pulled me into a deep kiss, sending a jolt down my spine that curled my toes. Heat ignited in my core, and once again, the familiar electric energy sparked between us. His calloused hands wrapped around my shoulders, and I melted. There was no other way to describe it. Calian made me melt with every touch and every kiss. Yet…We weren't Dragonmates. And one day, he'd find her. She'd be beautiful and smart. She'd be funny and kind. She'd be strong.

She wouldn't be me.

I broke away from him. "I'm sorry. I…uh…need some rest."

"Um, yeah. Okay," Calian mumbled. "I'll see you in the morning?"

I did my best to smile though it didn't reach my eyes. "Of course."

Calian turned on his heels and walked down the hall. When he was out of sight, I opened the door and threw myself on my bed, not bothering to undress. I stared at the ceiling for some time, but eventually, sleep consumed me.

*   *   *

I stood at the edge of the vast Arden Forest. I didn't know how I'd gotten there, but I didn't care. The air around me was cool and peaceful. The trees swayed with the gentle breeze, and the insects played their songs.

A powerful voice echoed through the trees, both comforting and compelling.

"Emera," it said, "I see your inner struggle. Doubts cloud your mind. I have come to put those doubts to rest, my child." Startled, I glanced around, but I was alone.

Terror claimed my voice. "Stop playing games, Amram,"

I croaked.

Amram stepped out from the trees. "Emera, darling."

I wanted to scream. I wanted to run. Again, he had slithered into my thoughts. Why couldn't I—a Chaos Dragongoddess—keep him out? I had killed his daughter, another powerful Chaos Dragon. Why wasn't my power enough to kill him, too?

"I am an ancient god," Amram replied, "and you do not yet possess the strength that I have. Your time will come. With practice and determination, you will be just as powerful as I am. Maybe more."

He was trying to win me over, but I wasn't going to fall for it.

"What do you want?"

"Out of the three Chaos Dragons, I am the embodiment of wisdom. I know your deeds, your sacrifices, and your unyielding dedication to humanity." He took a step forward, so I took a step back. I wasn't going to let him get any closer.

My heart raced. "What do you want?" I asked again, this time with a stronger, more confident tone.

"I offer you my guidance, my power, and my eternal support. Join me, and we can vanquish any darkness that plagues this world. We can ensure a brighter future for everyone," the god crooned.

"Except the humans."

Amram cocked his head to one side. "Why do you love them so much? You're not one of them. You never were."

"Because day in and day out, they wake up and greet the sunrise with hope. Hope that one day, they'll be treated as equals to Dragonborns. They always contribute, never complain. They thrive on family and culture, and they lead with their heart, not their magic. The heart of a Dragon is strong. But the heart of a human is stronger."

Amram didn't say anything more after that. Instead, he squinted his eyes and vanished.

Alone, I sat down on the soft green grass and admired the trees and the forest beyond. In my heart, I knew that one day they would burn.

CHAPTER FIVE
EMERA

"Is it not obvious?" Erjon asked.

"Not to some people," I snapped. The man really knew how to annoy me.

"You're trying too hard," Calian said.

"You think?" I yelled and slammed my fists on the ground. A large crack split the earth beneath me, and a deep rumble rose from within. The crack expanded into a slightly larger crevice.

Erjon sighed. "You must remain calm." My eyes hurled daggers at his smug face.

"I. Am. Calm," I said through clenched teeth. "At least, I

was. But then you both had to open your big mouths."

Calian laughed. The sound normally curled my toes and stoked a heat within my core, but this time it made my anger flare. In seconds, the grass beneath his feet lit on fire. He jumped with a slight shriek and began to stomp out the flames. It reminded me of a dance the elders performed back in Medora. It was quite an amusing sight.

Erjon now stood beside me, offering a hand to help me stand. "Hostility will only feed your frustration," he retorted. I smacked his hand away and stood. A smirk spread across his smug face.

"I'll show you hostility," I barked. He had the nerve to laugh.

We'd been at it all morning in the clearing that was located between two mountains away from the City of Ilmari. Calian felt a secluded area away from the city would be less distracting. Erjon and Morwen agreed. I had no say, so we had packed some belongings, food and drink, and rode the horses until we had reached a more desolate area with only the animals and the sounds of nature as our company. It was cooler within the mountains, so the gorgeous gown I'd worn at last night's dinner was replaced with my usual black skin-tight pants, black boots that hit below the knee, black gloves, and a long-sleeved purple tunic with an attached hood. The tunic was cinched in at the waist with a black leather corset belt.

Morwen was dressed similarly, but her tunic was a striking blue without a hood. Her dark shining hair was pulled back into a tight braid whereas mine fell loosely around me. I had already attempted to push her out of my head numerous times, but I failed time and time again. I was exhausted, more so since Amram had entered my mind last night.

"Let's try again," Morwen said delicately. She grabbed my hand, and her water magic flowed through her into me. The tranquility subdued my festering annoyance for Erjon and Calian until I finally felt ready to proceed again.

I inhaled, and the pungent smell of pine mixed with damp mountain air filled my lungs. Exhaling, I watched my breath turn white when it met the cold. My magic stirred once more, so I pulled on it like I was lifting an anchor from the ocean floor. But the anchor was too heavy.

"She's struggling," Calian said. He stood several feet away with his hands on his hips. He looked just as handsome as ever, dressed in all black with leather boots, gloves, and a wool cape tied around his neck. He used to wear red, but ever since he discovered he wasn't the Dragonheir of Vukan, he stopped.

I glanced at Erjon who nodded. He looked fine in his attire that matched Calian's, except that his was gray. Yeah, so he was handsome as well, but I wouldn't give him the satisfaction of telling him.

My brows creased from irritation, holding hostage the sweat that formed on my forehead. I needed my brain to focus. Focus. Focus. Focus!

"Shh," Morwen said and waved Calian off. "She just needs you two to leave her be for a moment."

"Morwen…" Erjon started.

"Erjon," Morwen interrupted. Her voice was direct, yet calm. No other words were exchanged between them. Erjon nodded his head and backed away. I needed to know Morwen's secret on how to silence Erjon with just his name. Now that was power.

"Let's try something different, Emera. I want you to imagine your Dragonmagic is a living being."

"A…living…being?" I asked slowly. Had I heard her correctly?

"Yes, a living being," Morwen said. "When I first started using my Dragonmagic, I had difficulty manifesting it quickly, and because of that, it wasn't as powerful." Morwen paced in front of me, her hands clasped together. "But then, I started imagining my Dragonmagic as a living Water

Dragon swimming within my body. Now, when I call it, I do so as if it is a friend and ally. My body is its ocean, and it swims within me." Morwen stopped and faced me again. "I want you to imagine your Dragonmagic in the form of a powerful Chaos Dragon. Let it be your friend. Let it be your ally. Don't force it to do your bidding."

What Morwen said kind of made sense. And it was definitely better than Erjon's advice. Seriously. Telling anyone to remain calm would always have the opposite effect. One would think Erjon was smart enough to know that.

"Close your eyes," Morwen said.

My eyelids slipped over my pupils, and I saw nothing. I steadied my breathing so I could maintain a grip on reality. Lately, when I closed my eyes, Amram's face stared back through the darkness. Sure enough, the outline of his human self took shape, and I choked down a ragged breath. The beating of my heart became thunderous, drumming so hard that my chest hurt. Did he know what I was doing? Was it going to be him this time?

"Focus, Emera. Hear my voice. Stay with it."

I nodded slowly, focusing on Morwen's voice. The outline of Amram's body faded into nothing, and I was left alone in my head.

"Good, Emera. You're doing good," Morwen assured me. "Now, I want you to dive deep within your Dragonsoul and uncover your Dragonmagic. Not just the threads of it. Reveal to yourself the source of it. That source is your inner Chaos Dragon."

"My inner Chaos Dragon," I murmured.

A shadowy outline of a body lingered behind my eyes. It took me a moment to realize that the shadowy body was me. I took one step after the other and ventured deep into my mind, searching for any remnants of my magic embedded within my subconscious. After looking in each dark corner of my mind, I discovered a tiny sparkling gem. I grabbed hold of it and turned it within my palm, inspecting the various shades of purple emanating from it. The purple glow wrapped around my body, and I materialized. My shadowy body was no more.

"I have it," I whispered.

But no one responded. A hand snatched the gem away from me. I looked up into Amram's smug face.

Darkness fell around us, and he stalked forward, tossing the gem into the air and catching it.

"This is interesting," he said. "In your attempt to practice casting me out of your mind, you've stumbled upon your Dragon form."

I put more distance between us. Was he here to finally kill me? Would I be able to get him out of my head?

"How long before you realize that you are not yet strong enough to banish me from your thoughts, Emera? You should know that you don't have the power to do so." The god slowly walked up to me, and for a split second, I contemplated running. But I wouldn't give him the satisfaction, so I stood my ground with my chin held high. I would not back down. I would not surrender.

"Maybe not now, but one day I will," I growled.

"That is if you are still alive," he mused. He lifted his hand and rested his palm on my cheek.

"I will die fighting."

"Of that, I have no doubt...So young...So brave. And you look so much like your mother." He dropped his hand and turned away from me. I thrust out my hands, and fire magic flared from my palms. The god looked back over his shoulder at the same moment that I threw my fire at him with as much force as I could muster. But the fire missed its mark. Amram had vanished instantly.

"But what if you didn't have to die fighting?" he whispered. I jumped from his sudden appearance behind me. He was close. Too close. His breath was hot and sticky on the back of my neck. He let out a deep and predatory chuckle.

"I don't know what you mean," I said.

His hand slid up my back over my shoulder and grazed my collarbone as it traveled upward. He wrapped his fingers around my neck and pulled me closer to him. "Join me," he breathed into my ear.

My heart beat furiously beneath my chest, and my breathing quickened; the cadence of the rhythm was erratic. "Never," I choked out.

"We could be...everything."

"We will never be anything."

Amram chuckled once more, sending a tremble down my spine. His fingers released my throat, and he dropped his hand back to his side. I turned to face him. Gods he was handsome. No one could argue against that. My cheeks warmed from embarrassment thinking about it. I needed to get away as soon as possible, but I couldn't. I was at his mercy in my mind.

He took my hand and clasped it within both of his. "Maybe this will help," he said and vanished.

The darkness lifted, and I stood alone and silent once more. Turning over my hand, I opened my palm and revealed the sparkling purple gem. My inner chaos. Morwen's attempt at teaching me how to push Amram out of my mind somehow led me to the jewel I held.

Amram mentioned this being my Dragon form. Shifting was not the intended result of today's lesson, but if I could do it, then I'd have another advantage against fighting Dragons…and Amram.

With the use of my earth magic, I squeezed my hand with such strength that the gem broke into tiny shards. But when I inspected my palm for cuts, there weren't any. The shards had embedded themselves in my skin, and I watched with complete fascination as they sank deeper into my flesh. Once they had disappeared, a faint purple glow pulsed to life from beneath my skin, growing brighter and brighter before traveling throughout my body. The sensation was like nothing I'd ever experienced before. It was unexplainable. Euphoric, even.

"Wow," Morwen said, snapping me out of my mind. I peered up from my hands to see her standing beside me once more. Her expression hadn't changed, which told me she didn't know Amram had spoken to me. I wasn't going to tell her just yet. At the moment, I was too concerned with the fact that I was glowing.

Calian inched closer. His face was etched with skepticism, and I could feel his concern. The feeling was so overwhelming that my magic began to falter. The purple glow started to dim.

"No!" Morwen said while clapping her hands in front of my face. "Focus. Do not let your inner doubts consume your magic. Let it go. I am going to enter your mind. Try to push me out."

"Push it out," I whispered. Morwen still thought I was trying to push her out of my mind. But I wasn't. I was trying to push something else out.

So, I did.

With a deep breath, I relaxed and let my magic fill every part of my body. The glow faded, but purple smoke poured from my skin and permeated the space around me. I could no longer see the others because the smoke—which had become thick and crackling with energy—had swallowed them whole. The steady beating of my heart now raced beneath my chest in anticipation—and fear—of what was happening.

The change began with a subtle tremor coursing through my veins like an ancient force had awakened from within me. My skin tingled, and my scales rippled. From my existing scales, new ones emerged, rolling over my skin until I was completely covered in them. They were deep violet, and glistened despite the sunlight being blocked out by the smoke. However, the initial fear that took hold of me let go, and I welcomed a profound sense of anticipation. I was born for this. I was a Dragongoddess.

My limbs elongated, morphing into powerful forearms and legs with sharp black claws that could easily slice through stone. My bones stretched and became thicker. My shoulder blades formed powerful wings that when opened, were deep purple and then transitioned into an iridescent green. If someone looked close enough, they'd see specks of blue, red, white, and silver mixed in.

My spine expanded and curved, forming a destructive tail. Each vertebra grew serrated spikes that could cut through flesh. Simultaneously, my neck lengthened, allowing my head to rise above my shoulders. It bore a crown of sleek horns that looked regal yet dominating.

The smoke dissipated, and I discovered that the transformation wasn't just physical. Each of my senses were more lethal. My eyes glowed, and I could see farther into the distance than I had with my human eyes. My hearing was attuned to the faintest of sounds. I could detect the tiniest insect moving on the ground, or the smallest bird humming in a nearby tree. My nose detected aromas with more precision than an Earthean Tiger. I wondered if I would also be able to taste better than before. The idea excited me, and I couldn't wait to test out my new taste buds.

A surge of magic ignited within my colossal body, and it

begged to be released. I opened my mouth, looked to the sky, and from deep within my core, a thunderous roar erupted. It was accompanied by an immense explosion of fire that startled the world around us. Birds took flight from the trees in a panic, and small creatures ran for cover.

With my powerful wings unfurled, I ascended into the skies. My Dragon form embraced the freedom of the open air. I soared through the wispy clouds and reveled in how soft and cool they were against my scales. I dove down toward the mountains below and back up toward the sun. I felt invigorated.

I was more alive and freer than ever. My eyes darted downward, scanning the serene landscape below. When I looked back up, a foreboding black mass in the distance.

A Dragon? My pulse quickened as I flew closer to it. It was a Dragon. Was Amram here?

A whisper entered my thoughts. *Emera, I am everywhere you are.*

A wave of exhaustion rippled through my mind and body, causing my wings to give out. The uneasy feeling, coupled with a potential threat in the distance, forced me to dive back toward the others. The ground shook once I landed, and I almost fell over.

"That was incredible!" Calian yelled as he ran toward me.

Morwen clapped. "Well done, Emera!"

"Good," Erjon added. "Now we can—"

"Wait!" I screamed. Only, it wasn't a scream. It came out as a booming roar.

Morwen held up her hands to stop Calian and Erjon from saying another word. "I believe she's trying to communicate."

I dipped my snout to confirm Morwen's statement. With careful concentration, I opened my mind to hers. Valda was able to communicate with me through telepathy since we were both Chaos Dragons. Surely, I'd be able to communicate with Morwen, whose secondary power was telepathy.

I saw a Dragon, I said.

Amram?

Maybe. Whoever it is, they are between us and the city. We must warn the queen. We need to evacuate the city.

Emera, please remain calm. I can see the panic in your eyes.

We must act quickly, Morwen.

I didn't say we shouldn't. But we also need to be level-headed or more lives will be lost.

I know whose lives will be lost! I've seen it. I let out a deep growl.

"What is she saying?" Calian asked.

Erjon shifted his weight and crossed his arms. "Withholding information is reckless, Morwen."

"I am not withholding information. I want to ensure I get every detail. Emera saw a Dragon between our location and the city."

Erjon's face turned pale, and I felt his terror. Pure, unadulterated terror. "We must get back to the city," he murmured. Our eyes locked, and I nodded. Color returned to his face while he calmed himself.

"It doesn't make sense. Why would a Dragon be hovering in the air and not destroying the city?" Morwen asked. She made a good point. What was a Dragon doing so far from the city?

Calian mounted Dhruv quickly. "We don't have time to deliberate. If what Emera says is true, then we're wasting time. We need to move now." He kicked his heels and took off toward the city. Morwen and Erjon nodded at each other and did the same.

Zari, hurry to the city! Would she be able to understand me?

Of course, my Kahina.

I sighed with relief—which probably sounded like another growl—and lifted back into the sky. I hovered over my friends in case they needed help against an aerial attack since they didn't have the ability to become Dragons themselves. I mentally prepared myself to fight in the sky. I would do whatever I could to protect my friends while making sure the City of Ilmari wasn't burned to the ground.

I took to the air. As I flew, the Dragon grew larger and larger. I finally made out who it was. It was…Valda. Wait. Valda?! How? She was dead. But the body of the Dragon looked exactly like hers. I gulped. It had to be her.

She hovered over the large opening within the trees. She hadn't noticed me yet since she appeared to be concentrating on whatever was happening on the ground, so I glided down to the others and landed before them. This time, my legs gave out, and I fell to my stomach.

Dhruv halted immediately. Morwen's and Erjon's horses stopped just behind Dhruv.

A Dragon is ahead, hovering over a large space between the trees. But…No…It can't be.

Who? Morwen asked. Who is it?

Valda.

That's impossible.

I…I…I don't know. I killed her…Didn't I?

"Could you two fill us in on what you're talking about?" Calian barked.

"It appears that the Dragon Emera saw is Valda."

Calian snorted. "Impossible."

I could be mistaken. Whoever it is, it's concentrating on something on the ground. They are hyper focused.

Morwen looked back and forth between Calian and Erjon. "The Dragon is engaged in something below him. Emera doesn't know what."

Erjon scanned the area, his face serious. "I know why the Dragon is here. And it's not good."

CHAPTER SIX
EMERA

"A resurrection ritual?" Morwen asked with horror written all over her face.

"Precisely," Erjon said. "Amram is raising his army, which we knew would happen. There are numerous burial sites scattered across the kingdoms where Dragons killed other Dragons during The War of Three. If he can resurrect them all, another war is inevitable."

"Why doesn't he just destroy the kingdoms himself?" Morwen asked. Amram was supposedly powerful enough to do so.

Erjon rubbed his temples. "A good question, and one I intend to answer when I dive into the archives within the palace."

Morwen squinted. "But if you had to guess?"

Erjon sighed. "I hate guessing."

Calian snorted.

"But if you had to," she pressed.

Erjon inhaled and exhaled slowly. "Then I would say that being resurrected took some of his power, and he needs his army to help him until he has all of his chaos magic back."

That's a good guess, I thought.

Calian jumped off Dhruv. "We need to concern ourselves with what's in front of us so that we can get back to the castle and alert the kingdoms of what's happening."

"Surely, Em is powerful enough to defeat the Dragon." Despite her best efforts to remain in control of herself, Morwen's voice shook with fear. I knew her. I was not from fear of her own death, but from fear of not seeing Fin again.

I will make sure that you get back to him.

Morwen nodded.

"It might not come to that," Erjon said. "We just need to stay undetected and focus on returning to the palace."

"We need to get closer," Calian argued. "We need to see how this is done so that we can prevent other resurrections from happening."

Erjon lifted an eyebrow. "Preventing future resurrections

is impossible. As I said, burial sites are spread throughout all of the six kingdoms. We cannot feasibly guard all of them."

Calian paced back and forth. "True. But maybe we can slow them down until we have a chance to defeat Amram."

Erjon opened his mouth, probably with some negative comment, but Calian interjected. "No, I don't know how, but we've got to try."

Letting the men discuss our exit strategy, Morwen dismounted her horse and walked toward me. "Are you okay?" she asked.

Yeah, I'm just tired.

Maybe you're just not used to being in your Dragon form.

Maybe. I thought for another moment. *Maybe being in my human form won't be as tiring,* I told Morwen. *Not sure how to transform back, though.*

Go back to when you first transformed. Think about how that happened. Try it in reverse.

Easier said than done. I crushed a gem, and it sank into my skin.

Morwen's wrinkled nose and furrowed brows meant she was thinking of some brilliant way to envision me transforming back into my human form. I brought my head lower in anticipation of the brilliant word she would say.

I have nothing. Only you can do this.

Perfect. Well, then. Here goes nothing.

Instead of retreating into my mind like before, I focused on the ancient-like energy that had filtered through my body. I tuned out all my surroundings, focusing intently on locating it. My magic became vines, growing rapidly and searching for a life-force. They twisted and turned, weaving themselves in and out of my body. Suddenly, they found it. In my mind, I saw the purple gem. It had burrowed itself within my heart, planting itself within the essence of my human self. A smile spread across my scaly lips, exposing the razor-sharp teeth I now possessed.

The vines grabbed hold of the gem, but they did not crush it as I had done before. This time, the vines morphed into a slender tail and wrapped around the gem, providing a cocoon to protect it. Knowing that it was safe there, my soul eased. I focused on my human memories and emotions that intertwined with the ancient power of the gem, and I knew at that moment, shifting back into my human form required me to grab hold of those memories and guide myself back.

With a surge of purple magic swirling around me—cutting me off from my view of the world—I began to shrink in size, dwindling from my towering Dragon form to the less fearsome version of myself. My new scales retreated under my skin, leaving behind the ones that trailed from my temples and down my arm—the ones that identified me as the Dragonheir of Nimerah. My magnificent horns that crowned my head receded, as did my long neck. My rough skin became thinner, whiter, and smoother, revealing small freckles that decorated my body. My once menacing tail curled around my body and shrank until it disappeared while my intense snout and large eyes took on a more human shape.

As my transformation progressed, my beautiful wings of violet and green folded inward and sank back into human shoulder blades. My spine shortened, and the spikes compressed into my back. Limbs that once bore sharp claws retook their former shape. I was now more slender and agile. I was in my human form again.

It took me a moment to readjust. I breathed in the scents that floated around me, felt the cool breeze against my bare skin, and listened to the symphony of nature's sounds. My senses were dulled, but I smiled, nonetheless. Being a Dragon was fun, but I felt lighter and less fatigued.

The smoke cleared, revealing me to the others. A smirk spread across Calian's face, and he turned his attention to the sky. One of Morwen's eyebrows lifted as a sly grin tugged at the corner of her mouth. Erjon looked bored.

"What's wrong?" I twisted and turned, straining my neck

to see if I still had any remnants of a tail or spike sticking out. I didn't find one. Instead, I found my naked butt. I gasped and attempted to cover my private areas quickly.

Calian kept his eyes on the sky, Morwen rushed to the bag strapped to Zari, and Erjon folded his arms, scoffing at my panic. "It's foolish to be embarrassed of your body, Emera. A woman is a woman no matter how tall, short, small, or large she is."

"And more than that," Morwen added as she returned with a simple night dress, "you were just a Dragon. Your body is capable of great things. You should be proud."

I was grateful for their words, but I refused to display all of myself to them.

"Is she covered?" Calian asked with a cough.

"She is," Morwen said after I slipped the dress over my head and let it fall over my body. It was silk—no doubt made for a princess. It was a pale blue, but it wasn't see-through, so that was good.

Calian mounted Dhruv and guided him toward me. Zari followed behind. "We remain as close to the path as possible. No need to get lost in the mountains. We travel as silently as we can manage."

I hoisted myself up on Zari and patted her neck.

Calian sighed. "Let's move out."

Dhruv proceeded quietly—well, as quietly as a horse can go—along the path. When we closed in on the area where I saw Valda hovering, we slowed to a stop. Looking left, then right, Calian nudged Dhruv toward the south side of the path which was lined with thick foliage. Large bushes and other shrubbery only reached the back of the horses, so we had to dismount and walk alongside them.

"They probably aren't here," I whispered. "They surely left during my transformation."

"Your transformation only took seconds," Morwen whispered back.

"That's not possible," I whispered.

"Do you know what the word silent means?" Calian hissed.

Erjon sighed softly, clearly just as annoyed as Calian. When we got back to the city, I would challenge him in the training ring and knock him on his back with such force, he would struggle to sigh ever again. But my voice of reason interrupted my aggressive thoughts. *Give him a break, Em. You know why.*

He quickened his pace to catch up to me and leaned into my ear. "I know what you saw. You need to squash any emotions toward me and focus on what lies ahead."

I stuck out my chin. "I don't know what you mean."

"Hmph. I can feel your emotions, Emera. Your sympathy. It's mixed with your irritation with me. Get them under control, or you'll get us killed."

I fumed.

"Now you're just angry. Cool it."

My magic took control and flooded my veins with tranquility. It washed over me, and I breathed a deep sigh. I would deal with Erjon later.

Calian's hand shot up, signaling us to stop. The horses stopped moving. Morwen breathed deeply, and I closed my eyes. After a few seconds, I parted my eyelids and glanced back at Erjon. His face was a picture of calm despite his harsh words to me. But were they really that harsh? Because he was right. Emotions got people killed.

Erjon scanned the area and faced me. When our eyes met, he tilted his head slightly and nodded. I nodded hastily in return and brought my hand to my chest. It rested there, rising and falling with each heavy breath I took. After a minute of ensuring we hadn't been detected, Calian motioned us toward him. Zari, Dhruv, and the other horses remained where they stood while Erjon, Morwen, and I joined Calian's side. We crouched low and sneaked closer to the clearing beside us. I pushed down any feelings of fear that I had. I needed to be brave.

We all peered through the thick brush that kept us hidden. Calian cursed when he recognized the Dragon that hovered over the ground.

"How is that possible?" he seethed.

"I don't know," I whispered.

"We'll figure it out later," he huffed. Calian radiated heat from his anger at seeing Valda alive.

The Dragongoddess remained hovering as I'd seen her before. But she wasn't alone. Standing on the ground below her was Anwir—former Dragonmaster. His arms were held out in front of him with green magic flowing from his outstretched palms to the flat ground that was void of grass or any plant life. The magic circled the area of dust and dirt below him. It was a grave.

Calian's nostrils flared. "That son of a…"

"Stop," I said, cutting him off. He inhaled sharply and held his breath for a few seconds before releasing it. "Breathe. Focus. Keep your mind at ease." Now I sounded like Erjon.

An incantation mixed with smoke poured from Valda's snout, but the words were of a language I'd never heard of. "Arthar, mir'kyn. Arthar et lenz," the goddess said. "Arthar, mir'kyn. Arthar et lenz."

Keeping my voice barely above a whisper, I asked Calian,

"What is Valda saying?"

"You mean growling? I don't know. I don't speak Dragon, Emera."

"Not growls. The words. Don't you hear them?"

"No. All I can make out is her growling and hissing."

Morwen leaned into me. "Emera? Do you hear something?"

"She's talking. She's actually saying something. But they aren't regular words. They're different. She's saying Arthar, mir'kyn. Arthar et lenz.

Valda's voice boomed throughout the sky again. "Arthar, mir'kyn. Arthar et lenz."

"She said it again."

We all looked at Erjon. "Why do you assume I know what that means?" he sighed.

I shrugged. "Because you act like you know everything."

His face remained unchanged, but the corner of his mouth curved upward slightly, and amusement sparked in his eyes. I preferred the Erjon that enjoyed a good teasing.

"Fine. She's speaking in the ancient Dragon language. The language is all but dead."

"Get to the point," Calian said impatiently. "What is she saying?"

"Awaken my brother. Awaken and live."

Upon Erjon's words, the ground trembled beneath us. A warm hand squeezed my own then weaved its fingers through mine. Calian's hand. His gaze remained straight forward and focused on the commotion before us, but I could tell his mind was restless. The muscles in his jaw twitched, and he squeezed my hand a little tighter without even realizing it. With my magic, I reached my empathic tendrils toward him. They snaked from my hand into his, and I had to bite down on my lip to keep from reacting.

In connecting with his emotions, I inadvertently connected with his mind. His thoughts were scattered, running in erratic patterns. He was trying to make sense of the situation while planning on how to escape or how we'd fight back. For the first time since I'd met him, he wasn't sure what to do. And that terrified him because he always had a plan. He always had a backup for the plan. In fact, I'm sure he had a backup for the backup for the plan. But not this time. He was in uncharted territory.

You'll think of something. I trust you, I said to him. I knew he couldn't hear me, but I needed to say it anyway. Ever since Elio—the true Dragonheir of Vukan—had taken Calian's place, I had put my trust in only myself. It was time that I let that go and allowed myself to depend on the others just as they depended on me.

A shift in the air caused us all to be on high alert, so I withdrew myself from Calian's mind. The earth below Valda cracked and fissures spread quickly. An intense rumble beneath our feet caused us to lose our balance and fall over. I fell onto Calian who quickly grabbed the back of my head and my lower back. He held me tightly against him as dust, dirt, and rock showered down upon us. We stayed there for a moment longer until the tremors ceased. As the dust settled, we got back on our knees and looked to where Valda had completed her ritual. A heap of bones lifted into the air from the crack in the ground. They began to swirl, circulating around one another before eventually connecting to one another and forming the skeleton of a Dragon. The skeleton lowered back into the opening of the ground.

Valda spoke one last time. "Mer flahk tosor flahk."

"My flesh to your flesh," Erjon translated.

A light breeze picked up, and a combination of dust and dirt poured into the opening. Valda lifted her forelimb and sliced her tail. Blood dripped into the opening where the bones of the Dragon remained. The wind picked up, shaking the grass and trees. Then everything around us became silent and still.

A colossal Dragon the color of crimson blood emerged from a large opening. The Dragon pushed itself up and shook off layers of his grave. Its forearms were tipped with dagger-sharp claws and its horns erupted from the crown of its head. It was smaller than Valda, but its eyes glowed with an intensity that mirrored hers. Its jaws were lined with teeth as long as dinner knives, and its mouth opened wide to reveal an inferno of fire. With its wings stretched wide, it ascended into the air.

Valda watched in triumph as the Dragon rose. "Rovar, Hadeon. Mir'kyn. Mir'kror. Mir'destruktor," she said.

Erjon translated again. "Rise, Hadeon. My brother. My warrior. My destroyer."

The edge in Erjon's voice didn't go unnoticed. Something about the way he said Hadeon's name. And that Valda called Hadeon a destroyer. I didn't like the sound of it. Both Dragons lifted higher into the sky until they were concealed behind the clouds.

"We need to leave," I said. We needed to get to the city. I didn't bother explaining; it would only delay us longer. Instead, I stood and ran back toward Zari. The others followed me quickly, not bothering to conceal their movement. "We need to leave," I repeated louder once we were back on the path.

"Agreed," Calian said. He mounted Dhruv and pulled the reins, turning Dhruv back toward the direction of the city.

"We've seen enough."

"I will transform and go after them. You get to the city."

"Be careful," Calian said.

I nodded and reached deep within my power to start the transformation. But when I did, another wave of exhaustion flowed through my bones, and I staggered forward.

"What's wrong?" Morwen asked with worry.

"I don't know. Transforming seems to take a lot of energy from me, I guess." I glanced at Erjon, but he just raised an eyebrow. He didn't answer.

"I'll just ride Zari for now for a brief rest. Then I'll transform again," I managed between quick breaths. "Zari's fast, so I won't be far behind them."

"Go as fast as she can take you," Calian ordered.

I nodded and took off. As we approached a fork in the path ahead, a man clothed in black pants and boots but no shirt, stepped out from the bushes. Zari halted with a loud whinny and raised onto her hind legs to keep from colliding with him. I fell off her back and onto the hard ground. My chest hurt from the impact, and I coughed in response. I struggled to sit up, so I rested back on my elbows to catch my breath while Zari remained in a protective stance in front of me until the other three caught up.

Once Calian had arrived, Zari's anxiety eased a little, and

she moved to the side, revealing the stranger before us. Standing in the middle of the path was a man a little older than Calian. He leaned from one side to the other, tilting his head to study us. His fiery red eyes darted back and forth between us all before settling on me. A wolf-like grin spread across his face, exposing pointy teeth.

"It's been so long," he drawled, his expression cold. He looked straight ahead at Calian. Calian's forehead creased, and his eyebrows knitted together.

"I don't know what you're talking about," Calian responded gruffly. Dhruv grunted and kicked at the ground, readying himself to charge.

The man snorted. "Pity," he said.

"Emera, my dearest friend."

The hairs on my arms stood up straight, and my pulse's rhythmic heartbeat became rapid and uneven, struggling to keep pace with my thoughts which ran wild in my head. Quick shallow breaths escaped my lips and sweat beaded from my forehead and my hands began to tremble. My elbows gave out a little, and I fought to stay upright. I knew that voice.

Valda stepped out from the trees and stood beside the man on the path, her black silk gown sweeping the ground as she walked.

CHAPTER SEVEN
CALIAN

Seeing Valda alive and well made me want to blast a blaze of smoldering fire at her smug face. But my head told me to remain calm. Emotions killed people, and I'd never forgive myself if my friends lost their lives due to my inability to control my temper. Dhruv sensed my inner turmoil because he, too, was restless. The steed kicked and snorted, making it known he was ready and willing to fight. He was the best godsdamn horse any man could have.

Valda stepped past the stranger. I immediately slid off Dhruv and ran to Emera, putting myself in between them. If Valda wanted to get to Emera, she had to get through me. I was nowhere near as powerful, but I'd put up a fight. One good enough for Emera to escape.

The Dragongoddess cackled. "Calian Westbow. You're looking good." Her eyes flashed with amusement, and she widened her smile. She swiped her tongue over the top row of her white teeth. I wanted nothing more than to knock them out.

Keep your cool, Cal, I told myself.

Although he wasn't there—thank the Dragongods for that—Fin's voice filled my head, warning me to stay level-headed. But what I'd come to find out was that I couldn't do that when Emera was nearby. It didn't matter that we weren't Dragonmates. Her life was more important than my own.

"I can't say the feeling is mutual," I retorted. I let my Dragonmagic flow wildly within me like a caged beast ready to pounce.

Anwir stepped out from the trees and joined the other two. "Now, Calian, my boy. It would behoove you to be polite when you're in the presence of a Dragongoddess. I know I taught you better than that."

"I'm not your boy," I growled.

Anwir's grin widened, and his eyes flashed green. "Now that is the truth, isn't it?" He took a few steps back, giving me the space needed to think about what he'd said. He meant it to be a loaded statement of unknown context. I looked at Valda, but her expression remained the same. Why didn't she attack? The man behind her continued to be silent as well. Just more secrets about who I was. It infuriated me even more.

With gusto, I hurled a ball of fire at Anwir's head. Anwir dodged, but not quick enough. The fire connected with his shoulder, and he threw himself to the ground, howling in pain. He frantically rolled back and forth until the flames went out. A plume of smoke rose into the air from his scorched clothes.

"I really hope I left a mark," I jeered. I called to another flame and let it dance in my palm.

Anwir whipped his head around and glared, which I met with a sneer. This exchange of expressions seemed to upset him even more. He stood and discarded his jacket which now had a large hole. His white silk shirt also had a hole, exposing his scalded flesh. He discarded that, too. Then he threw out his hand, and a swirl of dust circled around me, cutting off my vision from him. But the dust only circulated a couple of times before they dropped to the ground. My eyes focused on Valda, and I snarled at the goddess.

"I'm so over your little spats," she said while her hand guided the last of the dust to the ground.

Morwen cleared her throat, drawing Valda's attention away from me and onto her. Her back was straight, and her shoulders were relaxed. She maintained a commanding presence with a relaxed expression. This woman was no longer Morwen, Dragonheir of Anahita. She was Princess Morwen Elderbrook, a diplomat of the six kingdoms. "Are you here to kill us?" Morwen asked, getting right to the point. My shoulders tensed as I waited for the answer. I had no fear of death. But the others? I just couldn't let that happen. I wouldn't.

Valda waved her hand lazily. "The thought has crossed my mind."

Anwir snickered in response, and the stranger's face finally changed. His eyes looked past me and landed on Erjon. I knew that look. He was sizing up his competition, and by the twinge of his mouth, he'd decided that Erjon would be his first victim. The man's eyes then drifted to Morwen and squinted slightly, indicating she would be his next kill. I hated to admit it, and I never would do so aloud, but between the four of us, Erjon and Morwen just weren't as strong.

The stranger's eyes slid to mine, and we locked onto one another.

Me next, I thought. I flashed my teeth. *I won't make it easy for you,* I thought.

Finally, his gaze tore away from me to Emera–the strongest of us all. She stood now, brushing the dust off the silk night dress she wore while her eyes remained locked onto Valda's every move. Her purple chaos magic crackled at her fingertips. But I couldn't help but notice the strain on her face.

I shifted my focus and studied Anwir who was also taking an interest in Emera. It wasn't difficult to notice that the flimsiness of her dress hinted at her womanly figure. The fabric clung to her curves. Small cuts and holes in the fabric, which had been ripped open from her fall, exposed her smooth ivory skin decorated with tiny freckles. Anwir's nostrils flared as he audibly swallowed his desire. Disgusting. Flames burst from my palms, and I stepped in front of her, shielding her body from his prodding eyes.

"Look away," I demanded. "Or you'll lose more than clothes. You'll lose limbs."

"Do it," Valda said with amusement in her eyes. "I'd love to see it."

Anwir pressed his lips together tightly, holding hostage the words he was desperate to say. One day, I'd make sure that he was no longer alive to say anything. I didn't relish the thought of taking another man's life, but for him, I'd make an exception.

Emera put a hand on my shoulder, anchoring me to the present and away from my murderous thoughts. Her body heat warmed my back and the electric feeling I constantly yearned for was back. How in the hell was she not my Dragonmate? It was like a sick game the gods played on us.

"I've got this," she whispered. Godsdamn right, she did. Chaos magic started to build at her palms.

"It's amusing that you think so," Valda purred.

Emera paused at Valda's choice of words. Her jaw muscles tightened, and she clenched her fists, extinguishing her magic. After a few deep breaths, her shoulders relaxed. It appeared that shifting took more energy out of her than I'd thought.

Valda took note, and her eyes flared with joy. "Did you enjoy my father's gift?" she asked Emera.

Emera didn't respond immediately, but after a minute she replied, "I would have discovered how to change on my own."

"Of course, you would have. He just sped up the process. Wasn't it nice to have someone help you that actually knows what they're doing?" She looked at me and winked. Emera's fingers dug into my shoulder, commanding me to stay. She knew me well.

A smile tugged at the goddess's lips. "Come with me, and he can show you everything."

Emera stepped around me. "First, you wanted to kill me. Now, you want me to join you?" she pressed, her voice firm. That was my girl. Dragonmate or not.

The goddess shrugged like she expected that to be her response. "Father's orders." She turned to the stranger. "But since he isn't here, maybe Hadeon would like to have a little fun?"

Hadeon nodded curtly in return. That wasn't a good sign. I reached for Emera's hand right when Valda snapped her fingers. Thick purple smoke filled the air, covering her completely and blocking our view. It was just like the smoke that had enveloped Emera when she transformed into her Dragon form earlier. When the smoke cleared a little, Valda was already in the sky. I searched the area for Anwir, but he was gone. Of course, he was. He was a coward, and I was a fool for thinking he wasn't. But there was no time for complaining about the past. Hadeon was the present, and he was a problem. I intended to deal with the problem on my own so that Emera could get back to the city.

"Zari, take Emera back to the city!" I commanded over my shoulder. Although I couldn't speak to Zari like Emera could, I knew she'd understand me. Emera needed to get to the city, and Zari was the fastest horse I'd ever seen.

But before mounting Zari, Emera pulled me close to her and grabbed my face with both of her hands. "I need to go after Valda."

"Can you shift? I saw your struggle earlier. Any type of magic seems to tire you."

She rested her forehead on mine and whispered. "I can do it. Let them help you." She meant the others.

I pulled her in and kissed her. It was raw and passionate. A kernel of yearning formed in the pit of my stomach. If she died, I would never be the same again.

She pulled away, stepped back, and ran into the woods. A trail of purple smoke started to follow her. Her transformation began. I hoped she'd be able to manage it.

The air shifted around me, bringing with it a cloud of dense red smoke that enclosed around us all. After a few moments, a thunderous roar filled the forest, and a large Dragon stepped out from the smoke. We were in the presence of the Dragon that Valda had resurrected.

Hadeon towered over us all with sharp claws digging into the ground, his body radiating malevolence and power. His scales were deep red, the color of the blood he'd likely spilled from his enemies during the war. Jagged spikes protruded down his back, and his wings were tattered and torn, adorned with scars from countless battles. He was a descendant of the Dragongod Vukan, which meant he'd betrayed Nimerah and his father, the only gods I inherently trusted. It made me loathe him even more.

When I peered into Hadeon's eyes, pure evil and a hunger for vengeance greeted me. His eyes gleamed, and he opened his mouth, revealing rows of dagger-like teeth that were honed to perfection for the purpose of ripping flesh and shattering bone. From deep within his throat, a mix of smoke and flame coiled together. This moment was personal for him, yet I didn't know why. He wanted me dead. And although I was prepared to die, it wouldn't be at his hands...or claws.

"No!" I yelled and blasted an explosion of hot flame toward the beast just as his mouth emitted an eruption of fire.

As our flames intertwined, he let out a low snarl. But he stood his ground and attempted to overpower my flames. We could have been there for an eternity if it weren't for a wave of water that rose above me and fell, distinguishing the fire between me and the Dragon.

Morwen stepped forward on my right side, her eyes glowing a sapphire blue. Then Erjon–with his silver eyes– stepped up to my left, his hands at the ready with swirls of wind circling them. Dark clouds rolled in from the east and lightning streaked across the sky. Thunder boomed as the clouds connected with each other. Erjon's magic was impressive, but it wouldn't be enough. My energy fully replenished—not that I'd lost much—I brought forth a scorching fire that flickered in the blowing wind.

What we thought was another bout of thunder turned out to be a roar of a Dragon. Emera. Above the tree line, a magnificent violet Dragon lifted into the skies and immersed itself in the clouds. Emera was going after Valda. I admired her bravery. In fact, I loved her for it. Involuntarily, my hand placed itself over the pair of purple Dragonwings branded over my heart. Emera was my mate, regardless of whether she had a matching pair or not. I vowed to tell her those words when I saw her again.

Intense magic took hold of me, forcing my attention away from the Dragon in the skies and to the one standing in front of me. "Focus on the situation at hand," Erjon barked, and he withdrew his empathic magic from my body. He was right. At this moment, we had a Dragon to put back in its grave.

Erjon pushed his hands out, and a gust of wind went with them. The wind was so strong, Hadeon staggered backward, lost his balance, and stumbled to the ground. Erjon raised his hand and brought down a bolt of lightning into Hadeon's hide. I never knew that Erjon had the power to call down lightning, but Ilmari was the goddess of air and that meant the sky. It seemed like there was more power to the Dragongoddess than I had thought.

Hadeon roared in pain, but the lightning only stunned him, unable to completely penetrate his scales. His eyes glinted with fierce intensity while he shook his head to steady himself. He was furious.

Flames traveled down my arms, ready to be unleashed in streams of searing fire. "You couldn't have antagonized him any better, Erjon. So good going with that. We need a plan now! Any suggestions?"

"Can you create a ring of fire around him?" Erjon asked.

"Of course."

"Morwen, can you bring forth a powerful wave of water into his mouth?"

Morwen's eyebrow rose. "I can," she answered.

"We must time this perfectly. When I give the word, Morwen must first make sure that he cannot fly. Calian will trap him within the flames. Then, Morwen, when the beast opens its mouth, propel your water deep into him. I will do the rest."

By the time Erjon's plan—whatever it was—was set in

motion, the Dragon was back on its feet. I ran to Dhruv and hoisted myself up as quickly as I could so that I could ensnare the beast. I grabbed Dhruv's reins just as I witnessed Hadeon lash his tail into Erjon's stomach, sending my friend backward into a tree. Erjon cried out in pain from the impact, slid down the tree trunk he'd been thrown into, and went still.

"Time for Plan B, I guess," I told Dhruv. Dhruv snorted. He knew I didn't have a Plan B.

The Dragon moved toward Erjon for the kill, but Dhruv whinnied to get his attention. Gods, I loved my horse. I patted him to show my approval of his quick thinking.

Hadeon whipped his head toward me, his eyes possessed by unrelenting anger. Why this Dragon had it in for me, I didn't know. And I didn't have time to sit down and have a conversation with him.

Dhruv charged, but Hadeon was prepared. He flapped his massive wings, creating gusts of wind that forced Dhruv back. I held on tightly to the reins as Dhruv struggled against the wind until his knees buckled, and we tumbled to the ground. Hadeon–thinking Erjon and I were subdued–turned his attention to Morwen. I looked up from where I'd landed on the ground to see him take two ground-rumbling steps toward her. Morwen lost her balance and fell to her knees just as the Dragon lunged forward, catching only air between its jaws. Morwen, now laying on her back below the beast, threw up sharp icicles that pierced his wings. He roared in pain and retreated backward. The Dragon attempted to fly, but the icicles were so heavy, he couldn't lift his wings.

"Now!" Erjon yelled. He managed to crawl back to Morwen with his hand stretched out, blowing a fierce wind into Hadeon that forced the Dragon to stumble back further away from us. Dhruv was already upright and waiting for me, so I mounted him again. He ran around Hadeon whose eyes widened with a mixture of confusion and pain. As we circled him, I blasted towering flames onto the ground, cutting Hadeon off from us except where Erjon and Morwen stood. Hadeon was trapped. So far, Erjon's plan had worked.

Hadeon let out a low growl, exposing his sharp teeth like a cornered animal. His long neck vibrated, and it would only be seconds before a blazing fire erupted from his jaws. Morwen stood ready, her hands already dripping with moisture. When Hadeon opened his mouth wider, Morwen blasted water down his throat. Erjon's hands began twisting, forming wind in a circular motion around Hadeon's snout, snapping it shut and holding it closed. Hadeon fought to open his mouth and expel the water that filled his lungs. But he couldn't. The Dragon dropped to the ground and convulsed furiously. We stood silent as the Dragon drowned.

"That took three of us," Morwen said beside me. "Imagine an entire army." As much as she tried to hide it, the pain in her voice was there.

My eyes remained locked on the dead Dragon. "Then we better figure out a way to stop any more of those rituals from happening."

CHAPTER EIGHT
CALIAN

"Go after Emera," Erjon said, breaking the silence between the three of us.

I grabbed Erjon by the shoulders and pulled him close. "Get back to the palace. Warn Queen Eteri," I ordered and pushed him toward his horse—a little too roughly.

Morwen stepped toward me. "Take Zari. She is faster than your steed. I'll follow Erjon."

I didn't think twice. I ran to Zari and leaped up on her saddle. Without a command, she raced ahead. I'd always known her to be faster than any horse I'd ridden, but I still wasn't prepared for the speed at which she could run. The trees and mountainside became a blur, and the wind stung my face. After just a few minutes, the surrounding trees thinned out until there were no more left to offer me protection. The outline of the City of Ilmari was visible in the distance, untouched by flame or smoke, so I searched the skies for the two Dragons. Erjon's storm was still overhead, a cacophony of lightning, thunder, and wind.

In the open sky, Valda burst through a wall of gray clouds with Emera following closely behind her. They weaved back and forth, missing each lightning bolt that highlighted the outlines of their bodies in the dark atmosphere. They clashed in mid-air. Valda spewed torrents of searing flames. Her fire was strong, but Emera didn't waver. The warrior within her retaliated with blasts of icy breath, creating clouds of mist and sleet. Valda dove downward, hoping to lose Emera, but Emera followed without hesitation. Valda stopped abruptly, and the sky trembled as their colossal forms collided. Waves of chaos energy rippled through the air.

Twisting and turning, the Dragons spiraled through the sky. Valda continued to spew flames while Emera blasted frost. My mouth gaped open from the awe of the Dragons and bursts of steam that clouded the sky. The air echoed with the thunder of their roars, and the wind howled in response to their struggle.

Valda suddenly dove at an angle toward the nearest mountainside, and Emera trailed her. Just before Valda's impact of the jagged rocky terrain, she twisted upward, passing Emera and rising higher into the sky. Emera's reflexes weren't as quick, probably due to the exhaustion of transforming. I cursed at myself. I shouldn't have let her shift.

Then, to my horror, Emera soared into the side of the mountain. Her tail whipped back and forth, trying to wrap itself around any large tree or a boulder, but there was nothing to anchor her. She clawed desperately at the mountain but failed to slow down her fall. My eyes widened in terror when her body smashed through trees and hit the ground.

"Run, Zari!" I yelled. Terror seized my throat and closed it, making it impossible to breathe. "Please be alive, please be alive, please be alive," I pleaded to Vukan. Even if I wasn't his heir, he was the only Dragongod I felt connected to.

Zari sensed my panic. Although she ran at the fastest speed possible, her body was tense. With a determined purpose, her hooves pounded the earth in a rhythmic cadence of power. Her muscles rippled beneath her sleek coat, and with each stride, she propelled herself forward. She was the living embodiment of speed.

Seconds became agonizing minutes which felt like days. We finally reached the spot where Emera had landed. But there wasn't a Dragon to be found.

I slid off Zari and frantically searched through the broken trees, lifting and throwing away limbs. A sharp pain in my chest forced me to pause and catch my breath. I couldn't find her. Where was she? My Dragonmagic blazed to life, and I clenched my fists to keep from lighting the bushes and trees on fire.

Focus, Cal, I thought, and I suppressed the need to unleash my fire.

The ruffling of leaves and a slight cough sounded a mere ten feet from where I stood. Emera crawled out from underneath a pile of torn branches and got to her feet.

"Calian," she mumbled, and her body swayed before she stumbled toward me. I reached her just in time to catch her as she collapsed into my arms.

"I'm here," I whispered and kissed the top of her head. She was naked, bloodied, and bruised. My heart ached at the sight of what Valda had done. I scooped her up and tried to inspect the damage, but it was difficult to make out the extent of her injuries because of the blood that covered her body. The heat I'd suppressed earlier ignited beneath my chest.

Worried that I would hurt her more, I laid Emera down on a large patch of grass and took deep breaths to push down my fear and anger. Those two emotions were a dangerous combination for me, and I couldn't risk hurting her further.

I ran my hand through my hair; something I'd done since I was a child to help steady myself. It wasn't helping. My thoughts were frantic as panic settled in. Where was Fin when I needed him? He always knew what to say. Even Erjon would be helpful. But neither of them was there to help, and I needed to act fast. Emera's breathing was now ragged. She was dying.

Memories flooded my mind as I recalled the night in the camp when Emera had drunk Stormshade. I had been quick to blame her and Morwen. But the truth had been that I was scared. Scared of my growing feelings for her. Scared of her dying. Scared of opening myself up.

I'd always had a hunch that I wasn't just the Dragonheir of Vukan. Fire magic wasn't the only power I possessed. I could heal myself, and even though I couldn't read someone's mind, I tended to know what the person was thinking. I was stronger than almost all Dragonborn—at least those I'd met—and if I was persistent enough, I could tap into the other elements. I could cast light in a darkened room or create a small rain shower. Dragonmaster Anwir had always surmised that it was because of my duty as Emera's deliverer and future general. Ragnar must have given me some of his magic. Something told me there was more to it—more to me—than that. The only other person who knew of my additional abilities was Fin. I vowed not to tell anyone else, but the more my feelings grew for Emera, the more I wanted to share everything with her.

Regardless of what Dragonmagic I had; it wouldn't be enough to heal her fully—I wasn't that powerful. "I'm going to need your help again, Em," I whispered. I held my hands over her heart as I'd done that night and prayed to the Dragongod Endrit. Would he help me save her?

A faint luminescence emitted from my fingertips, casting a gentle glow that hovered over Emera's body. With a heavy breath, I thrust all my Dragonmagic into it. My magic responded to the call, building up through my body, and trickling down my arms like shimmering threads of energy. The light grew brighter and brighter, just as it had done before.

The light bent and weaved, flowing like liquid silk while it worked. It was a warm sensation. As it touched her skin, the light gradually eased her pain and comforted her. My magic sought out all of Emera's ailments. I attempted to make the magic as gentle as possible, but truth be told, I didn't know how. Deep down, I hoped I had the power needed to heal her.

"I need you to take this light, Em. Take it and all my magic. Heal yourself. Please," I pleaded, and tears stung my eyes. I didn't know what it was about this girl, but the thought of losing her sucked the air right out of me.

The light faded along with my magic. "Emera. Hold onto it! Live!" With one last push, I gave the rest of my magic to her. The healing light glowed brightly, and Emera stirred, her features relaxing as if a weight was lifted. Color returned to her cheeks, and her breathing deepened into a steady, rhythmic pattern. My luminous threads withdrew themselves. Her eyes fluttered open just as mine closed, plunging me into darkness.

*　*　*

Darkness surrounded me even after I opened my eyes. I sat upright, flames ready in my palms.

"Please do not be afraid."

The darkness lifted suddenly, and a strange woman stood before me. She was a beautiful woman with black hair, pale skin, and black eyes. She wore a black gown, a pure manifestation of night. We were back in the palace of

Ilmari—my chambers to be exact. But my senses told me we weren't really in my chambers. Everything looked perfect, but anyone who knew me knew that my bed chambers were never perfect. Clothes would be in random piles on the floor, chairs would be positioned awkwardly, and I wouldn't have multiple blankets. Like the numerous ones that now covered me. I pushed them off me and onto the floor. I could feel the sweat dripping down my back.

"Who are you?"

The woman didn't answer. My patience was thin. I needed to get back to Emera to see if she was okay—if she was alive. Because if she wasn't…I swallowed a large gulp that formed in my throat and pushed out the thought that I'd failed saving her life.

I got up from the bed I'd been lying on, but fatigue seized my bones and forced me back down to the bed. I sat for a moment and concentrated on replenishing my strength. Then the voice filled my head again. This time, I could hear her clearly. It was Emera's voice.

Deep breath in and slow release. Deep breath in and slow release. You are in no danger.

"You were weakened when you saved her. You spent a lot of energy ensuring she lived. Give it a moment, and your energy will return."

"I will ask again," I replied between deep breaths, "Who are you?"

"Who I am is irrelevant at this moment. It is what I need that matters. What I need is for you to take Emera back to the Kingdom of Water. For one, Nimerah is dying. Only Emera has the power to heal her. Secondly, my uncle won't strike until he knows Nimerah is dead, so he is searching tirelessly for her while his minions resurrect the dead. Time is of the essence." The woman walked to the balcony window. When she pulled back the curtain, my suspicions were confirmed. The Mystral Mountains should have been sitting beneath a full moon in all their glory. Instead, I saw a shimmering lake below a sparkling night sky painted in hues of dark purple and blue with speckles of black mixed in. The woman glanced cautiously to the left then right before closing the curtains.

"This is the Dragonplane of Existence," I said. I stood once more, but I took it slower. I planted my feet firmly on the floor and balanced my weight. My head didn't spin this time and my body felt lighter.

"Very perceptive."

"Why are you telling me this? Why not Emera?"

The woman clasped her hands and crossed to the chamber door. "Because he is watching her every move."

"Amram."

"Correct. Emera's mind is compromised."

I nodded, not caring to ask for her name again. The mention of Amram being her uncle along with her appearance was all the information I needed. I stood in the presence of Tamasvi, the Dragongoddess of Darkness.

"The Kingdom of Water, you said?"

"Yes."

"Emera already thinks Nimerah is near Medora."

"A wise assumption. Nimerah did favor the islands near there."

"I don't suppose you know exactly where Nimerah is?"

"Sadly, no. She withheld that information for my safety." She opened the door and peaked out. She closed it in a hurry and rushed toward me, her hand rising toward me. "You must return to Emera."

"What are you doing?" I asked as she got closer. My shoulders tensed and flames crackled at my fingertips.

She pressed two fingers to my forehead. "Do not be afraid, Calian Westbow."

CHAPTER NINE
EMERA

"You look terrible." Senna opened the curtains to my room, exposing the midday sun. I winced. The golden rays reflecting off her white fighting leathers stung my eyes. I'd been sulking in the darkness of my quiet room, trying to hide from my shame.

"So nice of you to say," I mumbled.

"Someone needs to give you a swift kick in the butt. You need to get out of here. You've been in here for a couple of days."

"Well, the next time you fly into a mountain and have to

walk back to the city naked, how about you come find me and tell me how you feel," I snapped. I quickly covered my mouth, embarrassed for my brazen words. "I'm sorry."

Senna tipped her head back and laughed, clearly unbothered. Her curls bounced on her shoulders with each breath and escaped her lips. "Good! Hold onto that spirit."

I rolled my eyes. "Who sent you?"

She feigned shock. "I'll let you know that I came of my own free will. You need someone who will tell you like it is. So, look. This whole thing with Amram being stuck in your head is only going to get worse if you hide away sulking. Instead, you need to channel that energy into something that will make you stronger. Put on some clothes and meet us in the training ring."

I opened my mouth to argue that we were trying to find a way to keep Amram out but I knew it would lead to arguing, and I didn't have the energy for it.

She stood and strode to the door and paused after opening it. "It's going to sound harsh, but you've got to pull yourself together. We're counting on you."

"No pressure there."

"Pressure is sometimes a necessary means to discovering your strength."

I leveled my gaze. "Did Erjon feed you that line?"

Her mouth spread in a devious grin. "You're strong, Emera. Start acting like it."

She closed the door behind her just as the pillow I threw at her head hit the wall. She didn't know the fatigue that transforming had caused me, and the whole situation angered me. When my Dragon mother had given me her blessing at the cave, I had transformed into a confident Dragongoddess capable of overcoming anything. But now? Amram stole that confidence. What happened on the mountain didn't help. One minute, I was flying after Valda. The next, my power gave out.

The only way I'd get back my power and confidence would be to pull myself out of the pitiful hole I'd dug and be who I was born to be. To do that, I needed to master putting up mental blocks—our original goal. I needed Morwen.

I changed out of my plain gown into a set of form-fitting fighting leathers; a gift from Queen Eteri. The leather was so dark the entire ensemble was almost black. But in certain lighting, one could make out the deep purple hue. The sides were laced from under my arms to my ankles, and a thick belt wrapped around my waist, adorned with holsters for small blades.

I weaved the strands of my thick red hair into two intricate braids just like Avani taught me. I looked like a warrior.

Now it was time to act like one.

The hallway outside my room was drafty. Little sunlight was visible due to the lack of windows, and the sconces on the walls weren't lit. The cool air roamed freely, and the leather that clung to my body wasn't enough to protect me from the chill temperature. Fire magic ignited within me and spread throughout my limbs, creating a cocoon of warmth. I was warm, but I was still uncomfortable.

"Emera!"

And in an instant, Morwen's voice provided the comfort I needed.

"I've been looking for you," she said. She looked stunning as ever in plain black pants, riding boots, and white tunic. "We are all meeting Calian and Fin in the ring. We have another day before the Winged Warriors are back, so Calian thought it would be beneficial for all of us to train together."

She took my arm in hers, and we continued toward the grand staircase. "I have more news. I was sword fighting with Fin when he mentioned something regarding our attempts to push Amram from your mind. It was quite interesting and may prove useful."

"Well, let's hear it. What does Fin think I should do?"

"He mentioned that we should not be using Dragonmagic

to push Amram out. We need to solidify a barrier so that he cannot even get in."

"How do I do that?"

We rounded the corner to the palace's grand staircase, which was my favorite part of the castle. It was the focus of the palace, constructed of smooth marble with swirls of varying shades of gray. Its steps—which widened out the further one went down—were covered with a dark gray velvet runner that matched most of the furniture in all the chambers. Whenever I walked up it, I imagined myself ascending into the heavens to see the Dragongoddess Ilmari. Funny how a staircase could bring a sense of peace.

A sly smirk crept up on Morwen's face. "Let us go find out," she said.

I pulled my arm from hers and playfully yanked her back. "Last one to the ring is a rotten Dragonegg," I yelled and took off running down the hall. I careened around a corner, knocking into a gray vase adorned with intricate etchings. I was lucky that a servant happened to be standing close by and caught the vase before it shattered. "So sorry!" I yelled and sprinted around him. The look on his face—he was clearly angered by my clumsiness—sent me into a fit of giggles. The laughter made running and breathing difficult. But I was determined to beat Morwen to the ring.

Other palace staff jumped out of our way, yelling at us to be careful. I didn't care. My accelerated heartbeat and the blood pumping furiously through my veins were exhilarating. I was actually having fun, and I really did miss having fun.

I ran past the kitchens, rounded a corner, leaped down some narrow stone steps, and pushed through the doors that led outside. Morwen was close behind. Her laughter indicated that she also enjoyed our game of chase. Once we'd cleared the palace gardens, the fighting ring came into view.

Calian and Fin were engaged in hand-to-hand combat…And both men were shirtless. I stopped dead in my tracks. Morwen slammed into my back, and I fell forward. Any air I had in my lungs was knocked out when my chest hit the hard ground. Morwen landed on top of me but rolled off quickly, mumbling her apologies among her gasps of air and laughter. I didn't care because I was too mesmerized by what I saw.

My gods, Calian was breathtaking. He was the physical embodiment of strength and power. His muscles flexed with every movement, and his broad chest rose and fell with each deep breath. His chiseled abdomen rippled as he twisted and turned from Fin's advances. It was a crime for anyone to look as good as he did. Between two swings from Fin, Calian caught me staring at him. A hint of a smile pulled at the corner of his mouth, and I turned away guiltily.

Sweat dripped down my brow from the sweltering heat. Okay, it wasn't from the heat because an ache of desire resonated within my core. It was the reaction I got whenever I saw Calian—shirtless or not. Unlike the electric feeling we shared, my body's new physical response to him was foreign to me. I didn't know how to manage it because it wasn't just desire. No, it clearly was more than that. Despite feeling older than my seventeen years—thanks to recent events—I couldn't define what was happening to me. I wasn't his Dragonmate, so none of it made sense. I thought about talking to someone, but I didn't know who. Morwen? It seemed like too scandalous of a subject for her. Senna? Avani? Yeah, maybe Avani. She never shied away from emotions or feelings.

"You've got to be quicker than that," Calian growled, and he shoved Fin back. Fin responded by throwing a quick jab, but Calian twisted his torso, escaping the blow. Calian then retaliated with a punch of his own, but Fin blocked it just in time. Their dance of physical force continued until Morwen cleared her throat. Her eyes were wide, and her lips were slightly parted, both indicating she also enjoyed the show as much as I did. Maybe Morwen was the right person to talk to about my…*feelings*.

Calian's attention was on Morwen and not the fist that connected with his jaw. He staggered back and fell. A foul word escaped his lips as he checked his mouth for bleeding.

"Language, Calian," Morwen warned, her eyes locked on Fin.

"It was a cheap shot," he argued.

Fin helped Calian to his feet, and they sauntered over to us. Fin kissed Morwen on the cheek. "Thanks for the assist, my love," he whispered. A pang of jealousy hit my chest hard. More and more I wanted to receive that kind of love from Calian. Not just kissing in the hallway. Real, unadulterated love.

"An unfair assist," Calian mumbled.

Please put a shirt on, I silently begged. Did I really want him to? Yes. No. Yes. I didn't know. "Please put a shirt on!" I blurted.

Calian's lips slid into a lopsided smirk, and he sauntered over. "Am I bothering you?" he teased.

"I'm sorry to disappoint you, Cal," I said quickly—too quickly. "I just thought you'd want some leather to protect you when you and I go at it."

Calian dragged a hand slowly through his thick hair and

down the back of his neck. He crossed over to me and stopped with only inches between us. His broad shoulders tensed, and he let out a heavy sigh. "Fine," he drawled. "Do your worst."

"Excuse me?" I didn't think he'd actually want to spar.

He took a few steps back and threw out his hands. Flames ignited within them instantly.

I, too, took a few steps back to further the distance between us. I threw out my hands, calling to my chaos magic. But nothing happened. I thrust my hands out again, willing chaos magic to appear. But again, nothing happened. Confused, I glanced up at Calian.

"What's wrong?" He closed his fists, and the flames went out.

I shook my hands furiously. "I can't bring out my chaos magic!" My voice trembled from the panic buzzing within me.

"What about your other magic?" Morwen asked from behind me.

I took a deep breath and called to my air magic. Circling my wrists, I conjured swirls of air.

"And the others?"

One at a time, I called to each element. Earth, water, darkness, light, and fire. My magic worked, but by the time

I extinguished my flames, I was out of breath.

Tears stung my eyes. "Something is wrong."

Senna entered the ring. "What's wrong?"

The rest of our group arrived trickled in behind her—you would have thought Avani woke up in the middle of the night, she was that irritated. We spread out and stretched, and I tried to hide the disappointment from not sparring with Calian. It was the first time we were all together in the training ring. Normally, we took turns using the ring to hone our magic since there were so many of us.

Calian and Fin looked at me. *Please don't say anything*, I pleaded silently. He nodded slightly, acknowledging my request and then turned to face Senna. "What's wrong is that Amram keeps invading Emera's mind. Until she can keep him out…"

"Which will happen soon, I have no doubt," Morwen interrupted, stepping beside me. She squeezed my hand, and I smiled in return, grateful for her confidence in me.

Calian nodded. "Until she can keep him out, we need to be careful. There's no telling how much he knows. We stay tight-lipped about any plans, and we train in the meantime."

"Tight-lipped around her, you mean?" Senna asked. "Sorry, Emera, but Amram isn't in our minds. Strategic plans still need to be made."

I swallowed the lump that formed in my throat. She was right. They couldn't tell me any plans. "Senna's right. It would be foolish to just sit around and hope the monarchies will take care of the threat. You need to formulate a plan should the time call for it. I'll remain on the outside looking in. Only tell me what I need to know."

"Agreed," Erjon said.

Calian stood with his legs widespread and hands on his hips. "Well, now that that's settled. Let's begin. Line up!"

We did as he said—Erjon was reluctant—while Calian and Fin paced before us in opposite directions. They both sized us up and down. I was anxious to hear what they had planned.

"We have to work together, or we will fail. Today, we will practice our Dragonmagic against each other to prepare for what will surely be an all-out war. It's not here yet," Calian stopped mid-sentence and looked at me, "but it will be." His commanding voice took control of us, and we nodded in agreement.

"Wait," Senna said, and she pointed toward Fin. "What is that?"

"A Chaos Amulet." Fin puffed out his chest. "I have it because I'm special."

Avani snickered just as Senna asked, "Where did it come

from?"

I groaned.

"Well," Fin began, "The soldier—the one named Jimmu—was wearing this when he tried to shove a blade into Em's chest."

Calian looked at me, and the muscles in his jaw twitched. Fin and I had told him how we got the amulet, but we may or may not have forgotten to mention that Jimmu attempted to kill me. "Go on," he said between clenched teeth.

"Come to find out, Em's magic was useless because he was immune. So, I did what any friend would do…I killed him."

Avani drummed her fingers against her lips. "Jimmu didn't seem all that evil to me," she said.

"Oh, he wasn't. It was the amulet. It had some bad magic…or something," Fin told her.

"Yet, you're wearing it?" Morwen said, her eyes wide.

I shook my head. "When Jimmu wore it, it was red. When he wears it, it's purple. We think it's intended for Fin."

Erjon stroked his chin. "A logical assessment."

"Why are we just now hearing about this amulet?" Senna stomped closer to Fin, her eyes holding steady on the amulet. "It seems like something important to mention."

Fin backed up, his hands up in surrender. "I forgot.

Honest! I put it away in a bag for safe keeping. Then we got here, and I just forgot."

Kedron left the line and stepped beside Fin. "I've seen one of those," he said. "In King Tellus's palace." He reached for the amulet, but hesitated. "What would happen if I touched it?"

"If Fintan is intended to wear it, reasoning suggests that what happened to Jimmu would be your fate as well," Erjon surmised.

Kedron drew back his hand. "If I could get Fin to Dhara, we might be able to confiscate the other."

Erjon raised his eyes, thinking momentarily. "It might prove difficult getting the other amulet out of Dhara since we do not know who it belongs to."

"We'd find a way." Fin winked at Erjon before turning to face me. "However, despite being Dragonheirs, you cannot rely on magic alone. None of us truly knows what Amram is capable of. If he somehow renders your power useless, or you come across a soldier wearing one of these…" he held up the amulet he was wearing, "…then you will have to use good old-fashioned fighting skills. Consider what else you can wield should your powers not work."

Unbeknownst to the others, Fin was doing me a favor. I could use my bow in the ring today under the guise of training without magic.

"I am certain you'd find a way." Queen Eteri entered the training ring alone.

We all glanced at each other, confused by her appearance. A charming smile met Erjon's bland expression. "Please. Don't stop on my account. I have yet to see what you all can do." She took a seat on a nearby wooden bench. For some reason, she made me feel uneasy. I didn't like the idea of being observed by a queen. I held Queen Eteri in high regard; surely, she was only here to assess how we'd fit in with her Winged Warriors if it ever came to that. Right?

"Em?"

"Yes, Fin?"

"Would you like to give it a go?" He pointed to the amulet. "Can't use magic."

"Not a problem." I teleported back to my chamber, grabbed my bow and quiver of arrows, and teleported back. I swayed slightly from the fatigue of using my magic, but everyone was too busy talking to notice. Fin had already strapped his arrows to his back. He stood his ground with an air of confidence that he wouldn't normally possess if he were facing me without the amulet.

Our fighting commenced, and I drew my bow with precision and let loose a volley of arrows in quick succession. Although his agility and reflexes allowed him to sidestep the arrows, the amount of them forced Fin to relocate to another area of the fighting ring.

Undeterred, I continued my assault, adjusting my aim with each shot. Fin grabbed a nearby shield to deflect the next barrage of arrows I sent careening his way. He reached back and released a few of his own. Fighting him was nothing like hunting wild animals. He was quicker and more agile. We each shot arrow after arrow. Finally, he let fly his remaining three one right after the other. It was risky, but I reached back, grabbed an arrow, and quickly sent it flying into his leg. Then I dodged his arrows just before Fin cried out, more so from the surprise of actually being hit than from the pain. I ran directly behind him and pulled the final arrow from my quiver. I swung it in front of his neck, grabbed the other end, and tugged backward. Fin coughed from the force of the arrow's shaft pressed against his throat.

"Do you yield?"

"I yield." There was no animosity in his voice. In fact, he sounded proud.

I lowered the arrow, and that's when Fin attacked. He spun around and kicked me in the stomach. My back hit the ground, knocking the air out of my lungs. My vision spun, so I squeezed my eyes closed and breathed.

"An enemy will never yield. You must have that warrior instinct, Emera." He reached out his hand, and I took it. Back on my feet, I bowed, accepting my defeat. I couldn't help but plaster a smile across my face.

We all looked at Calian. He looked toward the sky, noticing the impending storm that was rolling in. "We're done," he declared.

CHAPTER TEN

EMERA

"You need more than magic to keep Amram out of your head," Fin said. It was the morning after our whole-group training, and we—including Morwen—were sitting in a secluded area of Ilmari's stunning gardens. Fin had pulled me aside the previous night and requested a meeting so that he could help with my *mental problem*—the magic kind, not the crazy kind. To which he then stated that he wasn't equipped for that kind of torture. I'd punched him in the arm for that one.

The sun decided to sleep the day away under a thick blanket of gray clouds, so the mountain air was cooler than usual. The abundance of flowers didn't seem to mind, though. White Mountain Lilies mixed with Ilmarian Jewel Blossoms decorated the gardens. The gentle cascade of water fountains that flowed into wishing ponds eased my soul, creating a sense of peace that I desperately needed. Hopefully, Fin had a beyond amazing idea because we were leaving for Medora the next morning. To be honest, I had wanted to leave sooner, but Calian convinced me that an additional day of preparation was needed. I wasn't made privy to the exact route or locations we'd be traveling to. All I knew was that we were heading toward Medora.

I trusted they had a solid plan; therefore, I didn't argue. Besides, there was no telling who—or what—we'd encounter during our travel, so I agreed. Plus, Erjon added that it was unwise to leave Ilmari unprotected. For some reason even Erjon couldn't explain, Valda hadn't touched the city after our encounter with her.

The Winged Warriors were due back any minute from training in the higher mountains. Queen Eteri had sent them there after finding out Amram was alive. She'd called them back after we told her about Valda. I perked up at that because I wanted to get a closer look at their winged contraptions.

Fin cleared his throat. "Focus, Em. Instead of using just

magic to push Amram out after he's entered your mind, you are going to use your imagination to build a barrier around your mind, creating a wall to keep Amram out completely. No more waiting for him to get in. You need to keep him out altogether." The smile on Fin's face indicated his excitement. He was pretty happy with himself for this idea, and I knew that deep down it was because he was human. There was still the stigma that humans were inferior to us all, so I desperately wanted it to work. Being human didn't mean being less than. Fin needed to know that.

"A wall. I think I can do that."

"Once you think you have your wall intact, let me know, and I will attempt to penetrate the wall," Morwen said.

"Got it." I closed my eyes and imagined myself in an open field. The field represented my mind, a vast space filled with joy and wonder. My emotions blew like a wind over the plush grass beneath my bare feet. I looked as far as my eyes could see and, in the distance, I saw the darkness. The darkness wasn't like the one Tamasvi told me to find solace in. No, this darkness was painted with fear and anger. Amram preyed on those emotions, so I needed to build my wall to keep myself separated from them.

I stared straight ahead and mentally constructed a thick wall made of pure obsidian stone. It was small at first, but the more I concentrated the taller it grew. It then expanded and formed a barrier around me, and I stood at its center, pleased with what I'd built. "Okay, Morwen. It's up."

Despite being far away from the wall itself, a distinct pounding on stones filled my ears. Morwen was trying to burst her way through. I chuckled as she struggled to break through my stone barrier. I had succeeded, and I wanted to tell Calian about it so much that I turned my back to where she was trying to enter. I took two steps but was cut off when Morwen fell from the sky and landed right in front of me. "Oh, hell," I muttered.

I opened my eyes and was back in the garden. Morwen had a smug look on her face, clearly satisfied with her performance.

"How did you do it?"

"I went over it."

"That's not possible! I built that thing as high as a mountain! You couldn't have jumped over it."

"It took me a moment to draw the conclusion that Amram would fly over if he couldn't power his way through."

"So, what you're saying is that I can't just build a wall. I need to build something like a fortress."

Fin put his hand on my shoulder. "It appears that way.

And once you do, you'll need to always keep it up."

I heaved a sigh and rolled my shoulders backward a few times. "Alright. Let's try again."

"Making progress?" Calian walked down a set of smooth gray steps and took a seat on a nearby stone bench.

Fin and Morwen glanced at each other and then at me. I sighed.

"She'll get it. Let's try again," Morwen said.

I closed my eyes and tapped into my magic

I was in an open space. I looked toward the darkness in the distance of my mind and hastily constructed a wall. The wall grew higher and higher and then I began to build it around me. Once it was closed off, I connected all the walls.

"That's not going to work, Emera. But I applaud your efforts." The walls crumbled and Amram stepped through the rubble.

I bit the inside of my cheek. I refused to show fear. I was a warrior.

"When will you learn?"

In an instant, my mind turned dark, and I was looking into Calian's concerned face. "Em?"

My body started shaking, and I fell to my knees. Calian rushed to my side.

"Amram was there. The fortress didn't work. He

shattered it with barely a thought." I peered into Calian's dark eyes, and I found fear.

CHAPTER ELEVEN
CALIAN

I entered an open room furnished with a large rectangular table at the center. It was surrounded by six lavish plush chairs in dark gray fabric. Bright paintings enhanced the gray walls with pops of color.

"Welcome to my private meeting room," Queen Eteri said. The queen sat at the head of the table.

"What's through those doors?" I asked. The doors were made of a sleek silver wood with the Mystral Mountains carved into them.

"My bed."

I smirked. We definitely weren't going in there. I turned

and leaned against the wall, waiting for the queen to explain why she had summoned me.

"Ah, here they come," Queen Eteri said. The doors opened once more and the monarchs of the Kingdom of Fire, Kingdom of Water, and—surprisingly—the Kingdom of Darkness walked through the door with Erjon and Fin following them.

King Orpheus Tynan smoothed out his black jacket with silver buttons before sitting down in a plush gray chair at the table. He tucked a strand of pale-yellow hair behind his ear, revealing his obsidian black scales. His pale face showed no hint of emotion. One of the many reasons that he was a king shrouded in misconception. The name Kingdom of Darkness carried a negative connotation throughout the other kingdoms. Apparently, darkness automatically meant evil. But I knew better. King Orpheus was loved throughout his kingdom and known as a benevolent king. He was admired and respected for his compassion and fairness toward his subjects. He ruled with a strong sense of justice, which I admired.

I'd encountered him only a few times through my time as Captain of the Nimerian Guard. I'd visited the kingdom with Anwir and attended meetings with the purpose of maintaining faith and trust between the kingdom and the council. Looking back, the meetings were only a ruse for Anwir to gain access to the kingdom's palace and knowledge of whether or not Orpheus would ally himself with Amram. From what I remembered of his character; Orpheus wouldn't ally himself with a traitor god.

Queen Eteri motioned for a servant to bring forth the wine he carried on a silver platter. "I'm so glad you've come," the queen said to her peers as she took a goblet off the tray.

King Calder Elderbrook took a seat opposite of King Orpheus, a wide smile illuminating his dark complexion and sapphire scales. He rested his arms on the table, his bright blue jacket and pants with silver stitching complimented the gray tone of the wood. "We are glad that you've welcomed us into your palace, Queen Eteri." He raised the goblet he'd just received in a toast to the queen. He placed the rim to his lips and drank slowly.

My attention was drawn to the woman who sat next to King Calder. Queen Hestia of the Kingdom of Fire was a beautiful woman of advanced years. She crossed her legs, revealing that she wore red pants and not the skirt I thought it was. Her top was more fitted with flowing sleeves that matched the billowy nature of her pants. I ogled at her, never having seen a queen wear pants before. The fabric was sheer enough from below the knee that one could see the crimson scales on her legs. She caught me staring but said nothing. Instead, she wiped away a stray wavy black curl that fell over her eyes.

"It seems we are missing a couple of our peers," Queen Hestia said.

Queen Eteri took a drink of wine and sat her goblet down. "Unfortunately, I received word from one of my ambassadors that Queen Leora has opened her kingdom to the Dragongod Amram. My other ambassador insisted that King Tellus will follow suit."

"Most unfortunate," King Calder replied before glancing around the room and spotting me. He rose from his chair, crossed over to me, and wrapped me in a hug. I couldn't hide the surprise from my face. "Captain Westbow! My boy. I didn't see you there." His tone dropped as he pulled away from me. "How are you holding up, son? Morwen relayed all that has happened. It must have been difficult for you."

My heart warmed when he called me his son. I'd been around King Calder a handful of times as a liaison between Anwir and the Kingdom of Water. During each visit he made me feel like family. "No apology necessary, your highness. I must admit that the past several weeks have been an adjustment. And speaking of, I must inform you that I am no longer a captain. There is no use for that title now." I clenched my jaw. It was the first time I'd officially renounced my rank as captain.

"I disagree," King Calder said. "Anwir being a snake doesn't negate your rank as Captain."

"Ah, yes, the former Dragonmaster," Queen Hestia spat. "Where has he slithered off to?"

"I am told he remains close to Amram," King Orpheus said.

Queen Hestia started to reply but stopped, her body tensing. Her eyes clouded over, and she frowned.

"What do you see?" King Orpheus asked her.

The queen closed her eyes, and after a few moments, opened them. Her eyes were back to the dark brown they once were. Her gaze swept around the room and landed on me for a split second. Then she turned her attention back to the king. "The fate of our kingdoms if we do not act."

As if reading my thoughts, Queen Eteri spoke up, "Queen Hestia has Dragonsight."

I glanced at Erjon then back to the queen. "Excuse me?" I looked at Queen Hestia for an explanation. I'd heard of Dragonsight before, but it was just a tall tale that no one believed.

Queen Hestia's eyes bore into mine, and for some reason I couldn't explain, my magic flared in response. "When I was little," she began, "my parents died of a horrible disease that swept through my village of Sol. I was only four years old, so my brother did the one thing he could think of, and that was to take me to the church in the City of Vukan. The Dragonpriestesses took me in, not caring that I was human. In fact, some were humans themselves. On my tenth birthday, I discovered I had Dragonsight."

"Dragonsight," I repeated slowly. Queen Hestia nodded.

"Amram doesn't know," she said.

King Orpheus leaned over the table, resting his elbows on its surface. "A seer is rare."

Queen Eteri slid her eyes from King Orpheus to me. "Hestia can see parts of the future."

"Kind of," Queen Hestia added. "I can see what might happen."

"If this is true," King Calder said with skepticism, "Amram will see you as a weapon."

Erjon finally spoke. "Amram will know the possible outcomes of his decisions. He will take whatever path results in the most human deaths, and the queen can give him that knowledge."

Queen Hestia's expression remained unchanged. She knew. "I received another vision several months ago."

"What did you see?" King Orpheus.

Queen Hestia didn't miss a beat. "Fire. And death." Silence haunted the room. "I immediately told my spy about it. About the lives lost as a result of a Dragongoddess rising to power. I ordered him to offer Anwir his services so that he could eliminate the threat."

I pushed forward from the wall. My magic flared once more, but this time from anger. The flames in the fireplace behind me rose, the heat pressing into my back. "Elio. You ordered Elio to kill Emera."

The queen didn't answer. Instead, she held out her hand, motioning for me to sit in the vacant chair next to her. I hesitated, not wanting to come close to her. "Let me show you," she said.

I gave in and sat down. She reached her hand out slowly and pressed two fingers softly to my forehead. Suddenly, the room went pitch-black and eerily still. The only sounds present were the inhale and exhale of my own heavy breathing.

I stood slowly, blinking several times until my eyes adjusted to the darkness. My eyesight was better than most Dragonborns when it came to seeing in the dark, but it still wasn't clear. My eyes could make out the outlines of shapes, but that was about it. I had to rely on my magic, so I summoned flames from my palms and took another step forward. For several minutes, I put one foot in front of the other, each step echoing in the darkness as I maneuvered my way through. Soon, the darkness started to lift. Suddenly, a sickening crunch sounded beneath the heel of my boot. I glanced down, lifted my foot, and lowered the light so that I could get a good look at what I'd stepped on.

It was a sight from a nightmare. Hollow sockets of a human skull stared at me. A large lump formed in my throat, and I forcefully gulped it down. Slowly, I shifted my eyes away from the skull to what lay around it.

Bones. So many bones.

Human bones, Dragonborn bones, and Dragon bones littered the ground where I stood. The bones shattered under the pressure of my leather boots. Additional magic flared in my other palm, and I cast it into the sky. Light filled the open space, revealing an expansive room. Piles of bones were everywhere, and they weren't alone. Mutilated and charred bodies lay among them. The foul stench of rotting flesh burned my nostrils and seized my insides. The contents of my stomach forced their way up, and I doubled over and heaved. From the corner of my eye, I caught a view that froze my heart.

Gods, no.

I angled my head and looked upon the bodies that were

strapped to the walls. My friends were in front of me, stripped of their clothing and hanging on display like trophies. Their eyes were wide, frozen in a constant state of shock. Blood dripped from their gaping wounds, splattering on the cold stone floor in a steady pattern. Drip. Drip. Drip.

"That wasn't all."

I whipped my head around to see Queen Hestia standing in front of pure white light. She was draped in a vibrant red cloak which contrasted with the bones beneath her feet that creaked and shifted with each careful step that she took forward.

Tears stung my eyes, but I pushed them down. The queen waved her hand and the scenery changed, swirling around me and blurring my vision. Once I was able to regain focus, I stood among rubble and ruin. The destruction went on as far as I could see, indicating that I was standing in what was once a thriving city. The air that surrounded me was thick, so much so that I struggled to breathe. The acrid scent of burning wood and scorched stone mixed with another foul odor that turned up my nose. It was blood and rot. I kicked over a pile of scorched wood beneath my feet. Lying face down was Emera, her body marred and distorted.

I threw myself to my knees. I reached for her but drew my hand back. This wasn't real. This couldn't be real. "What is this place?" I croaked.

"I hoped you'd recognize it."

Confused, my eyes searched frantically left then right, looking for something—anything—recognizable. My eyes didn't catch it at first. It was my nose. I inhaled deeply the familiar scent of saltwater. I exhaled, and my shock and fear subsided, replaced with a volatile rage that filled every part of my body. In the distance I saw the silhouette of a once sturdy wooden door amongst the wreckage. The same door that opened wide during the day, inviting travelers from all the kingdoms to enter. The same door that closed at night, protecting the Edevane family.

Fire tingled at my fingertips, ready to explode. "I will not let this happen," I said through clenched teeth.

Queen Hestia, now at my side, placed her hand in mine and nodded. "I know you won't, my—"

In the blink of an eye, we were back in the meeting room. Queen Eteri was immediately at Hestia's side. Queen Eteri held her elder's hand while she wiped the sweat away from her forehead. Queen Hestia's eyes were shut tight. Her Dragonmeld had taken quite a bit of energy from both of us.

"How?" I murmured, massaging my temples.

"No time for questions," Queen Hestia breathed. "We have work to do. We must ready our kingdom's armies."

"And what about Nimerah?" Erjon asked.

Queen Hestia's eyes met mine, and I nodded. "That's our task," I told Erjon. "We will find Nimerah."

A smile spread over Queen Hestia's face. "We shall depart for our kingdoms tomorrow."

CHAPTER TWELVE
EMERA

The Winged Warriors were a sight to behold. Men and women of different shapes and sizes made up the legion, and there was a lot of them. The training ring couldn't hold them all, so some lounged on the grass outside of it. Others passed me on their way into the gardens, bowing as they walked by, and some flew in the sky. Just like Tuuli and the Zeph in Erjon's memory. A shiver ran down my spine.

They were all Dragonborns—for good reason—except for a handful of their superiors. Queen Eteri employed humans—almost half of the palace staff included them—but to see them in military positions was unusual albeit refreshing. Much of what I knew about the co-existence between Dragonborns and humans had been from stories when I was back home. I grew up resenting them. It was true that in most areas throughout the six kingdoms, humans were inferior because they lacked any magical abilities. I'd always argued that humans made up for that with their abundance of strength and intelligence. I'd never met a Dragonborn who was smarter than my father. As much as I'd never admit it, Erjon was the only one to come close.

Calian and I were almost to the training ring when a burly man with blue eyes and brown hair tied at the base of his neck landed right in front of me, cutting me off from my next step. I lost my balance and fell forward into his remarkably large arms. My face was buried into his rock-hard chest.

"Sorry, miss!" he said. His voice was deep and gruff. More than Calian's which I didn't think was possible. "It's a little windy today. Got caught in a current and…"

Calian scowled at the stranger. "Be more careful next time."

"I'll be as careful as the wind allows," the man replied with a cool smile. He folded his arms in front of him which showcased the muscles of his chest even more. He wore a large contraption behind him constructed of leather, metal, and large feathers. They must have once belonged to an

Airian Eagle. I'd seen a picture of one once in a book my father bought me. It contained many birds and other winged animals from all over the six kingdoms. He was fascinated with birds. A quick stab at my heart reminded me of how much I missed him.

Calian cocked his head to the side. "I don't care if the gods above are blowing winds as powerful as a Kaimana hurricane…"

"I flew into one of those once," the man interrupted. "It was fun. Too bad it was to save the Dragonass of a scrawny man-child." His grin morphed into an arrogant smirk.

My pulse quickened and adrenaline coursed through me. Was I going to have to break up a stupid fight?

Calian took a step forward. "Scrawny? Man-child?"

Seconds ticked away. The two men stood silently, sizing each other up.

Calian took a deep breath and the corners of his mouth widened into a toothy grin. "Gods! It's good to see you, Zepherin," he said.

Zepherin? Wait. I did a double take at the man's face. He was older, but it was him. The man was Zeph. How had I missed it? This man was Erjon's brother.

"You, too, Cal!" Zepherin exclaimed, and the two embraced. As I attempted to decipher what had just transpired between them, Erjon cleared his throat to announce his presence. Zepherin released Calian and threw his arms around Erjon. He lifted the Dragonheir into the sky and twirled. Zepherin laughed while Erjon looked bored. Like normal.

Zepherin finally put Erjon back on the ground. "Onny! I haven't seen you in years, brother." He slapped Erjon on the back, and Erjon stumbled forward. He stood up and ran his hands down his shirt, smoothing out the wrinkles.

When the two men stood side-by-side facing one another, I finally realized how much they looked alike. The unmistakable resemblance was uncanny. They shared the same skin and hair color. Their facial structures were exact replicas, including the same cheeks, nose, and lips. The only differences between them were their size and eye color. Zepherin was the warrior with blue eyes and Erjon was the scholar with gray eyes. Both were Dragonborns, but only one was a Dragonheir.

"It's only been three months, Zepherin," Erjon remarked.

Zepherin laughed. "There's that sparkling personality I've missed."

For a split second, Erjon smiled. Then it was gone.

"Ahem!" Calian stepped up beside Zepherin. "As enchanting as this reunion is, I have some things I'd like to discuss."

Zepherin straightened his back. "I suspected as much." He pointed to the western mountains where the sun sat suspended overhead. "We saw the Dragons over the western mountaintops a few days ago. One larger than the other. Both purple. We had to get our men out of the air as quickly as possible. None of us had weapons on us, so we took cover."

"The smaller Dragon was me," I said and raised my hand like a silly schoolgirl. I immediately regretted the decision and pulled my hand down quickly. My cheeks reddened with embarrassment, not only from raising my hand, but because I'd flown straight into one of those mountains. Had he seen that?

"Impressive," Zepherin responded.

"Yeah, sure." My response came out squeaky.

Zepherin stared at me for a minute. "Which one of you slammed headfirst into the mountain?"

Great. I'd just met the guy, and he was humiliating me in front of everyone. Not that anyone else was paying attention to our conversation, but still. It was mortifying. "That would also be me," I mumbled.

"Emera had just learned how to shift into her Dragon form. Should probably cut her a little slack," Calian commented breezily.

Zepherin slapped me hard on the back. "No worries, miss! The first time I flew with these bad boys," he said, pointing to his winged contraption, "I flew straight into a tree and plummeted to the ground. The most embarrassing part was that on the way down, my pants got caught on a branch and ripped. All the new recruits got a good look at all of me. If you know what I mean."

I stifled a giggle.

"It's okay," he said. "You can laugh. Just like one day, you'll look back to that mountain and laugh."

"I suppose so," I said, but I didn't believe myself.

Zepherin moseyed toward the garden. Calian and I followed behind while Erjon quickened his pace to fall in step with Zepherin.

I couldn't contain my curiosity any longer. "Do you mind if I ask how those work?"

"My wings?"

Calian snorted. "No, your arms, Zeph."

"I don't think you want me to show your girlfriend how my arms work," he called over his shoulder.

Calian's expression didn't falter at Zeph's words, but I blushed.

We were at the edge of the gardens, but instead of straight back into the palace, Zepherin veered left down a short path.

The path led to four stone buildings, all marked differently. We stopped at the building that said Weaponry above its entrance. "Come inside and let me show you," Zepherin said.

The interior of the small building was laden with numerous weaponry racks stocked with blades and battle axes. Numerous winged contraptions of varying sizes lined the walls with benches beneath them. I imagined a warrior had to sit on the bench to strap on or take off their wings.

"Our wings are constructed of a lightweight metal for the frame. But don't be fooled when I say lightweight. These babies can withstand the strongest winds—even the ones my brother conjures up for us." He elbowed Erjon who winced from the pain. I was delighted to witness the interaction between the brothers. It painted Erjon in a more identifiable light. Like how he was in his memories.

Zepherin continued showcasing his wings. "It follows the curvature of our shoulders and spine so that the weight is distributed evenly, making it comfortable to fly with. Each harness is custom made so that it stays snug against our bodies as we twist and glide through the air."

"Impressive," I said. They were truly fascinating.

He looked quite pleased. "Absolutely! And check out this wingspan!" Zepherin pulled a tiny lever on the right side of his chest. The wings unfolded, their tips almost reaching each side of the room. "Each wing has several sections that can fold and unfold quickly. We control them with these levers. There is one on each side of my very broad chest…" He puffed out his chest and winked. Calian groaned while Erjon rolled his eyes. "One to unfold the wings, and one to bring them back in."

I slid my attention from him to the others. "So, then…How do you fly?" I waited for Erjon to make some snide remark about me asking a silly question, but he remained silent. True, I already knew how they worked because of Erjon's memory, but wouldn't it seem suspicious if I didn't ask? To the others, it was the first time I saw the wings.

"We use our magic. We lock our arms to our sides with our palms upward and expel air. We can control air flow from our hands into the wings to lift us, and once we're airborne, we push the air down so that we can stay up. It takes a lot of practice to master the skill of flying." He collapsed the wings and sat on the bench, and Erjon stood behind him. Once Zepherin unstrapped his harness, Erjon lifted the wings with ease and hung them on the wall behind him. The wings next to Zepherin's were just as large, but the others on the wall to my left were smaller. And the ones on the wall to my right were even smaller than those.

As if reading my mind, Zepherin stood and pointed to the wings. "The stronger the Dragonborn, the larger the wings."

"And yours are the largest ones," I pointed out.

Calian barked out a laugh. "He'd like to think so."

I was confused. "Then whose are the largest?"

"Mine," said a feminine voice. We all turned to find Queen Eteri leaning against the entrance of the building.

Queen Eteri caressed a large set of silver wings with her delicate fingers. They were the most beautiful wings out of all the ones hanging on the walls. And she was correct; her wings were slightly larger than Zepherin's pair. It didn't quite make sense to me. Her body was much smaller than his, so how could she carry more weight?

"I began training at just eight years old," Queen Eteri whispered, and her eyes closed as she recalled a memory from long ago. "I remember stepping into the ring for the first time. The sun on my face and the breeze on my neck. It would take years of grueling physical and mental training before I donned a pair of wings. But it happened when I was twelve. And after that, more years of falling, colliding, and near-death experiences. It could make any grown man cry."

"I cried," Zepherin said with a shrug. "That first time I hit the ground from a fall. The first time I flew into a mountain. The first time I witnessed a fellow warrior's death." His eyes darted to Erjon who looked away quickly, not daring to meet his brother's gaze. No one else saw the exchange but me, and I watched Zepherin hang his head once he realized Erjon wasn't going to acknowledge him. The room remained still. They didn't know that I knew of Tuuli's death, and I would keep it that way.

The silence in respect for Tuuli's death lingered around us for quite some time.

Queen Eteri placed her hand on Zepherin's shoulder. "Death is inevitable in what we do, Mr. Coro," she replied, relieving the tension in the air. She glanced sideways at Erjon, but he didn't acknowledge her. The death of his sister affected him more than he let on. I bet it was why he suppressed his emotions.

"It is time we ready you for your journey east. I have faith that the weather will hold fair for you all. The kitchens have prepared food rations and plenty of water. I also visited the stables myself to ensure the horses are fit for travel. Your horse, Calian, seemed more than eager to leave."

I smiled at the image of Dhruv pacing back and forth, anxiously awaiting freedom from his confinement. Zari was probably grazing, enjoying her remaining moments of peace and reflection.

"Are we to head to Medora?" I asked.

Calian looked at me, hesitating to speak. His jaw tensed, indicating that he wanted to tell me, but Amram's intrusion into my mind prevented him from revealing any important information. I wasn't angry, just sad.

"Right. You can't tell me."

"I wish I could. It would make everything easier."

"Unfortunately, nothing is easy these days."

CHAPTER THIRTEEN
EMERA

"I was told you have a problem."

I turned from my breakfast to see Zepherin sitting opposite of me at the dining table. "I don't know what you mean." I mumbled.

He leaned across the table and clasped his hands together. "Erjon told me you're having trouble with your magic. Something about it weakening you."

I sat my fork on the table and sighed. "He told you that? Seems like private information."

"He's worried about you."

I threw my head back and laughed. "Erjon? Worried about

me?"

Zepherin leaned back in his chair and crossed his arms. "You find that hard to believe?"

"And if I said that I do?"

"I'd say you don't know him well enough."

"Ha! That's an understatement."

Zepherin stood from his seat. "Let's go."

"Go where?"

"To the ring. You can't use your magic because it weakens you, so you'll have to use other means of bringing down your attacker. Fin is waiting for us."

"Where's Calian?"

"Planning and scheming. That's all I'm allowed to say." He turned and headed for the door. "I'll see you out there."

I contemplated not following. I secretly had plans to visit the library in the hope that I could locate any valuable information on how to combat an evil Dragongod from poisoning my mind. Seemed unlikely, but what else did I have to lose?

Grumbling to myself, I followed Zepherin to the training ring. The sun was shining, but a dense fog hovered in the air. Zepherin thrust his hands out and conjured a mighty wind that forced the fog to retreat. With the ring cleared, he turned back to me.

We stood there staring at each other. In a way, he was a seasoned soldier sizing up the young recruit. "Alright, Em," he said, his voice gruff and authoritative. "Should your powers leave you completely, you'll have your bow and your physical strength to fight. Let's say your bow is knocked away from you. At that point, you will be forced to fight in hand-to-hand combat. Your wits and physicality are your only allies. Today, you're going to learn how to use your body effectively."

"And how many times have you been forced to fight with your fists and not your air magic?" I asked. Seemed like a valid question.

"Too many times to count. That's part of my training. You never know when an opponent will strike you with an arrow or blade laced with a toxin that renders your powers useless. Those do exist, y'know?"

I didn't answer because I hadn't known that.

"Sometimes, it's just you and your opponent. No magic, no bow, and no blade can save you. You have to save yourself." He lifted two fingers and gestured for me to step forward. I walked toward him until he motioned for me to stop. "First lesson is your stance. Your stance is your foundation. With a solid foundation, you will have balance and agility. Watch me."

He widened his legs into a sturdy fighting stance. His feet were should-length apart, knees slightly bent, and his weight was evenly distributed. He nodded, silently telling me to do the same. I mimicked his movements, albeit a tad awkwardly. I'd fought before, but I'd relied more on my magic, so actually taking the time to consider my fighting stance was foreign to me.

"Good. When you move, keep your knees bent and your body slightly low. You're already shorter than most of the challengers you'll face, so that's good. A smaller target is a trickier one. Second lesson is to always face your opponent with your arms up and ready to block whatever comes at you. Never give them an opening. Finally, stay light on your feet. Hand-to-hand combat is more than just throwing punches. You'll need to read your opponent's movements so that you can out-maneuver them. Always move with a purpose. Don't just move to avoid getting hit but to ready yourself for a counterstrike. Make sense?"

I nodded.

"Good." Zepherin suddenly lunged forward, swinging his right arm up to my face. His attack caught me off guard as I was anticipating another lesson. I bobbed and weaved just in time to avoid getting hit. I stumbled over my feet and almost fell to the ground. "Your opponent isn't going to tell you it's time to fight. You have to anticipate it. Let's try again."

After several more jabs from Zepherin, I started to feel more comfortable and each of my movements became more fluid with each dodge. Sweat trickled down my forehead, and my breathing started to become somewhat labored, but a smile spread on my lips.

"That's it!" Zepherin yelled encouragingly. "Now, let's work on you attacking me. It's important to know that success in hand-to-hand combat doesn't solely rely on your physical strength. You're going to face opponents that are larger than you. So, you need to take into account the best areas to take down an enemy which are the eyes, nose, throat, groin, and knees. The eyes will render their vision useless which gives you an advantage. Striking the nose can be painful and disorienting. A strike to the throat can disrupt your opponent's breathing and disable them. A kick to the knees can destabilize your attacker, and finally, the groin is vulnerable and can easily incapacitate your enemy."

"Eyes, nose, throat, knees, and groin. Got it."

"Okay. I'm going to attack. This time, don't just block it. I want you to set yourself up for a counterattack. Go for one of those areas."

"But what if I hurt you?"

"You can't hurt me." He stepped back a few paces. "But

I'd like to see you try."

"As would I."

My heart skipped a beat at that deep, gruff voice. I whipped my head around to find Calian at the entrance of the ring. His hair was more disheveled than usual, and the familiar curl tumbled over his eyes. He raked his hands through his hair to put it back in place. A fire ignited in my core. I ignored the impulse to run and throw my arms around his neck. With great effort, I turned my attention back to Zepherin. A lopsided grin was planted on his face, and he was looking directly at Calian.

"About time you showed up."

"I had other matters to attend to."

"That's an interesting way of saying you slept in."

"Funny."

Zepherin laughed. "Stand in for me!"

"Gladly," Calian said with a smirk. He jogged to Zepherin's side and took a fighting stance that mirrored Zepherin's. So, I was fighting Calian.

"It's one thing to fight me. You don't know me as well, so the chances of you being distracted are low. But if you fight the man whom you are so clearly in love with…Well…That's a different story." My face warmed from him saying I loved Calian. Calian smirked, so I dropped my smile and narrowed my eyes, determined to prove to Calian that I was strong; that I didn't need magic or a bow to fight him. And that his chiseled face and large biceps wouldn't distract me.

"Go!" Zepherin shouted. The air crackled with tension as Calian and I started to circle one another. There was no playful banter or teasing. My concentration was singularly on our sparring. What happened in the ring could eventually occur out on a battlefield, so I needed to focus. I kept my stance low and my arms held up.

Calian initiated the first strike, sending a powerful punch toward me. I twisted out of the way, and back into an open stance. Then his next punch came, and he connected with the arm that I drove up to block him. I staggered backward and pulled my arm into me, wincing from the pain. I straightened and pushed my shoulders back. Calian hesitated momentarily, his eyes softening with worry. I took that moment and lunged, sending a powerful hook into Calian's jaw that sent him reeling backward.

We traded blows with desperate intensity, neither of us striking our target. We were each fast, although Calian was undoubtedly faster than me. He sidestepped my punches with ease whereas I narrowly escaped his. After a minute of back-and-forth, Calian delivered a powerful elbow to my face that I wasn't able to outmaneuver. I fell to my knees in pain.

Calian leaned over me. "Are you okay?"

A gritty determination took over, and I shot out my leg, taking him down in one swooping motion. I got up and kicked my foot into his ribs. Calian let out a resounding growl. I went to slam my foot down into his gut, but he grabbed my foot and twisted it, causing me to crash to the ground beside him. We were both a tangled mess of limbs and dirt as the two of us fought for dominance. Punches were thrown and insults were exchanged. Finally, Calian pinned me beneath him. I squirmed beneath his strength, but his hands held my wrists steady to the ground. His weight pushed me down until my hips couldn't move.

Fire flashed in his eyes. My mind raced as I tried to figure out how to get out of his grasp. He raised back up and our eyes met. The electric spark between us jolted me to life while he lowered his head. "I've got you," he breathed. Our lips were mere inches away.

"No…You…Don't," I said. With all my might, I brought my knee up into his groin. A brief look of shock flashed in Calian's eyes before he rolled onto his back and cried out in pain. He brought his knees to his stomach and started coughing. Any ounce of victory vanished when I saw the two tears that fell down his face. What had I done?

Zepherin howled and clapped on the other side of the ring. "We're going to make a warrior out of you, Em!" he shouted to me. Meanwhile, Calian's hands, which were suspended over his groin, glowed fervently until he stretched back out on the ground. His chest rose up and down quickly. I crawled over to him.

"I'm so sorry. I'm so sorry."

Calian laughed, his voice rich and lighthearted. "No. Don't be. You fought, and you won."

"But I hurt you."

"You were supposed to. I can heal myself, remember?"

I leaned back on my heels. "That's why Zepherin wanted you to fight me. In case I did hurt you, you could heal yourself."

Calian nodded. Then he abruptly sat up and pulled me into his arms; his warmth becoming a cocoon of comfort. His fingers traced the bottom of my jaw, and then he lifted my chin. He pressed his lips into mine, and my mouth parted slightly. Our kiss deepened into a gentle exploration.

"Ahem," Zepherin called out.

Calian and I broke away from each other.

"Time to get a move-on. The world won't save itself," Zepherin said, shaking his head.

Calian wrapped his arm around my shoulders and held me close to him. "I think we'll stay here a bit longer. The world can wait."

CHAPTER FOURTEEN
EMERA

It was early morning when we left for Medora. The sun rose, and the sky transitioned through an array of mesmerizing colors. When we started our descent out of Ilmari and down the mountainside toward the hidden path Zepherin disclosed to us, the horizon was painted in hues of purple, blue, and gray. Now, the faint shimmer of the night stars faded, and the sun lifted higher. Its golden rays pierced the air and the colors lightened into red, orange, and yellow. The shadows on the ground rescinded, and the trees in the distance became more visible. I breathed in the air, relishing how crisp and clean it was.

I hope you slept well, my Kahina, Zari said.

Amram didn't show up unannounced, so I'd call it a win, I told her. I leaned forward and patted her neck. After my training with Zeph, I thought it best that I refrained from using any magic until we figured out how to stop Amram from getting into my head. That meant no flying and no teleporting.

My eyes rested on the purple leather cuffs that protected my wrists. They matched the leather of the armored vest I wore as well as the other bits of leather attached to protect certain areas of my body. The leather was designed to look like large Dragonscales. A hood with a mask were attached to the shoulders of my vest. The color was a dark purple—darker than the leather—and matched my tight long-sleeved shirt and pants. The hood had also been attached to a cape, but I had it removed so as to not interfere with my bow. The clothing was another gift from the queen. She'd insisted we all wear the newest armor to protect ourselves. Who knew how many Dragons Amram had resurrected?

Calian leaned restlessly in his saddle atop Dhruv, clearly uncomfortable. His eyes darted back and forth, constantly assessing the area in case of an ambush. Despite not being the Dragonheir of Vukan, Calian's leathers were still a dark scarlet red. They covered his broad shoulders, chest, and stomach. He had protective leathers on other areas of himself that matched the riding boots he wore. Daggers were strapped to his sides along with a large blade at his back. Erjon wore the same style of attire, only his colors matched his elements—gray and black.

"You might want to change that scowl on your face," Calian said.

"Excuse me?"

"You look like you're about to use your magic to hurl someone off a cliff."

"Wouldn't matter if I wanted to. I can't use my magic. Remember?"

"You're acting ridiculous. You can use your magic once we figure out how to stop Amram from stealing it."

"What did you just say?"

Fin whistled loudly. "Oh, Cal. Never tell a woman that she's acting ridiculous. That's one of the cardinal rules for a man's survival." Fin's clothes were his usual assassin-like attire. Lightweight, black, and adorned with a hood and mask like mine. He also wore a sleek black bow and quiver full of arrows.

"Maybe I'll stop acting ridiculous if you stop acting like…What did Zepherin call you earlier? Oh, yeah. A man-child. You're acting like a man-child. I'm not some helpless little girl."

"Man-child!" Fin shrieked. He threw his head back and laughed. His laughter turned into wheezing, and he grabbed his stomach to steady himself.

Calian rolled his eyes, clearly unimpressed by his friend's lack of loyalty. "Thanks, Fin. You're the best." He angled himself back toward me. "And I am not a man-child."

"I for one agree with Emera," Morwen chimed in. Her beautiful black mare fell in step beside Zari. Morwen tugged at the sleeve of her billowy black tunic and straightened the leather vest that matched the rest of her black attire. It didn't matter that Morwen was the Dragonheir of Water. She looked like the Dragonheir of Death. Beautiful, yet lethal. And the blade strapped to her back confirmed it.

Senna's horse—a muscular white steed—trotted just behind Morwen's mare. "Man-child is a mild way of putting it," she teased. On her hips were sleek white ropes, a shade lighter than the gray leathers she wore. I'd been informed that they were called whips. She had told me just before we had left Ilmari that those were the weapons her mother had given her. She wasn't an expert with them, but they'd be useful in a fight in case she couldn't use her magic.

Our banter was interrupted by Avani. She took her wavy hair out of its braid and shook it over her emerald and brown leathers. "Look there, in the distance," she said. She pointed to a large figure that loomed in the sky.

"Not again," I groaned. "We seriously need a map of these burial sites."

Valda hovered over a large area of dirt and dust at the bottom of the mountain, and below her was Anwir. It was another resurrection ritual, and there was no way around it.

There were too many of us not to be seen, so we tied up the horses and lowered ourselves to gather our composure.

"We can stay here and wait it out," Senna suggested.

"Or we can end this now," Avani argued. We stood waited while the others finished tying up the horses off the beaten path—it was Fin's idea to keep them hidden from Valda and whatever was out there with her. I let my magic flow from me and into Avani. With my empathic abilities, I soothed her soul from the pain she felt when thinking of Amram. She wanted to end Amram's life because she blamed him for her parents' deaths. And rightly so, considering it was the prophecy of Amram's arrival that triggered Valda to seek out all of the Dragonheirs. We'd surmised that Valda was responsible for the hanging of Avani's parents.

"I know you want revenge," I said with a quick gasp for air. "But we have to be smart about it." I'd see to it myself that Amram met his true fate if I had to.

Avani glanced at me. "I appreciate what you did, but don't waste your magic on me."

"Avani is correct. Stop using your magic." Erjon exited from the trees with Morwen and Senna following him. They stood beside us and stared at the large Dragon in the sky. I kept my eyes on the trees, waiting for Calian to emerge.

All at once, the beating of my heart quickened, my breathing became heavy, and my ears warmed.

"Arthar, mir'kyn. Arthar et lenz."

The words traveled with the breeze and drifted into my ears. I turned my head sharply toward the goddess that hovered over a dead Dragon's burial place. All of us crouched low to conceal ourselves as best as we could. It was difficult considering we were out in the open. Why were we out in the open? It seemed foolish now.

"Arthar, mir'kyn. Arthar et lenz."

"Awaken, my brother. Awaken and live," I whispered.

"You know what she's saying?" Avani asked.

The Dragongoddess continued. "Mer flahk tosor flahk."

"My flesh to your flesh," I translated.

Avani lightly pushed my arm. "Huh?"

"Uh…I did some light reading of a text Erjon gave me."

"Was it called How to Speak the Ancient Dragonlanguage in Just Two Days?" Avani pressed. "You told me the first time you ever heard the language was on the mountain."

I scrunched my nose. "I may have tapped into my magic to help me read a little faster." It had taken an enormous mental toll on me, but I wasn't about to tell her that.

"You can do that?" I jumped at Fin's voice.

"Apparently. Because I did."

"That's…" he paused, and I waited for him to say something like impressive or amazing. "Cheating. That's cheating," he finished and shook his head.

"I don't know everything. I just focused on the words I heard on the mountain and any others that might be involved in rituals. Erjon will have to translate everything else."

"Still cheating."

I brought my arm back, ready to punch, but I let it fall. Valda wasn't speaking. She was done with her incantation.

And that wasn't good.

The wind picked up, meaning the dead Dragon was being resurrected as we stood there. Correction. Dragons. We watched in terror as three Dragons lifted from the ground. Three. Dragons.

"Where's Calian?" I asked hastily. I didn't bother to crouch anymore, and I took off toward the horses. We needed to get out of there. There was no point in trying to wait it out.

"I'm here," he answered. Before I reached him, his eyes drifted to the sky, and his mouth gaped open. "What…the…Dragonhell?"

Kedron stepped out from behind Calian. His demeanor changed from relaxed to nervous in seconds. His shoulders tensed, and he released an audible gulp when he swallowed. He'd never seen a Dragon before. Senna hadn't either.

Fin ran up to us. "We need to leave," he said, his tone serious.

Before any of us could agree, a deafening roar thundered overhead. Large shadows loomed above us, casting darkness over the terrain. All of us watched as the three resurrected Dragons landed before us. Valda circled an additional time before she joined them. The ground shook mercilessly, causing all of us to stumble.

The air sizzled with tension. I called to my magic and let it form golden tendrils of my empathic ability. I pushed them out of me and let them wrap around my friends' emotions. Kedron was scared, rooted into the ground by fear. Avani was anxious, but she hid it well. Senna was in shock and like Kedron, remained rooted where she stood. Morwen and Erjon were calm, ready to face the Dragons head-on. Fin was nervous but willing.

Calian was…furious.

His eyes blazed red as he whipped his head to me. "Stop using magic."

"You felt that?"

"Every time you do it."

I felt the air coming in through my gaping mouth. "You never mentioned it."

"Didn't feel the need to. I have nothing to hide." He tore his gaze away from me and focused his eyes elsewhere. They were fixated on something. Valda? I pulled my magic back in and followed his line of sight. Atop of Valda was what held his attention: Anwir. Flames ignited at Calian's palms.

In the distance, the horses whinnied in fear. The Dragons made no movement in response, so either they didn't hear the horses, or they didn't care. My guess was the latter.

I reached out to Zari just in case. *Remain silent, Zari. Please do what you can to keep the other horses silent, too.*

I will do my best, my Kahina.

I tried to focus, but using my empathic magic weighed on me so much that I staggered back. I would have fallen over, but Erjon reached out and steadied me. I was surprised to see him by my side.

"Look at your scales."

I glanced down at my arms and noticed that the color of my scales were faded.

"You have to push your magic down deep," Erjon said. I was pretty sure he meant my empathic magic. "Lock it inside of you, and do not let it out. If you let it out, you can get yourself or someone else killed."

I wasn't going to lock away my magic just yet regardless if my scales were an indication of it fading. I reached behind me and felt for my bow, checking for the third time that I'd strapped it to me. It was still there, so I had means of fighting if my magic took too much effort. I looked around. We all stood together now, ready to face the Dragons—and possibly our deaths—together.

"There will be no fighting today," Anwir said. We all exchanged looks. What was he getting at? What game was he playing?

Anwir slid off Valda—I found it surprising she'd let anyone ride her—but they both disappeared in rising purple smoke. When the smoke cleared, Valda appeared in her human form beside Anwir, and she was surprisingly clothed. I had no idea how. She walked forward between the two largest Dragons. Valda glanced at one Dragon, bowed her head, and then repeated the gesture toward the other. Both Dragons lowered their snouts in response, clearly loyal to her. I could only imagine the hatred they felt for Nimerah. I wished she was with us.

Valda continued to walk forward until she was only twenty feet away from us. "But only if you agree to my terms." Just like I'd thought. She was playing a game. One that she made up, and only she knew the rules.

"We won't agree to Dragonshit," Calian spat. Human Emera would have winced at the curse, but Dragongoddess Emera did not. Because I agreed.

Valda clicked her tongue then smiled. "I'm afraid that won't do."

"You think we'll just give into your demands?" I asked.

She slid her eyes from Calian's to mine, and light sparked within them. "Oh, I do."

Morwen stepped forward. "If you do not wish to fight, then what is it you want?"

Valda raised her hands. "Ah. At least someone is level-headed. My terms are simple, Princess. Emera goes with me, and I let you all live."

"Are you forgetting that those three killed one of your precious Dragons?" Avani seethed. I didn't need my magic to know she was about to explode.

"You mean Hadeon? As unfortunate as that was, it was to be expected. Hadeon may have been known as my father's Destroyer during the war, but I knew the truth. He was reckless. His resurrection was purely a trial run. Once I knew it would work, I didn't care what happened to him. In fact, it's why I suggested to my father that we should resurrect Hadeon first. I wanted to see what would happen. It's not my fault that he didn't live up to expectations after that."

"So, you brought your soldier back to life knowing he wasn't strong enough?" Senna asked, appalled by Valda's disregard for the Dragon's life.

"Yes."

Senna gritted her teeth as she said, "And you don't plan on bringing him back?"

Valda inspected her nails. "I can't. One time only. He officially has no Dragonsoul."

Behind her, Anwir snickered loud enough for Calian to take notice. He started to take a step forward, but I grabbed his arm and pulled him back. "Not yet," I whispered.

"Do we have a deal?" Valda asked, ignoring Calian's reaction to Anwir.

"Absolutely not!" Senna yelled. Bright light shot out from her palms.

Valda chuckled, amused by Senna's outburst. "Did you know that when Endrit joined my father's side, it was because I promised him that I wouldn't kill Nimerah?"

Senna closed her hands. "Excuse me? How old are you?

Valda clasped her hands behind her back and paced a few steps back and forth. "Old. I've been waiting. But that doesn't matter. What matters is your legacy."

"What's that supposed to mean?" Senna asked.

Valda chuckled. "In the beginning, each of the original Chaos Dragons created their own two children. Father created Ilmari and Dhara, both beautiful Dragons with divine souls."

"You say all of that like we care," Senna spat. It seemed her fear had subsided, replaced by a growing confidence.

"Senna," Calian warned.

"Nimerah created Tamasvi and Endrit. See, your ancestor, Endrit, came to me because he was repulsed by the humans. They were unintelligent, crude, and soulless. They had no place in this world, and Endrit knew it. He still loved his mother, but he'd begun to disassociate himself from her due to their polarizing beliefs. As we all know, Endrit was a healer, which would be extremely useful in the war. So, I promised my father would spare Nimerah's life if he joined my father's cause."

"How is this relevant?" Calian demanded.

"Because my father kept up his side of the bargain," Valda answered, her voice strained from trying to keep her composure. "Nimerah lives, and Em's going to help me find her." She gestured toward me, and I all but blasted her with magic. I loathed the way she said my nickname as if we were still friends.

"I don't know where she is," I lied.

Valda's eyes flashed. "That is a lie." The three Dragons behind her lowered their heads and growled.

"Even if she did, she wouldn't tell you," Avani said.

Valda cocked her head to the side. "Is that so?" she asked.

Avani crossed her arms in front of her and nodded. A smile spread slowly across Valda's face in response.

"Eventually, Endrit turned his back on the cause. He betrayed his mother and then my father." She looked over her shoulder at the largest of the three Dragons. It snorted in response, steam shooting out from its nostrils. There was history between it and Endrit. I didn't need my telepathic magic to know that.

I grew restless because deep down something was wrong. What was Valda's point in telling us about Endrit? I contemplated asking. Why not? It was apparent that Valda loved to hear herself talk. But before I could ask, my attention was drawn to the spot where Anwir had been standing. He wasn't there anymore.

A scream pierced the air. Anwir held Senna tight to him with his left arm and a dagger to her throat. She squirmed and kicked, trying to break free of his hold on her, but she couldn't.

Valda's eyes narrowed, and she grinned wickedly. "I knew I needed to do something about him. It would be disadvantageous for Nimerah to have a powerful healer on her side…So I killed him."

On Valda's final words, Anwir plunged the dagger into Senna's heart.

CHAPTER FIFTEEN
EMERA

My ears rang, and my head spun. What just happened? Anwir…a dagger…Senna…dead? I shook my head. No. Senna had healing magic. She'd heal herself. Right? Unless…unless the dagger wasn't removed.

"You monster!" Avani's scream pulled me back to the present.

Meanwhile, Calian, Morwen, and Fin all spread out to give Avani and me time to get to Senna. Calian pulled his arm back to throw fire at Valda, but the second largest Dragon—a bright emerald with razor sharp horns all over its body—swiped its tail. Calian jumped back, but he wasn't quick enough. The Dragon's tail hurled into his stomach and threw him backward. The Dragon turned its attention to Morwen. She looked at me and then at Avani, who was already running after Senna.

Morwen stared intently at me, like she was trying to say something through her telepathic magic. I craned my neck, trying to hear her in my mind, but I couldn't. Panic seized my heart, but I couldn't let it take over. I nodded, pretending I heard her. She blasted water into the eyes of the emerald Dragon and ran off toward Calian. I held my breath and waited. Would the Dragon follow? It shook its head and then whipped his eyes to Morwen. The Dragon stretched out its massive wings and launched itself into the air, flying after her.

Good, I thought. I glanced at Erjon and then at Fin. They both faced off with the smallest of the Dragons, another green one. I wasn't surprised. Dhara and Endrit had joined Amram in the war. Most of his resurrected army would undoubtedly be green or white Dragons.

Erjon's arms were extended out with wind swirling in his hands. Fin already had an arrow nocked, the amulet glowing around his neck. Both men looked calm and in control, prepared for the attack. Erjon brought forth a tornado of wind, while Fin looked for the best vantage point.

Knowing they could handle the Dragon, I twisted around and raced after Avani but skidded to a halt when the largest of the Dragons—a shimmering white one—stepped in front of me. Then Valda stepped in front of it.

"Em, don't do this to them. Join me, and I'll stop all of this." She held her arms out wide as if anticipating me to run and embrace her. "No one has to get hurt."

Movement behind the white Dragon caught my attention, and I looked past Valda to see Kedron. Our eyes connected, and we both nodded simultaneously.

"I don't believe you," I replied.

My lungs opened, inviting in a deep breath to steady myself for a jump. But when I called to my power, nothing came. I couldn't jump. What was wrong with me?

Valda caught onto our plans and immediately twisted around, spread her arms out wide, and blasted Kedron's feet with ice. Kedron was frozen to the ground, and the ice was thick and strong. Kedron tried with all his strength to break free from his snare, but he couldn't. The stupid ice would take fire magic to melt it. I ran to him and attempted to release flames from my hands directly upon the ice. But again. Nothing came out. I shook my hands furiously. What in the Dragonhell was wrong? I cursed loudly, knowing

Senna didn't have much time. If I didn't get that dagger out…No. I couldn't think that way.

"Just give the word," Valda crooned, her eyebrow raised.

"No," I spat.

She shrugged her shoulders and dropped her smile. "As you wish. But remember this conversation. Remember that you had a chance to stop all of this." Instead of throwing magic at me to kill me, she used it to leap onto the Dragon's back. It surprised me. Why didn't she just kill me there?

The Dragon unfurled its wings and lifted into the sky. It maneuvered its massive body and flew overhead. With a quick turn, it landed on a ledge above the open space we all stood in. The Dragon and Valda were up high enough that our magic couldn't reach them. The ledge gave Valda a clear view of everything below her.

Kedron yelled through the cacophony of madness. "Don't worry about me! Go save Senna!"

"I'll be back for you!" I promised. Determination filled my limbs, and I sprinted forward just as Avani lunged for Anwir. With a wave of his hand, the ground rumbled and split. A wall of solid rock shot up from the crevice and formed around Senna and him. Avani hit the wall and staggered backward. But she didn't back down. She let out another rage-filled cry and gathered green energy into her hands. The rock formation split in two just wide enough for her to step through the crack. The amount of strength she'd displayed was remarkable.

A cry from Fin pierced the air, and I turned in time to see him propelled through the air. He landed on the ground, just shy of a protruding rock that would have ended his life. Fury spiked within me, and I quickly reached back for my bow. I launched an arrow toward the Dragon that had Erjon pinned beneath its claws. My aim was true, and the arrow struck the Dragon between its eyes. My arrow didn't kill him, but it gave Erjon enough time to free himself. He held out his hand toward the Dragon and closed his fist. The Dragon was confused at first, but panic soon registered within its eyes as it panted and roared, desperately trying to breath. Erjon moved out of the of way as it fell to the ground dead, its air having been sucked from its lungs.

Fin pushed himself up onto one of his elbows from where he had been sprawled out on the ground. "Well, that's one way to do it!" he yelled. He obviously regretted yelling out because he winced and held the side of his stomach. Blood oozed from his nose, but it was the only visible wound on his body.

For a split second, I contemplated running to him and healing his wound. But Fin shook his head. "No! I'll be fine!" That was all I needed to turn and run toward Senna.

Valda remained perched on the Dragon, watching the fighting unfold. She made no move to save her Dragons or intervene with our attempt to save Senna. She just watched, her demeanor unsettling. But my friend was dying, so I'd deal with Valda after I saved Senna's life.

With no rock wall to hide him—thanks to Avani—Anwir retreated toward the trees. Senna struggled to free herself, her arms flailing wildly and her feet kicking the ground as he continued to walk backward. His gaze locked onto Avani and me. Senna's eyes glowed a blinding white while her magic attempted to heal the damage to her heart. One arm continued thrashing wildly to dislodge herself from Anwir while the other pushed her healing magic into the wound. It was that bit of magic that kept her alive. Anwir maintained his hold, keeping the dagger firmly in place.

"It's no use," he snarled. He could have been talking to Senna, or it could have been Avani.

Avani stalked toward them. Anwir tried to throw up whatever magic he could muster, but it was no use. Avani blocked and dodged everything he tried.

Having had enough, she thrust out her hands. Her palms split open and unleashed thorny vines. They wrapped around Anwir before he could defend himself, and he cried out in pain. The vines weakened his grip on Senna, and she slumped to the ground.

My heart skipped a beat at the sight of her body. Senna wasn't moving.

While Avani closed the gap between her and Anwir, I ran to Senna. I turned her toward me and inhaled sharply. The light in her eyes was gone. They stared straight into the sky, lifeless. I choked back the tears that pooled within my eyes and pulled out the dagger, but Senna didn't flinch. I threw the dagger far behind me. Panic in the form of bile rose in my throat, and I gulped it down. My magic sparked to life, and empathic tendrils flowed out of my body and connected with hers.

I felt nothing. Her body was an empty shell void of life.

Fin came over. "Em…Is she?" he asked quietly.

Please, I begged. *Please let my light magic work.* I placed my hands on top of the wound and forced healing magic into her heart. The dam that held in my tears finally broke, and they poured down my cheeks. Senna, once twirling in Morwen's bed chamber, feeling beautiful in a gown made for a princess, was now motionless beneath my outstretched hands. Her eyes, once bright and lively, were open in an unsettling stillness. The wound Anwir inflicted was deep, and there was so much blood. My magic started to give out, the light beneath my palms flickering.

"No, no, no," I pleaded. "You can't give out now. You can't." I forced more magic to my hands, but the familiar exhaustion flooded my body. Erjon knelt beside me, gave me his hand, and I siphoned his magic from him. But it wasn't enough. My light flickered once more and then it was gone.

I sat back on my heels, gasping for air. A heavy pain pounded behind my eyes, and a worrisome realization dawned on me. My healing power, which had mended countless wounds when Valda attacked the camp, were ineffective against the gravity of Senna's condition... Because I didn't have it anymore. First, I couldn't hear Morwen telepathically. That meant my water magic was gone. Then, I couldn't teleport, so my darkness magic was gone. I couldn't melt the ice at Kedron's feet after that, so my fire magic was gone. And now, I couldn't heal Senna. My light magic was gone? What was happening to me? I looked at my scales. The purple color was even more subdued.

My brow furrowed in anger, and my heart beat rapidly with despair...and failure. Seeing Senna this way, and not having the magic to save her, made me feel utterly powerless. The tears continued to rain down my cheeks. My body shook from exhaustion. I was a Dragongoddess for crying out loud! Why couldn't I save her? Why didn't I have my magic?

With a breaking heart, I lowered my head and my hands. "I'm sorry, my friend," I whimpered. I could wish for a miracle, but I knew it wouldn't come.

"Emera!" Avani yelled. Anwir groaned from the pain of the vines that remained tight around his body. Blood stained his clothing from the sharp thorns that dug into his skin. Avani tugged the vines, and Anwir fell to his knees. "Is she okay?" she called out over her shoulder; her voice drenched with panic.

"I…I…" I didn't know what to say. How did I tell Avani that the woman she'd grown so close to was dead? How did I steal her joy like that?

Calian's hand rested on my shoulder, taking the spot where Erjon once sat. I didn't know when he'd returned or how. I didn't know if he'd killed the emerald Dragon or not. But what I did know was that Senna was gone because I couldn't save her. I hung my head and let the tears flow. Would the tears ever stop?

"My magic," I whispered and leaned back on my heels. He wrapped his arms around me, and I doubled over them. First Rehema and now Senna. Death was inevitable, but they had both been so young.

"No!"

Avani's shriek of pain sliced through the air, causing me to sit up. She flung her body over Senna and pressed her ear to Senna's chest. "Why is there no heartbeat? Why is there no heartbeat?" She sat up, grabbed Senna's shoulders and shook her. Tears streaked down her now bloodied cheek. "Wake up! Don't leave me! You can't leave me, too!" She stopped shaking Senna's shoulders and instead placed her hands on Senna's chest. Up and down, up and down, Avani pumped Senna's chest, desperate to get her breathing again. But I knew it was no use.

Avani stopped and dropped her blood-stained hands to her side. Her eyes, filled with pain and anger, cut into my soul when she looked at me. "Why didn't you save her?" she demanded, her voice low and volatile.

I eased my way out of Calian's arms but stayed beside him. I opened my mouth to speak, but nothing came out but ghostly silence.

Avani dove toward me, but Erjon used his wind to lift her off the ground and back about ten feet. Right when her feet hit the ground, she ran toward me once more, desperate to release her rage upon me. This time, Fin stepped in front of her. He grabbed her around the waist and held her tight, keeping her from advancing. Avani repeatedly pounded on his chest to free herself from his grip, but because Fin wore the amulet, her strength didn't work on him.

Why didn't you save her!" she screamed again.

Morwen, who until this point had stayed silent next to her mate, said, "That's not fair." But she was wrong. Avani's words were more than fair.

"She's the all-powerful goddess!" She jabbed her finger at me. Her words didn't sting. She was right.

"The dagger was in too long, Avani," Kedron added. He didn't know the truth. I had no healing magic.

Avani's anger dissipated a little, replaced with grief. "But you can…You can bring…her back to life," she pleaded through heavy sobs.

I shook my head slowly. "I…I can't do that, Avani," I whispered. I wished I could bring Senna back, but I didn't have that kind of power.

"That's not how it works," Erjon stated, maintaining the lie. He knew. He knew I was losing magic. "A life lost cannot be reclaimed."

Avani's eyes flashed emerald. "But she can!" She pointed to where Valda sat atop the white Dragon. She raised an eyebrow and angled her head. For a split second, the thought of asking for her help crossed my mind. If she could raise the dead, shouldn't I be able to as well?

"Valda is raising pure-blooded Dragons. Not Dragonborns," Erjon said.

Morwen took Avani's arm and pulled her into a comforting embrace. "Senna wouldn't want it. Her soul is at peace, Avani. Let her stay that way."

"But I'm not at peace," Avani sobbed. She buried her face in Morwen's shoulder and cried. My own tears had ceased falling. My eyes were dry, but they ached.

"Where's Anwir?" Kedron asked, standing where Anwir had been confined in Avani's vines. The vines that were no longer attached to her hands. Kedron picked up the dagger that I'd tossed away in a panic. So not only did I not save Senna, but I was also responsible for Anwir getting away.

Calian leaned into me. He cupped my face with his hands, and I stared into his dark eyes. "We will figure this all out."

Avani's tormented cries continued to fill the air. If we were to get out of here alive, she needed to calm herself. It sounded cold and heartless, but it was what needed to happen.

My eyes met Erjon's.

"I'll do it."

"Do what?" Calian asked.

I didn't answer. Instead, the remaining embers of my magic crackled within me, and I let my empathic magic resurface. Avani's pain hit me like a tidal wave. She was angry, sad, guilty, and even in disbelief. My throat cut off, and a knot formed in the deepest pit of my stomach. Despite her outburst toward me, she didn't blame me. She blamed herself. Oh, Avani. Senna's death was not your fault.

Erjon closed his eyes, and his breathing became more labored as he pushed his magic out to Avani. I imagined him wrapping his empathic tendrils around her like ribbons. Her demeanor transitioned. Her eyebrows that were furrowed with hatred, eased and lifted. Her mouth parted, letting out a sigh. Her fists unclenched, and her shoulders dropped slightly, releasing the tension she'd bottled up. She looked straight ahead.

Erjon opened his eyes, and he looked relieved. When I opened my magic back up to Avani, she was no longer angry. She was numb.

"What did you do?" Fin asked.

"I eased her Dragonsoul."

Morwen, still holding Avani, didn't like Erjon's answer. "You cannot suppress her emotions, Erjon. She deserves to feel."

"You are not wrong, Morwen. And I give you my word that I will give her emotions back at the most opportune moment. This is not it." He turned abruptly and walked away. Erjon needed space.

Kedron stared up at Valda, "She's laughing."

Valda closed her mouth and angled her head to make it clear that she was only interested in my next move. I hesitated, but only for a moment. I knew what she wanted, and if it meant that my friends would be safe for the time being, then I would oblige.

Putting one foot in front of the other, I forced myself forward.

"Is this what you want?" I yelled to the smirking goddess.

"Emera, no." Kedron grabbed my hand, but I shook him off.

Valda smiled, knowing that despite losing a Dragon—maybe two because I had no clue where the green one was—she'd won. I'd agree to her terms.

Calian cut me off. He tried to hide the fear and worry in his voice, but I heard it. I reached my hand up to his cheek.

"Find my mother," I breathed. He pressed his cheek into my palm. I let his warmth wash over me, providing one last bit of comfort before I bid farewell to him and the others.

"I can't heal you if you aren't with me," he murmured.

"I'll find a way," I assured him.

Valda teleported to me, grabbed me by the arm, and teleported back to her position on the mountain. She climbed up on the white Dragon and extended her hand, but I wasn't about to give her any satisfaction.

"Not going to fly yourself?

"Not when I have to maintain your safety. Don't want you falling off. It's a long way down."

I scoffed and brushed her hand aside then climbed onto the back of the Dragon. Her smile didn't falter when she said, "I knew you'd do the right thing."

My heart dropped at the sight of my friends' faces when the Dragon flew away.

CHAPTER SIXTEEN
CALIAN

Anwir didn't know it yet, but his death would be at my hands. And I had it all planned down to the smallest detail. It would be slow and painful. First, I planned to heat his inner temperature so high his blood would boil. My fire would spread through his entire body, turning his insides into ash. He'd scream in pain for hours before I'd end his suffering by running my blade through his heart.

"Calian? What do we do now?" Morwen asked. Her voice was soft and flustered, which chas unlike her. Between Senna's death and Emera leaving with Valda, she had every right to feel frightened. Her friend—our friend—was dead, and a goddess with immeasurable power had flown off into the sky with our enemy. What the Dragonhell was she thinking?

I ran my hands through my hair and looked up into the darkening sky. We'd remained in the area to…well…breathe and cope. The sun now sank into its bed as the moon rose to guard the night. We were now a day behind schedule, but traveling through the night seemed—as Erjon would say—illogical. We were all in shock, which would compromise anyone's ability to think straight in a moment of combat. I cursed Anwir's name and kicked the dirt. Dhruv did the same. He might have snorted, but I knew he cursed the slimy Dragonmaster's name. I looked at my steed and nodded. We'd find a way to kill the traitor.

"Calian?" Morwen's repeating of my name was followed by a cool sense of tranquility. My jaw loosened, and I unclenched my fists. When I glanced down, Erjon's hand rested on my shoulder. Any other time I'd be furious that he'd used his power on me. But not today. I welcomed the peace.

"We will rest for the night."

Fin sighed. "We've been here all day, Cal." He shifted his weight and shrugged. "I know how much Senna meant to all of us, but we have to consider the bigger picture, here. We need to get to Medora before Amram does. It's not a matter of *if*. It's a matter of *when*."

"Fintan's reasoning is sound," Erjon added. "Now that Emera has gone with Valda, we must act quickly."

I shook my head. "We will rest here and move in the morning." I had no intention of moving no matter how right they were. They could call me stubborn, but I wasn't going to do it. I looked over my shoulder to where Avani lay curled up beside Senna's body, sleeping. We'd wrapped Senna in whatever blankets we had and placed the nicest stones we could find on top of her. The thought had crossed my mind to ask Avani to create a hole in the ground to bury her, but I'd decided against it. "Besides, Avani isn't ready."

"She'll never truly be ready," Fin continued. "People are going to die. She needs to come to terms with that."

Morwen smacked Fin on the arm. "Fintan!" she hissed.

"Look, being insensitive is not my intention. Senna made it her life's mission to defeat Amram and save humanity. She'd agree with me wholeheartedly. We need to get to Medora."

He had a point. Senna would be angry with us for stopping on account of one person's death. Even if it were her own.

"I agree with Calian." We all turned our heads in the direction of Kedron's voice. "Avani needs this night." His eyes drifted into the sky. "Tamasvi commands it."

I frowned, unsure of what to make out of his statement. But he was the Dragonheir of darkness. He knew more about the Dragongoddess Tamasvi than I did. Maybe she had some healing magic I was unaware of. Regardless, I wasn't going to argue. He was on my side, and I needed that right now.

"So, it's settled. We'll rest tonight and head out tomorrow at dawn." I closed my eyes and waited for Fin to debate me on this, but he didn't. When I opened my eyes, he and Morwen were already walking hand-in-hand back to their horses. Dhruv was off doing gods knew what, so I sat on a fallen tree trunk on the far side of the clearing.

Avani tossed and turned, occasionally mumbling in her sleep. Morwen and Fin were huddled together next to a fire. Erjon and Kedron had both gone off in opposite directions to relieve themselves. That left me with nothing but my own mind chastising me for my ineptness. Why hadn't I studied the history of the war more? Why hadn't I mapped out the ancient Dragons' burial sites? Maybe we could have avoided the area to begin with. I closed my eyes, hoping I could drift into nothingness for a little bit before having to ride out in the early morning.

*   *   *

A twig snapped, causing me to wake up suddenly. "Who's there?" I croaked out into the foggy gray morning. Pieces of a horrific nightmare remained visible in my mind, so I shook my head to rid myself of them. Then I rubbed my eyes until my blurred vision became clearer. The sun peaked over the trees, but the fog of the early hour made it difficult to make out who or what was walking toward me. I called to my magic and formed a flame in my palm. But the flame did nothing to help with the lack of visibility.

"Answer," I demanded.

The figure drew close. As it did, I took a few steps forward and extended my arm. With a final step, a familiar young face was illuminated by the fire I held.

"Queen Hestia? What are you doing here?" Despite my best effort, I couldn't hide the relief in my voice. At least it wasn't Anwir or another of Amram's resurrected Dragons.

"I thought I would be more useful helping you than hiding in a palace," she said.

"You shouldn't have come." Why in the world would Queen Hestia think it was okay to leave her kingdom? "We've already lost someone," I continued. "I cannot guarantee your safety." I didn't want to imagine the death of a queen on my hands.

"I'm going with you."

"That would be unwise."

Queen Hestia's face remained neutral while her eyes bore into mine. "You cannot go against an order from the queen."

"Watch me." The words escaped me before I could stop them, and I flinched, waiting for the queen's retaliation. I'd let my frustration get the best of me, and the result was that I'd just disrespected a queen. A brief memory of Anwir slapping me with horse reins for disobeying him flashed through my mind.

We stared at each other for a few moments. When it was clear she wasn't going to reprimand me, I turned and left her standing there. I let the embarrassment stir within my chest as I scanned the area, looking for Dhruv. My horse snorted loudly from the trees, giving away his location. Fin was awake, tending to his horse Shadow—a slender black steed with a gray mane. Morwen's eyes fluttered open just as I walked by her; the exhaustion on her face indicating she'd awoken from a fitful sleep. Kedron was nowhere to be seen, but I wasn't concerned. Even though he teleported places occasionally, he was always prompt. I didn't know where he teleported off to, and I didn't ask. It wasn't my place.

Erjon snored deeply from where he slept on the ground next to Avani. My stomach dropped at the sight of her sleeping peacefully next to Senna's grave. Erjon's hand rested on her arm. Knowing him, he was making sure his power kept her mind at ease so that she got some sleep. He might have subdued her pain, but I bet deep in her heart, she still felt the burden of loss. I couldn't bring Senna back, but I'd be damn sure her murderer was taken care of.

"Slow and painful," I muttered to myself.

"Captain."

I sighed. "Please, your highness, go back to the palace."

The queen ignored my request. "You need me," she said.

"Doubtful." I muttered. I picked up my pace toward Dhruv.

"Queen Hestia." Morwen bowed. She looked more refreshed than when I'd first seen her. Her hair was pulled back, and her clothes were smoothed out. "May I ask why are you here?"

"To help us with that Dragonsight, I hope," Fin said.

I exchanged a confused look with him before asking, "How did you know that?" It was a dumb question because I knew the answer. Sure enough, Fin winked at me, confirming my suspicion.

By this time, Erjon appeared at my side. "You weren't supposed to be in that room," he told Fin.

Fin shrugged. "Think of it like a party…Except I wasn't invited…And nobody knew I was there."

I threw Fin a foul gesture, and surprisingly, Queen Hestia laughed. "Dragonsight is not fortune telling." I was caught off guard by how nice she was. Why hadn't she at least scolded me?

"Dragonsight?" Morwen asked.

"Yes." The breeze picked up slightly, blowing her dark wavy hair around her. A stray curl fell over her eyes, and she ran her fingers through her hair to brush it back. The motion was oddly familiar.

Morwen addressed me with fire in her eyes. "That would have been helpful information."

The queen watched carefully, and Fin looked sideways, but I still maintained eye contact with Morwen. Erjon looked bored. Arguing was beneath him.

Morwen glanced at Queen Hestia. "Your highness, I apologize. It's just that…Well…" Morwen turned to me. "You knew the queen had Dragonsight, yet you didn't think to ask about our trip?" Her top lip quivered. "Senna might still be alive, and Emera might still be with us."

"I did ask her."

Maybe I shouldn't have admitted that. Morwen's eyes narrowed as she walked straight toward me and slapped my face. It was the angriest I'd ever seen her.

"The vision didn't show Senna dying. It only showed

Emera leaving."

Morwen looked at Queen Hestia who nodded. "My visions don't always tell the entire story."

"Emera's headstrong and stubborn," I said. "At some point, she was going to take Valda up on her offer to save our lives. To save *your* life. I just didn't think it would be so soon. My plan was to find Nimerah first, and then I'd talk to her about joining Amram."

Fin grabbed his mate's hand. "It's not like any of us wanted her to go with Valda. But you can't blame Cal."

I opened my mouth to explain, but I decided to stay quiet this time. Morwen had been upset when Rehema died, but the look on her face now was something different. Anger mixed with sorrow and fear.

"Why do you always keep secrets, Calian?" she whispered. It was a fair question.

"Because sometimes, secrets save lives."

I knew that deep, aggravating voice well. "I was wondering where you'd gone off to, Kedron," I said over my shoulder. Looks like a stray followed you back." Zepherin came into my peripheral view, but my eyes remained locked on Morwen.

Erjon stepped forward. His right hand lifted slightly at his side, and Morwen's demeanor began to soften. She blinked a few times before her face flushed with embarrassment. She let out an audible exhale.

"Oh, Calian. I am…I just…"

"It's okay, Mor. We've been through a lot lately."

Fin pulled her in for a hug. Any tension she still harbored melted away in his arms. Then he guided her away from the rest of us. I closed my eyes and prayed to Anahita to give Morwen peace. When I opened my eyes, I nodded at Erjon. This was the second time he'd stepped in to do what I couldn't.

"A stray, huh? That's rich coming from you," Zepherin joked once the tension in the air dissipated. We embraced, and I realized then how much I'd missed my old friend. Zepherin and I had known each other ever since Anwir had declared me captain of the Nimerian Guard. We'd worked closely together on several training missions. It was how I'd met Erjon.

"When I saw the queen, I thought that maybe something was wrong at the palace," Kedron replied.

At the mention of something being wrong with Queen Eteri's palace, Erjon's back stiffened. Zepherin strolled over to his brother and wrapped his arm around Erjon's shoulders. "Everything is fine, little brother." Relief softened Erjon's expression.

"So why are you here?" I asked him.

Zeph laughed. "Tired of me already?"

"No, you're staying," Fin chimed in. He sauntered over without Morwen. "Everyone here is so serious." They shook hands, and I permitted my mouth to tilt into an awkward smile. Zeph and Fin were my brothers. I'd die for those men.

"Well, none of you have a say in the matter. I'm here as her escort." Zeph gestured toward Queen Hestia whose brow raised slightly. Something told me she didn't need an escort.

He turned to the queen. "I was ordered to find you and stay by your side. There are wild animals out here, your highness."

Queen Hestia looked at him point blank. "I could handle them on my own."

I admired her tenacity.

"And please," she continued. "I hate formalities. My name is Hestia."

"Yeah, no. That's going to be weird," Fin said. He wasn't wrong.

I cleared my throat, ending the conversation. We needed to leave. "Erjon, wake up Avani. We need to move out." I hated barking orders, but we couldn't waste any more time. That sounded harsh. Recovering from Senna's death wasn't a waste of time. But it was time to move on. The queen's vision had also shown Nimerah alone, so for now, Amram didn't know the Dragongoddess's location. My task was clear: continue to Nimerah while trying to come up with a plan to find Emera.

Everyone made their way to the horses while Erjon nudged Avani delicately. She stirred and lifted herself up on her elbows. She blinked several times and rolled her head from side to side, stretching out her neck. We all watched her closely as she stood. I glanced at Hestia and Zeph. Like the rest of us, they remained silent and let Avani have her final moment with Senna.

The air around us stilled. Nothing but the songs of the birds filled the space around us. Avani closed her eyes briefly. When she opened them, her gaze lowered to Senna's grave beside her. She released a ragged breath, and her shoulders sagged slightly. For a few minutes, time ceased to exist. Avani bent down beside the pile of rocks that covered Senna's body and placed her hands on the ground. Bright green magic flowed from her and into the earth. The ground rumbled slightly beneath her palms and tears fell from her eyes. They dropped onto the grass below her. The earth beneath Senna's body opened, and she lowered into the ground slowly.

I prayed silently to the Dragongod Endrit to comfort his

heir when she arrived in the Dragon Empyrean. When I opened my eyes, the opening closed over Senna, sealing her beneath the surface. Avani held her hand steady as grass and wildflowers bloomed where the rocks had been. Lightenion Sunflowers blanketed the ground, marking the resting place of our dear friend. When the flowers stopped growing, Avani wiped her eyes and stood. She nodded, and it dawned on me that she not only had unmatched physical strength but immense mental strength as well. She wasn't completely herself—anyone could see that. But there was a fight within her to finish what Senna had worked for. It made me appreciate her even more.

The others took their turn hugging Avani while I readied Dhruv for the long journey ahead. Zari came up and nuzzled my arm, letting me know that she was still with us. Despite Emera not being here, she'd remained. Yes, I knew she was a horse. But Emera treated Zari like she was more than that. I understood because Zari was loyal like Dhruv.

"You're lucky we have an extra horse," I told Hestia over my shoulder. And with that, I mounted Dhruv and headed east toward Medora.

CHAPTER SEVENTEEN
CALIAN

We rode east until the sun hung directly overhead. We'd entered the Arden Forest earlier that day. It wasn't necessarily the route I wanted to take, but riding north of the City of Dhara meant we'd travel through the Blayr Plains. Trees were scarce throughout the plains, making it impossible to hide should any Dragons attack. In the forest, we at least had the trees to blend in with and a running river to guide us. We'd follow it south of Dhara to remain undetected by King Tellus Hollowman's forces.

When we'd first set off that morning after Senna's burial, Zeph confirmed that King Tellus received payment from

Amram for a Dragon's destruction a while back. Safe to say that Dragon was Valda. And "a while back" was when we fought her in Dhara. Gods that seemed like so long ago.

It was the information needed to prove that King Tellus allied himself with Amram. Kedron and I planned to seek out an ally within the city when we stopped to let the horses rest. While the others refreshed themselves by eating and sleeping, we would teleport into the palace kitchen. Kedron claimed he had an informant inside the palace—a family friend—and that they would help locate the other amulet. I didn't question Kedron's reasoning for transporting into the kitchen. I just assumed it was a place he and this other person met often. Kedron had proven time and time again how valuable he was to us, so I would just go with it.

When we finally reached what appeared to be a good place to stop, everyone dispersed to their own areas for resting.

The area was a hidden glade with tall trees forming a protective circle around us. Sunlight filtered through the canopy, providing the right amount of warmth from the cool, verdant shade. Everything about the glade reminded me of Emera, and my heart twisted in my chest. The air smelled like her, a mix of wildflowers and the earth.

A small crystal-clear stream wound its way through the

glade. Its babbling waters reminded me of Emera's laughter—a smooth melody to me. The horses quickly located the stream and lowered their heads to sip from its refreshing water.

None of us said anything for a little while, which I found incredibly soothing. After the events of yesterday, I wanted peace.

Morwen—who'd apologized over and over again for her behavior by the mountain—kept close to Avani. In my mind, Morwen shouldn't have apologized. Tensions were high, and it was normal for anyone to be burdened with heavy emotions. It didn't matter that she was the Dragonheir of Water with the ability to flood her soul with tranquility. Everyone lost their shit every now and then. Regardless of my feelings, I accepted her apology.

Now the two women lounged in the shade while Erjon tended his horse and Zeph sat on a fallen tree. Hestia wasn't with him. When we stopped, she'd gone to meditate to the gods and goddesses or whatever it was she did to conjure visions. Apparently, the connection was clearer when the meditating was done alone. I still hadn't asked her how she had Dragonsight since she was human. The more I was around her, the more I didn't care. No one else seemed to care either.

"I should be going with you." Fin said as he approached.

"I need you here in case things go badly," I replied. I took off a riding boot and inspected my hidden dagger.

"I'm an expert at sneaking around. Your muscles are too big to hide behind anything. You have a hard enough time keeping them contained in that shirt of yours. Seriously. You need a new tailor. The proportions are way off."

I refastened the leather strap so that the small dagger was secured at my ankle. "I think I will take that as a compliment."

"You might be large and in charge here, but there, you'll stick out like a sore thumb." He leaned against a thick tree and crossed his arms. He had no intention of letting this go.

"I see what you're saying, Fin. Really, I do. But I don't think Kedron can teleport us both."

"That's not an issue." Kedron appeared out of thin air by the tree, startling Fin so much that he stumbled over a tree root.

"How many times have I told you not to do that?" Fin said, bracing his arm against the tree to regain his balance.

I snorted. "Kedron might be the only person alive that can scare you, Fin."

"I don't know about that. Have you met my mate?" Fin pointed out.

"That's fair," I responded, and Kedron nodded in agreement. Morwen was frightening when she wanted to be.

"I can take you both. You'll hold onto one hand while Fin holds onto the other."

"See!" Fin all but screamed.

I crouched down by the stream, cupped the cool, clear water into my hands, and splashed my face. It was a brief comfort. When I straightened back up, Fin was gone. He walked toward Morwen, his pace indicating he was on a mission. I rolled my eyes because I knew what he was doing. He was going to convince her that he'd be more useful on what he would probably label *the scouting mission*. He had a label for everything.

Kedron and I waited for him to return. If Morwen agreed, there would be no arguing with Fin. If Morwen disagreed, there would be no arguing with Morwen. The fate of *the scouting mission* was in the hands of the Dragonheir of Water. Soon enough, the foolish smile planted on Fin's face gave away the verdict.

"Let's do this!" Fin called out on his way back.

It didn't take much effort to convince the others to remain at the rest stop. Zeph yawned and nodded before he splayed-out on the ground, welcoming the opportunity for a long nap. Morwen kissed Fin good-bye and then walked to the stream to shield Avani while she bathed in the stream. Hestia had returned. She and Erjon were deep in conversation about Dragonsight, so I'd taken the opportunity to ask if she saw anything regarding this trip.

Her eyes clouded over for a few minutes. When they cleared, the queen smiled. "Your mission will be successful." Her smile faded slowly. "But it will come at a great cost."

"That seems like the opposite of successful."

The queen shrugged just as Kedron took hold of my hand. Then we made *the jump*.

The last time I'd jumped, I had been recovering from the drugs Anwir had given me. I didn't remember the experience. This time was different. I was momentarily disoriented as if a rush of vertigo had twisted my sense of space and time. The world around me shifted and shimmered. It was like the reality around me was being rewritten.

There was a tingling feeling, almost electric, that coursed through my body. It started at the tips of my fingers and toes and spread upward and outward. I was weightless, and I heard nothing. The familiar world dissolved into a blur of vibrant blue hues that swirled around me. Then those blues suddenly went pitch black. Being a shadow of the night, Fin probably found the sensation exhilarating, but I found it alarming. The darkness swallowed us whole, and the air was sucked right out of my lungs.

The jump was only a split second, but the process felt like an eternity. When we arrived in the palace, the light poured back in. I suddenly reconnected with the ground in a resounding jolt. My heart raced and I blinked several times to gain my composure.

After we appeared in the kitchen, I reached out my arm to grab the nearest solid object and gasped for air. Fin stumbled backwards into a large cauldron, choking and coughing simultaneously. Good thing the fire beneath the cauldron was out.

Kedron looked at both of us like we each had two heads.

With one hand on my knee and the other clutched to the end of a table, I looked up at him, inhaling air like a newborn babe. "It's not as easy as it looks, is it?"

"I guess not," Kedron said. He offered his hand, and I took it, standing up and straightening my back. After a couple of pops, it felt better. If I could limit my jumps with Kedron, I'd die a happy man.

"That…was…amazing," Fin said between breaths. "Oh…and…someone's coming." He was bent over with his arm reaching out, pointing to a door across the kitchen. It creaked open slowly, and two people could be heard on the other side of it. We all dove under the table. In any other circumstance, I'd be tempted to fight, but a brawl would only draw attention. We needed to be stealthy.

"Two voices," I whispered. We were only meeting one person, so we stayed hidden.

"Kitchen staff?" Kedron suggested.

I shook my head. "We were told they'd be at the chapel."

"Maybe Zeph's scout wasn't as informed as he'd said," Fin whispered.

The strangers opened the door fully, but they were met with darkness. Kedron had used his magic to blacken the room. My breathing quickened. I felt like I was back in *the jump*, void of air.

"Just breathe," Kedron murmured.

"I am!" I hissed.

"Shh!" Fin kicked me, and I winced but didn't dare make another sound.

"What in the Dragon'ell is goin on 'ere," said the closest voice. Whoever it was stumbled around, bumping into the table and everything else. The man was so noisy, I wanted to set him on fire. Pans and other kitchen utensils fell, clanging loudly when they hit the stone floor. "Lemme get the fire a'goin, and we'll..." I waited for the man to finish, but instead, there was a loud thwack and a grunt followed by a thud. An object connected with my nose, and I bit my lip to stay quiet. Something warm trailed over my lip and down my chin. Blood. Wonderful. I would have healed myself, but every time I did that, I glowed. It was silly. Glowing like a star. No. I would bleed out before I gave away our position.

"Psst! Keddie!" the voice whispered hastily. "Are you there?" The voice belonged to…a woman?

The darkness lifted, and the object that had hit me was a man that now lay unconscious on the floor. He was large with a round belly and hairy arms. I guessed it was his bald head that hit my nose since there was blood on it. I lifted my hand to my nose, let my magic flow through me, and healed the wound. When I got out from under the table, Kedron was hugging a petite woman—smaller than Emera—in a tight red gown with long hair so light, it was almost white. I looked from her to the man that lay unconscious on the floor and then back to the woman.

"You can pick your jaw off the floor, Cal," Fin teased. I didn't notice my gaping mouth. I was impressed that such a small woman could take down such a large man. Emera could, of course, but she was a goddess.

Fin held his hand out to the woman. "Fin. Archer extraordinaire," he said.

I snorted, but the woman ignored me. She took his hand and shook it ever so slowly, and her lips spread in the most lustrous smile I'd ever seen. Her heart-shaped face, supple red lips, and hypnotic dark eyes could stop a man in his tracks. "Nyx," she said. Good gods. The woman's sultry voice could melt any man's heart. She turned and held her hand out to me.

"So that's how you did it," I said, not bothering to take her hand. Whatever spell she'd cast on the man left him barely breathing on the floor. I was not about to fall victim to that. Fin was on his own. "Lured him in here with a promise of intimacy and then you just…"

Nyx dropped her hand and her smile vanished instantly. It was so fast; one might not even remember if she'd been smiling at all. "Not everyone is gifted with natural magical abilities." There was venom with every word. She was beautiful and captivating. A true succubus.

"That's fair," I replied.

She looked me up and down. Once satisfied, her smile slowly returned, like she had been joking the entire time. It was then that I studied her face more closely. Her hair and eyes reminded me of someone.

Nyx beckoned us toward the door. "We must hurry. King Tellus's kitchen staff will be back. The spell will wear off shortly."

She was a witch. What kind of people did Kedron get himself tied up with?

As if I'd voiced my thoughts aloud, Nyx argued against the label. "I'm not a witch by the way. I'm a sorceress. There's a difference."

I widened my lips into a fake smile, leaned against the table, and crossed my arms. "I didn't say you were."

Nyx nodded and pointed to her head, "Yes, but you were thinking it."

I didn't drop my smile, but the embers within me sparked to life. This woman was going to get under my skin. "And how is it that you know what I'm thinking?" I growled.

She swayed over to me and stood so close; we were almost touching. "Because I'm good at reading people," she breathed.

I carefully grabbed her shoulders and pushed her back.

"She's one lucky gal," Nyx purred.

"Who is?"

"Your mate."

"I don't have a mate." I hated to say it, but it was the truth. As much as I longed for Emera to be my mate, she wasn't.

Nyx threw her head back and laughed. Just another weapon in her man-killing arsenal. "So, you say, Cal."

Heat blazed behind my eyes. "It's Calian."

Nyx glanced at Kedron and gestured to Fin. "It seems like your friends call you Cal."

"True." I leaned toward her. "My *friends,*" I snarled.

She turned on her heels and headed for the door. "Ah, but we're going to be great friends," she said over her shoulder. She waved her hand, beckoning us to follow her as she sauntered out of the kitchen. The three of us followed closely behind her. We turned left out of the kitchens and sneaked quietly down the narrow hallway, our footsteps light and stealthy. We rounded a corner and headed down a flight of stairs. At the end of the stairs was a small wooden door. Nyx stopped in her tracks and spun on her heels.

"Where are we?" I asked.

"A closet," she replied, deadpanned.

I glared. "And why are we at a closet?"

"We're going to get disguises?" Fin asked. "This just keeps getting better and better."

Kedron opened the door once it was clear that Nyx wasn't going to. Being all chivalrous, he motioned Nyx in first and Fin and I followed her in.

I surveyed the closet. It was pretty bare for the exception of a couple stools and a pile of clothes that Fin rummaged through.

"The king has many Dragonpriestesses that follow him everywhere. He doesn't know any of their names, and quite frankly, wouldn't recognize a single face. He wants to appear like a holy man, but he's all about wealth and power. Rumor is that he's in cahoots with the resurrected Dragongod. I paid off three of them because deep down, they hate him. They were glad to take a day off. Discreetly, I will add."

"I don't think I can pull this off," Fin said jokingly, holding up a robe and cowl with no mask.

"You can't," Nyx replied, "But he can." She gestured toward me.

Fin howled with laughter. Kedron punched Fin in the shoulder, a command to quiet down. Kedron didn't typically resort to violence, so Fin shut his mouth. Kedron meant business.

I threw Fin a smirk before turning back to Nyx. "If you're talking about shape-shifting, I don't know that I can," I said coolly, folding my arms over my chest and leaning back against the door. "I haven't shifted in a very long time."

Nyx put a hand on her hip. "You can. And you will. There's only one hood here without a mask, and it's all yours."

"You seem so confident about that."

"It's just another of my many talents," she teased. "Now get dressed, Dragonpriestess."

"Funny," I grumbled.

"Well, what are you waiting for? Shift." She was insufferable.

With a deep breath, I closed my eyes and focused on the transformation. It had been a while since I shape-shifting magic take over me, so I needed to concentrate. My body seemed to ripple. My limbs shortened and became slenderer as I took on a woman's physical appearance. My broad shoulders softened, and my facial features morphed, taking on more delicate and feminine contours. My short hair lengthened past my shoulders in dark waves. Even my height shrank. I stood shorter than Fin.

Fin pressed his hand to his heart. "Oh, Cal. You're breathtaking." He proceeded to wipe away a fake tear.

"Funny," I quipped with my now soft, feminine voice. Why was it so high-pitched? It was almost squeaky. Wonderful. "Throw me some clothes. It's chilly."

The clothes I wore were now too big. Their looseness allowed more air to slip through the gaping holes. I intended to continue wearing them, though. As soon as I shifted back into my regular self, they'd fit again.

Nyx tossed me a robe, and I put it on without hesitation.

"Well, you look lovely," she said.

I glared at her, and she just laughed in response. Why did I let her talk me into this? She was a sorceress. She probably cast a spell on me. Yes, that was it. It was the only logical suggestion for why I'd subject myself to this torture.

"I look stupid," I muttered in my high-pitched voice. My limbs were itchy from not shape-shifting in years, so I stretched out, arching my back and pushing out my chest.

"Please don't do that," Fin said with a chuckle. He fastened the mask of the hood he wore and smoothed out his emerald robe. I envied him for having a mask, and I didn't. But Nyx risked her life getting these robes, so I couldn't complain. Aloud, anyway.

Kedron leaned against the wall; his arms crossed in front of his chest. He and Nyx would scour the palace looking for the remaining amulet while Fin and I infiltrated the throne room during King Tellus's meeting with his advisors. Today's topic of conversation: Amram. At least, that's what Nyx claimed was on their agenda. She was a master at getting around discreetly. She was the female version of Fin except she was an expert at stealing information, and he was an expert at stealing lives.

CHAPTER EIGHTEEN
EMERA

The Dragonrealm of the Dead was nothing like I'd expected. I expected darkness, unmarked tombs, and a world ravaged by drought. Instead, the landscape was covered in a glistening white snow that sparkled with an array of colors beneath the setting sun. The wind pierced my exposed skin, so I lifted my cowl higher to protect my lips. The wind danced around us, singing an evocative lullaby from long ago. Ancient stone buildings peaked out from their snowy blankets, giving me a slight glimpse of a forgotten world. The Kingdom of Air had snow; the highest peaks of the mountains were covered with it. But those were nothing in comparison. The scenery before me was out of a dream—or a nightmare disguised as a dream.

The realm was hauntingly beautiful.

The white Dragon that carried us glided to the ground and landed gracefully in front of a stone bridge with intricate carvings made to look like scales. The bridge extended over a frozen river below that flowed and weaved through the Obsidian Mountains. I attempted to guess which mountain Erjon had pushed me off of, but they all looked the same aside from their varying heights. That moment seemed years ago considering all I'd been through.

Valda didn't bother to speak as we slid off the back of the Dragon. She didn't need to. Because if she had, I'd punch her. She was responsible for Senna's death. As was the man who greeted us.

"How the hell did you get here?" I hissed.

Anwir smiled. "I have my ways."

As angry and heartbroken as I was, I needed to remain calm. So, I took a deep breath and focused my attention on the snow beneath my feet. The crunch from my feet hitting the packed snow had a loud cadence to it.

The Dragon transformed behind us into a tall naked man with flowing brown hair and vivid white eyes. He wasn't particularly muscular, but rather lean and toned. The man was built for speed and agility compared to strength and physical power. He appeared older than Amram, but not by much—a few years at best. Our eyes met, and I looked away sheepishly, my cheeks warm with embarrassment. I hoped he didn't think I was *looking*.

Valda and Anwir engaged in quiet conversation while I slowly shifted my eyes back toward the stranger. He walked away in the direction of a lone tree. I strained my eyes to see the object of his attention. It was an enormous chest covered in snow. The man swept off the snow, opened the chest, and pulled out clothes. He shimmied into tight white leather pants and a billowy white shirt before stepping into white leather boots. From the chest, he pulled out pure white metal armor. The armor was thin, and my guess was so that the wearer could move swiftly. He lifted the breastplate over his head and secured it in place. The last of his armor consisted of leg coverings and gauntlets. I thought he was finished, but he finally pulled out a bow and quiver with various sized arrows.

This Dragon wasn't Amram's warrior, he was Amram's archer. I gulped down a knot of worry that formed in my throat. How skilled was this archer? Would he best Fin in a sudden death fight? The Dragon marched toward me, a pleased expression on his face.

"Glad to see it all still fits, Gawen," Valda said. The two shook hands. I snorted because their greeting was a very human thing to do. Then again, how would Dragon friends greet each other? Coil their tails around each other? The three of them turned toward me. I so desperately wished I had my chaos magic. There'd be nothing left of them if I had. Accepting that I wasn't going to speak, they started over the bridge.

Where the bridge ended, a flight of stone stairs began. Two staircases ascended upward with a towering statue of a headless Dragon between them. Looking at the statue's curvature, the scales, and the size of the Dragon, it wasn't my mother. So, this must have been Ragnar. And I assumed it being headless was Amram's doing. On each side of the Dragon were fountains, but no water sprouted into the frozen pond below.

My eyes followed the path of the staircases. They met and opened into a courtyard above the statue. When I finally set foot on the beaten stones of the courtyard, I was met with weathered stone and intricate mosaics, framed by the palace behind it. Dragon motifs were carved into the stone I stood on and into the towering stone columns and archways.

The landscaping was barren, but I imagined that at one time it was a harmonious blend of nature and artistry with lush gardens that provided a tranquil setting for meditation and reflection. Winding pathways all met at the stairs leading into Ragnar's palace.

The courtyard, even void of life, exuded a sense of timeless magic. I couldn't help but feel Ragnar's presence even though I knew there was no essence of him in existence. But the place still held a sense of wonder and reverence in his name. It truly was a boundary between the unnamed world and the divine.

Anwir fell in step beside me. "This courtyard was built in Ragnar's honor. He was the harbinger of Dragonsouls. Now Amram resides here." He spoke to me as if he hadn't just killed my friend.

I bit the inside of my cheek to keep from pummeling him with my fists.

"As you can see, Amram beheaded Ragnar's statue," Anwir breathed, inching closer to me. "He was a traitor to our kind. I am delighted that you've accepted that truth." His green scaly hand reached for my hair, but I slapped it away before he was able to grab any of it.

"You forget your place," I hissed, my voice laced with venom.

Valda stopped abruptly up ahead and turned on her heels. "Is there a problem?" It was a genuine question. And it was aimed at me, not Anwir.

"Can you leash your lapdog?" I asked in return. "Because if he touches me at all, he's going to lose a hand." I looked directly at Anwir. "Or a head."

Valda raised her hand. Anwir lifted into the air, his eyes widened in fear, and he started to protest. "I'm sorry. She's just so tempting."

I cringed from his words and looked away. Bile tossed in my stomach, so I swallowed hard to keep it from coming up.

"Emera," Valda purred. "How would you like me to punish him?"

What did she just ask me? Did I hear her correctly?

Anwir's face paled. "I'm sorry. It won't happen again," His fear was justified.

I cupped my hand around my ear. "I'm sorry. I couldn't quite hear you."

A wicked grin transformed Valda's face from being irritated to amused. She held Anwir suspended in the air.

Anwir's forehead creased as his brows furrowed together. When he realized I wasn't going to budge, he repeated himself slowly. "Emera, please. It won't happen again."

"Do not dare address me as Emera. We are not on that level of informality." I stood straight and nodded to Valda. She lowered her hand, and Anwir fell to the ground. He cried in pain when his knees hit the stairs beneath him. When he looked up, pure hatred flashed in his eyes. Good.

"I'm afraid your begging will not help you next time," Valda said with a slight wave of her hand.

"Oh, no," I replied with a glance over my shoulder. "There won't be a next time." Because I was going to kill him.

We entered the wide double doors of Ragnar's Sanctuary. It took a moment, but my whereabouts finally came into focus. I thought we'd enter a large room, but instead, we stood in a small hallway with lit sconces fastened to the stone walls. Whereas the outside was bright and serene, the inside was shrouded in darkness, illuminated by the flames on the wall. The air was damp and the drip drop of water echoed throughout the hallway.

Valda lifted her palm and called to her light magic, projecting it into the air until we were no longer masked in darkness. The hallway led to another set of double-doors. When we neared them, the intricate carvings of what had to be the ancient Dragon language became visible. This door was the barrier to what I assumed to be an inner chamber. Maybe that chamber would appear more welcoming than where we stood.

Valda placed her palm on a symbol—an engraved picture

of a key—at the center of the door. "Vylar, mir'draconar."

"Open, my friend," Anwir whispered behind me.

The doors opened, and I stepped into a vast chamber bathed in an ethereal glow. Large violet crystals hung from the ceiling, casting a soft purple haze onto the walls and the floor. The chamber was circular with murals on the walls that told of the unnamed world's tumultuous history. Cast in vibrant light at the center of the chamber was a large throne made of smooth obsidian stone. The stone was crafted to look like Dragonscales. The feet of the throne mimicked the appearance of Dragon's feet, and atop the high back was a Dragon's head looking downward with its wings closed below it. The angle of the wings made it appear as if the wings were draped around whoever sat there.

Valda leaned into my ear and whispered, "Go ahead and look around. I know you want to."

Hatred for her scorched my throat, and I swallowed it down. Part of me wanted to be stubborn and remain where I was. However, the other part of me knew that exploring the chamber for anything advantageous was the best course of action. I walked forward without so much as a glance at the throne. It was the structure behind it that caught my attention. At the farthest end of the chamber, a large human-shaped statue of pure violet gemstone stood proudly in front of a blazing fire. I'd never seen a stone of that color before. It was mesmerizing.

And so was the fire. The flames whipped and crackled behind the statue, emitting flickering shadows that danced upon the statue's domineering shape. It was as if the figure itself was moving. Tiny sparks burst from the flames like stars, soaring briefly into the air before they fizzled out.

My eyes drifted to the statue's base which was the same smooth obsidian stone of the mountains. Etched into the stone were engravings written in the ancient Dragon tongue. The words looked familiar, having been written in the book Erjon had gifted me. I knelt down and traced the words with my fingers, letting my soul connect with the magic of the language.

Drakonar Skalzor ~ Hilvar Mirkyn, Hilvar Drakonar ~ Stronkar vel cradunzor yulnol eyekuldanar et tolun.

"The Dragon Slayer. Half Human, Half Dragon. Bravery can birth the dawn of equality and hope," I whispered. What was more beautiful than the promise of a world with equality and hope?

I looked up at the statue and tried to recall any distant memory of a Dragon Slayer being taught in my history classes. Although the statue was of a pure violet gem, it was clearly a man with scales. So, a Dragonborn. That was a

Dragon Slayer? There was something incredibly familiar about the features of his face, like I knew him somehow. But it was impossible. He was a man of the past, and I was of the present.

The warrior was adorned in armor from the neck downward. His stance spoke of unwavering readiness as it held in its grip a pure obsidian blade—a real blade. His posture exuded power, and he looked like he could break free of his stationary prison at any moment. Upon the armor were intricate patterns and textures I'd never seen before. Attached at his shoulders was a flowing cape, adding an element of magnificence.

"A Dragon Slayer." I said to no one.

"His identity is a mystery, even to my father," Valda said, disdain dripping from every word. Her voice made me jump. I was so engrossed with the statue that I'd almost forgotten where I was. "Which I find incredibly infuriating," Valda continued, "considering he is the one that killed my father."

Too bad the Slayer hadn't killed you, too, I thought. I found it suspicious that Valda claimed she didn't know the identity of the Dragon Slayer. Then again, anything that came out of Valda's mouth was suspicious.

"My father was able to share his final moments with me through a Dragonmeld when I resurrected him."

I waited with bated breath, hoping she'd share anything else. If the man really killed Amram so long ago, then maybe learning more about him would help us figure out how to kill the god again.

Seconds passed, and I'd almost given up hope when Valda placed her palm on the side of my head. In an instant, I was taken into the past.

The land was shrouded in mist and filled with death. The fearless Dragon Slayer, clad in his armor, stood atop a hill, the outline of his body a stark contrast against the crimson-tinged sky. At his side, his hand firmly gripped a long blade. He stood among the dead, Dragonborns and Dragons lay scattered on the battleground.

I—a lonely soldier—stood among the dead, searching for the god I followed into battle. A deafening roar shook the trees at the bottom of the hill. A Dragon—Amram—loomed menacingly overhead. His wings were stretched wide, casting a shadow that seemed to swallow the Slayer whole. Amram dove at the Slayer, his jaws gaping wide, exposing the rows of his razor-sharp teeth.

But the Slayer held his ground, unshaken by the impending attack. He raised his blade, and as if it were responding to his command, the blade glowed with a brilliant violet light. Its sharp edges hummed with power.

In a flash of movement, the Slayer leaped forward, his boots landing squarely on Amram's snout. Amram's fiery breath, a scorching inferno, engulfed the Slayer. But the Slayer didn't cry out in pain. His armor must have been enchanted or held magic of its own—or he wore an amulet. When the fire cleared, the Slayer and his armor were unscathed. With a twist of expert agility, the Slayer flipped through the flames and landed upon Amram's head.

"Lyor mornulzor lith crulon vun lukar ol sahnar cradunzor mustari vel gavarnar et tolun," the Slayer growled.

Guided by his hand, the Slayer thrust the blade downward. The blade struck true, slicing through Amram's scales and penetrating deep into the god's skull. Amram let out an agonizing roar, one loud enough to shake the mountains. He thrashed wildly, trying to dislodge the Slayer's blade.

But the Slayer, undeterred, held on to the hilt of his sword. With every ounce of strength, the Slayer carved a searing rift from Amram's head to the back of the Dragon's neck. The god's eyes, once ablaze with fury, dimmed and flickered out like dying stars.

As the god let out a final, mournful cry, he fell to the ground. His colossal body quivered as he drew his final breaths. The Slayer, having rode Amram to the ground, stood victorious upon Amram's still-warm body. He withdrew his blade from Amram's skull, wiped the blood on the dead god's scales, and then sheathed it. He drew in a long, exaggerated breath, took hold of his helmet with both hands, and carefully lifted it from his head.

"Lyor mornulzor lith crulon vun lukar ol sahnar cradunzor mustari vel gavarnar et tolun," she murmured.

I was back in the sanctuary, standing in front of the statue with the Chaos Dragongoddess at my side. A curse formed at the tip of my tongue. If she'd kept me in there longer, I would have seen who the Slayer was.

"May your death be a warning that even the greatest power must heed the call of balance and the promise of life," she translated in our modern language.

"Pretty powerful words to say to a god," I said, smirking internally.

"I can appreciate the eloquence of his words, especially at the moment they were spoken. But the blade through my father's skull?" She let out a heavy sigh, not finishing her thought. Little did she know that the vision just given me the hope I needed. If the blade killed Amram before, surely, it could do it again.

"He's dead." It came out more as a statement and not a

question.

"No Dragonborn, not even if he's a powerful Dragon Slayer, can live as long as we can," she replied with a hint of a smile. Like we were best friends in a secret society of gods, and it was a common joke that we could outlive humans. I didn't find it humorous. And we definitely weren't friends.

I didn't smile, struggling to keep my anger at bay. I needed to play the game. I needed to figure out how to kill Amram and Valda.

"Very true," I agreed. "So, what? You keep this statue as a trophy?"

Valda chuckled. "Hardly." She drug her fingers down the blade. "There was a ceremony commemorating the Slayer and his blade. This statue was created as a reminder of who and what killed the powerful Dragongod Amram. Maybe if they hadn't forged the statue with the blade, then it could have been used to save the Slayer himself…before my soldier thrust a blade into his heart." A couple of minutes passed before she let out a sigh. "It's also a shame because this is an immaculate blade that I wouldn't mind using myself."

"Can't you just remove it?"

She turned to me suddenly, her eyes lethal. I'd touched a nerve. "I tried," she seethed and left me standing in front of the statue. She took her place on the throne. It struck me as odd that she sat there so comfortably. "It's getting late, and I am exhausted. Anwir will show you to your chamber. And if he so much as breathes wrong, you have my permission to kill him."

"I appreciate the sentiment, Cousin, but I don't need your permission."

Valda's eyebrow shot up when I called her Cousin. "You're scheming already?" A sly grin spread across her face.

I ignored her question. "Where's Amram?"

"Oh, don't worry. Father will join us soon."

I struggled to keep my knees from shaking as I walked toward Anwir. "I look forward to it," I called out over my shoulder. Then I followed Anwir through a side door on the west side of the sanctuary.

CHAPTER NINETEEN
EMERA

I followed Anwir through the west door into another cold, damp hallway. This one was larger, with the heads of each Elemental Dragon protruding from the walls. The hallway opened up into a small rounded chamber with three doors. He stood beside the one across the room.

"This is yours," he snarled.

"Thank you," I snapped. "Whose are those?" I pointed at the two remaining doors.

"Mine," he said, pointing to the door behind him, "and that one…Well, you'll find out soon enough." He smirked, and I wanted nothing more in that moment than to throw him back into the stone wall. But I remained focused. As much as I hated him, I needed to play the game. For Rehema. For Senna.

"I look forward to it," I replied through clenched teeth.

His smirk faded, and he trudged away down the hall. The door to the sanctuary slammed behind him. The tension in the air faded, but my smile didn't. Anwir wouldn't be lurking around me anymore, so I had more freedom to explore the sanctuary and devise a plan on how to get the information I needed and then get out. I wasn't staying. The only potential problem—besides the Dragongoddess in the next room— was the stranger who slept in the room next to mine. I assumed he or she was foe and not friend, so I'd have to work my way around them. And I'd have to use my human wits and fighting skills since my magic had left me. It seemed forever ago since I truly unleashed my power.

I opened the heavy door. As it creaked open, a luxurious chamber revealed itself. Plush purple velvet covered the obsidian stone chairs that sat in front of a roaring fire. At the center of the northern wall was a four-post obsidian stone bed with silk violet bedding. After closing the door behind me, I strolled to the bed. The thick cover was soft, and the silk sheets beneath it were smooth to the touch. Before I knew it, my feet had left the floor, and my back connected with the center of the bed. I sprawled my arms out, instantly relaxing into the opulent fabric. My whole body was weary, so I figured closing my eyes wouldn't hurt. After about a minute, sleep pulled me into its realm of darkness.

*　　*　　*

I bolted up after what seemed like hours of sleep. I was well-rested, but guilt panged my chest. What was I doing? My friends were out there without the comfort of a bed. And here I was, sleeping the night away in a lavish bed. I hopped off and explored the room.

Everything in the room was well-kept and made of obsidian rock which meant it was expensive. The obsidian mountains were hard to mine. A human's ax couldn't penetrate the rock, and I'd never heard of a Dragonborn being able to split it apart. Granted, I was only made privy to the conversations of the travelers that entered the apothecary. Ah, the apothecary. The mere thought of it stung. The more I learned about my new life, the more my old life faded into a distant memory. Before my Dragonmother's blessing, I could hear my parents' voices in my head, but now I could only see them. And even their faces were somewhat blurry. I missed them terribly—especially my father. So much of my life had changed since I parted ways with them, including the deaths of two people whom I grew to love. I held in a breath and vowed to get rid of Amram once and for all.

I walked along the walls of my room, my fingers grazing the refined stone walls and opulent tapestries of black, purple, and gold. One of the tapestries was a little lopsided, and it bothered me. I tugged down on one corner, but it didn't budge. A little more strength, I guess? I reached down for my magic from the Dragongoddess Dhara and tugged again. I'd used a little too much magic because the entire tapestry came crashing down on me.

"Good gods," I huffed and called to my strength magic once more to help me push it off. But nothing came. "So now I've lost my earth magic." At least I wasn't fatigued anymore. After several minutes of twisting, tugging, and pushing, I freed myself from the tapestry. My leathers were now covered in dust, but with a twist of my wrist and a little air magic, they were spotless. I glimpsed the area where the tapestry had covered...and gasped.

Behind the tapestry was a small wooden door. Did I just discover a hidden room or hidden exit? My excitement disappeared as quickly as it had surfaced. Surely, Amram or Valda knew the door was here. It didn't matter that I came here of my own free will. I was still their prisoner regardless if they pretended that I wasn't.

I breathed in several times and exhaled to steady my thoughts. If I was to be caged in this glorious room, I might as well explore a little. Gripping the handle, I pulled. And I pulled. And I pulled.

"This would be a great time for more earth magic." I gritted my teeth then clapped and rubbed my hands together. This would take a lot of muscle. I placed both hands on the handle and pulled. The door didn't move an inch. I braced my leg on the wall and pulled with all my might, but it still didn't budge. "Ah, hell!" I cried out. "What's the use of having a secret door if you can't open it?"

My eyes and hands searched the surface of the door for any clues. Maybe there was a secret word engraved in the wood? Maybe if I pressed a certain area just right, it would open? Maybe…Yeah. It all sounded stupid.

I pressed my back against the hidden door and slid to a seated position to rest my arms. Level with my line of sight was the head of Ragnar carved into the foot of the bed. I closed my eyes, rubbed them, and opened them again. I wasn't seeing things.

"Don't look at me like that."

The eyes of the carving sparkled even though it was void

of any jewels in the place of its eyes. I crawled to the bed and traced the outline of Ragnar's head. There were faint swirly details around it that looked awfully familiar. I'd seen them somewhere. But where? Wait. It was the door! The door had the same swirly markings. Valda had pressed her palm to the door to the sanctuary and said…Gods! What had she said? I clenched my fists and pounded the air. What had she said?

"Vylar, mir'draconar. It means, Open, my friend."

I angled my neck to see Amram standing at the door. "You again," I muttered under my breath. My hand instinctively shot out, but no magic accompanied it. "Haven't you grown tired of this? I know that you know Nimerah's whereabouts."

The god laughed. "I only know as much as you."

"Then you should leave me alone and go find her."

He walked forward and sat on the bed. "Oh, Emera. Why do that when I know you'll eventually lead me to her?"

"Good luck with that. I'm here as your prisoner. How can I find her if I'm trapped?"

The god conjured a single flame in his palm and watched it dance between his fingers. "I'm sure you'll find a way." He stood from the bed and walked over to the silent fireplace. In one swift motion, he threw his flame into the small logs. After a few seconds, the logs accepted the flame, and the fireplace roared to life. Amram then wiped his hands across the mantle, disturbing the dust that clung to the wood. Particles flew into the air and hovered over the tall black candelabras. Despite the flames that whipped back and forth, the room was still a little drafty.

"Is there anything else you need?"

"Not yet." He smiled, flashing his perfect white teeth. "Stay warm. I know these rooms can get quite drafty." The god snapped his fingers.

I was surrounded by darkness. I closed my eyes and opened them. Finally, the room came into view, but now I was back beneath its luxurious covers, having woken from my sleep. Amram was gone, but I knew I hadn't been dreaming. He was haunting me again.

I rolled out of bed for a second time, only now I was in the present. The flames were still alive in the fireplace which gave me pause. If Amram was only in my mind, then how was the fire still going? Had he really been here? We were in his domain after all. An eerie chill ran down my spine, so I shook it off.

I kneeled at the foot of the bed and located the outline of the Dragon. I repeated the words in the ancient Dragon language. "Vylar, mir'draconar."

There was a faint click and a hidden magical

compartment protruded out. Inside was a sleek obsidian key on a silk pillow. It had a distinct, intricate design that set itself apart from any other key I'd seen. Overall, the shape was reminiscent of a skeleton key. Perched on the key's bow was a lifelike figure of Ragnar. Well, I assumed it to be Ragnar. Two small violet gemstones served as the Dragon's eyes and its scales were individually etched, indicating that the key took time to create. The Dragon's tail coiled around the key's shaft and stopped before reaching the key's bit. The bit was thin with two key words on each side of the shaft, resembling open Dragon wings.

I stood and almost tripped over a chair from excitement. The air around me buzzed with a magical energy as if the room itself knew what was about to happen. With a shaky breath, I inserted the key into the slender keyhole of the hidden door. I turned the key, and as it rotated in my hand, the Dragon seemed to stir. Its gemstone eyes glowed a soft, ethereal light. The buzzing of air stopped, and in its place was a cool breeze. It flowed through my hair, tangling the blowing strands.

Click.

I held my breath and attempted to open the door once more. This time, I succeeded. I withdrew the key. I didn't want to put it back in the bed. At some point, Amram would see that key, and he'd figure it out faster than I did. I had no choice but to conceal it on my body. After I found a good enough hiding spot for it, I gently closed the door behind me. My light magic flared to life, but I didn't cast it above me. Instead, I created a glowing orb in my palm. It radiated just enough light for me to see that I was in a tunnel. The light expanded a few paces ahead. It was important to be as discreet as possible in case I encountered someone—or something—at the end of the tunnel. The orb could go out quicker than if light was all around me.

The tunnel was quite different than my room. The moist stone walls were weathered by time with cracks decorating their shapes. The tunnel was narrow at the entrance, but as I ventured further down it, it widened, revealing alcoves that beckoned exploration. The passage finally opened up, exposing a large chamber. It wasn't the expansive size of the chamber that made me pause, it was what the chamber possessed.

Books. And more books. And scrolls. A lot of scrolls.

I'd stumbled my way into a library. The space felt simultaneously open and enclosed. Tall archways connected to rows of tall shelves, harboring ancient tomes covered in dust. More crystals hung from the ceiling, catching the light from the lit sconces on the walls that came to life as I entered and projecting magical patterns of light and shadow across the floor. The air was thick with the scent of old parchment and a musty fragrance from the ancient tomes. Surprisingly, it all calmed my spirit and uplifted my senses.

The shelves stretched from the floor to the ceiling, lined with a variety of tomes, scrolls, and leather-bound manuscripts. Many of the spines were labeled with runes that hinted at the knowledge contained within. The shelves curved and spiraled, creating a winding maze.

Once vibrant tapestries decorated the walls, yet again depicting the history of the unnamed world. Scenes from the battles of old and the deeds of the ancient Dragons danced across the fabrics. As I passed by them, I noticed that each one told a different story, but they didn't just display the beginning, middle, and end of the war. No, they told of the smaller battles and the rise of human rebels. The detailed tapestries were a testament to the library's connection to the past and its role in preserving it.

My ears picked up on the constant humming of energy that pervaded the atmosphere. Runes and symbols decorated the shelves, radiating faint glimmers of enchantments. Would I be able to take a book from the shelf? What magic would I need to possess? It all seemed a bit exhilarating and dangerous. I felt slightly invigorated. If I couldn't escape the palace all together, I could at least escape down here during the night. Being a Dragongoddess had its advantages. I could go several nights without sleep. That meant I had plenty of time to steal away down here. Maybe the information I wanted was tucked away within the books that lined the shelves.

I seemed to glide through the stacks until I'd arrived at what appeared to be the heart of the library. In the center stood a grand oak table, covered in sigils of magical significance. The table seemed to serve as a space for study and contemplation, which was exactly what the individual sitting at the table was doing. He glanced up from the papers he was reading. His long black hair was tied behind him which emphasized his high cheekbones and thin nose. When I approached, he looked up from his reading. His eyes glowed red.

"Hello, Emera."

I gulped. "Hello, Elio."

Why couldn't I catch a break?

With a quick wave of my arms, I hurled air magic—the only magic I still possessed—at Elio's head. He dove from his chair to the floor. The gust of air hit the table, picked it up, and slammed it into the wall. Shards of wood and pieces of papers flew into the air, obscuring my view of Elio. As the papers glided to the floor, Elio ran behind the nearest bookshelf. I darted left just in time to watch Elio transform from a man into a sinuous, shadowy creature that slithered to the floor. Like a demon snake. It was quite gross, actually.

I advanced on him slowly. His eyes gleamed as he calculated my next move. I had no idea if he still maintained his own personality in a form like that. Maybe he'd be just like any other creepy snake-looking magical creature. Those existed, right?

"It seems like you've taken the form of your true self, Elio. A slimy slithering snake."

Elio shifted again, this time into a young boy. The form was unnerving, because the shape of the boy's face and the curl of his hair reminded me of Calian—but a younger Calian. Elio took this form to throw me off, but I reminded myself that it was him. "I know what you're doing, and it won't work. Hiding behind the mask of a child, even if it looks like Calian, isn't going to save you."

The young boy's eyes grew wide with fear. Despite telling myself it was Elio, I hesitated—a stupid move. Elio threw flames shaped like daggers at my head. I barely turned away in time, plastering my back against the bookshelf. Heavy tomes fell from the shelves onto my head.

I dropped to my knees as more books fell upon me. A

warm liquid trickled down my forehead. I reached up my hand, and when I pulled it back, blood coated my fingers. My anger spiked, and my remaining magic begged to be unleashed. Air magic burst from my body, expelling the books off of me and into the air. Some of the books hit a group of scrolls, and they tumbled to the floor. I struggled to stand; the familiar fatigue was back. How much longer would I have my air magic?

"You better cool it with that magic, Emera. If Valda finds us, we're both dead." Valda. He'd said Valda not Amram.

"I'll take you on hand-to-hand if you want," I taunted.

"No, thanks." His voice echoed off the library walls, so I couldn't quite place his exact location. Instead of running around frantically trying to find him, I paused. I needed to tap into my hunting skills that my father taught me. That meant taking in my surroundings. I glanced upward and noticed a second level of books. There had to be a staircase. If I found it, I could go up to the second level to have a better vantage point. And I needed that vantage point to find him and make him pay for what he'd done.

Which was what, exactly? Orchestrate Rehema's death? That was Valda's doing. Calian being in chains? That was Anwir's doing. Come to think of it, he hadn't done much. In fact, he'd warned us about Valda at the caves. So, what was he trying to accomplish?

I rounded a bookshelf, coming face-to-face with the black spiraling staircase. It was quite the contrast against the wooden shelves and tables. Its steps were crafted from gleaming, obsidian stone. It was polished to a mirror-like shine. Each of its rounded edges were smooth. It was both elegant and foreboding. It fit the ambiance of the entire palace.

Beneath the first twist sat a large cabinet with a bust of the Dragongod Ragnar atop it. The cabinet couldn't hide a man, but it was spacious enough to hide a child. Elio could have hidden in there. It was worth a shot before I went up the staircase.

I crept slowly as to not make a sound. I leaned over and reached for the handle.

Suddenly, I was knocked down from behind. Elio's body pinned me to the ground. I cursed loudly. I should have seen that coming.

Elio held my arms behind my back as I struggled to free myself from beneath him. "I am not your enemy," he said between pants. He was out of breath. Good. That meant I'd worn him out a little. He probably wasn't used to so much fighting being employed as a spy. Being a shapeshifter, he probably devoted most of his time to sneaking around dark alleys and hiding in the shadows.

I called to my air magic, but it didn't come. I was officially out of all my magic. I took a glimpse at my scales. I still had them, but they were void of color. With a surge of adrenaline, I thrust my head back into Elio's face and heard a resounding crack when my skull connected with his nose. Elio's grip on me loosened, so I pushed myself up off the ground, causing him to stagger backward. His back hit the staircase, and he slumped to the floor. A small dagger fell from his hip and bounced to my feet.

"Not my enemy, huh? That's rich." I picked up the dagger and stalked toward him. Blood streaked from his nose. Good. I wasn't going to show mercy.

Elio held up his hands in surrender. "Wait! I know what's going on with your magic. I know why it's gone."

CHAPTER TWENTY

EMERA

There was no way I heard him right. "Um…I'm sorry." I leaned my left toward him to make sure I heard him correctly. "What did you say?"

"I know why you don't have your magic anymore, Emera." His casual use of my name irritated me. The way his arms dropped to the side and how he slightly twisted his wrists didn't go unnoticed either.

"Watch it," I snarled. "Or I'll throw this dagger at your head."

He stopped rotating his wrists and sat in an empty chair next to the stairs. He looked around the library. His shoulders sagged forward, and he sighed heavily.

My mind continued to buzz with the revelation that he might know what was happening to me. "How do I know you're telling the truth?"

"You don't."

He was right. I didn't. But did I care? I was desperate to learn what Amram was doing to me that I'd risk it.

"Amram is siphoning your magic from your mind."

"Excuse me?" I inhaled and exhaled several times then leaned against a bookcase adjacent to the chair Elio sat in.

"That's why you don't have your magic anymore. He's taking it from you every time he enters your mind."

I slid down the bookshelf to the floor, feeling defeated. It all made sense. And it all made me very angry.

"You need to get to Queen Hestia. She can help."

"Why? Why are you being nice all of a sudden? After what you've done."

He leaned back in the chair. "You blame me for your friend's death, but I was not responsible for that. And Calian would have been killed had it not been for me. Valda wanted to end his life there and then, but I convinced Amram that Cal would come around. So, he went into the dungeon instead." He paused, pinching his nose and inhaling deeply to steady his erratic breathing. "You have to understand.

Hestia is a pragmatic woman who only thought of saving her people. She thought that eliminating you would ensure her kingdom's safety."

I considered his determination to convince me that he wasn't the enemy while he swept his gaze around the library. "It took me days to find this library. Then more days to locate the texts you blew off the desk. Thank you for that." He stood and made his way back to the desk at the center of the library.

I followed closely behind, my senses on high alert. "But the council led people to believe that the prophecy was to resurrect Amram for the good of the six kingdoms, not to destroy it. How did she know Anwir was lying?"

Elio crouched down in the mess we created—okay, that I created—and sifted through the scattered pieces of paper. "Queen Hestia hates Anwir. Which makes sense because she's a human."

Had I heard him correctly? "She's…a…what?" I'd never met the queen before.

"A human."

My mouth gaped open. A human queen was unheard of. Dragonborns ruled the six kingdoms, not humans. They held a higher status throughout the unnamed world because of their Dragonmagic. It was impossible that a human queen would have control of a kingdom of Dragonborns. I paced back and forth, letting down my guard in order to process this new information.

"I didn't think it was possible for a human to rule a kingdom?"

"She's not just any human. She's a sorceress," he answered while continuing his search. He spoke clearly, but he was obviously distracted. His hands moved with haste, quickly discerning which papers contained the text he desperately needed. Some pieces of paper he held up to inspect more closely while others he discarded without thought.

"I didn't think those existed," I mumbled. A fleeting feeling of irritation heated my cheeks. We were back at the fact that valuable knowledge of the world was hidden from me. My parents were just trying to protect me, but in the end, I was cheated of the information needed to navigate my life as a goddess.

Elio seemed to have located what he needed. He dropped to his knees, cleared an area on the floor, and laid the papers out in a row. "They're rare," he said. "Sorcerers and sorceresses are born to a Dragonborn and human couple. Their blood doesn't activate completely, so they can't produce magic from their body, but they can manipulate it through other magical resources."

Other magical resources? "Like an amulet?" I asked. My body hummed with excitement. This would explain the amulet Fin can wear, and the one I kept on me at all times.

Elio stopped and sat back on his heels. "Yes, like an amulet. Queen Hestia wears one when she needs to appear like a Dragonborn. She only does it when meeting with ambassadors from other countries. The people of the Kingdom of Fire don't care that she's human, but I'm sure it also helps that she has Dragonsight."

"Dragonsight?" I'd heard of it, but it seemed like the stuff of fairytales.

"She can see the future. Not always clearly, and futures can change, but it's helpful when dealing with enemies."

"Like an evil Dragongod."

"Exactly."

My heart was giddy. For the longest time, I'd heard stories of how humans were less than. Even though my parents were well established in Medora and had a great reputation, they were still second-class compared to the Dragonborns in the town—including Nile Ford and his family. I scoffed at the thought of Nile's name. I wished he could see who I truly was. Maybe when Amram was defeated, I'd find him…And show him.

"You're smiling."

"Am I?" I dropped the expression on my face and pursed my lips. Elio chuckled and went back to his work. Our entire encounter was weird. First, we'd been fighting. Now we were…not fighting. I didn't know what to make of the situation. Wasn't I supposed to hate him for trying to infiltrate the camp and kill me? The answer was simple.

No.

I couldn't be mad at the queen or him for their actions. My life was nothing compared to the countless others who occupied the kingdoms. If killing me had meant saving them, then the queen's plan was justified. I was not more important than anyone else. It just turned out that Valda was alive and kicking which no one saw coming.

"What important information are you piecing together?" I asked.

Elio paused, recognizing that he was still missing a portion of text. "A prophecy," he muttered.

"Good gods, not another one," I drawled.

"I don't think you're going to mind this one," he replied between laughs. "Ah! There it is." He grabbed the remaining paper he needed. I was impressed that he was able to put it all together considering the chaotic mess I made. A twinge of guilt hit my chest. I looked at the ceiling and sent a silent prayer to Ragnar, asking for forgiveness. I didn't know how or when, but I'd replace that desk.

"Take a look." He moved to the side, making a spot for me to read the prophecy.

I crouched down below and read the words written in the language of the ancient Dragons. "In the age of embers, when the stars align, a Dragon Slayer born of chaos will rise. With an unyielding heart, and immense courage, the Slayer will face the Second Chaos Dragon beneath darkened skies. With the swing of a magical blade, forged from chaos itself, the Slayer will pierce the fiery heart of the Dragon god. The Dragon god will reign no more, and the unnamed world will be freed from its chains. Thus, the prophecy is fulfilled, and the unnamed world will flourish."

"That's the second part of the original prophecy."

There it was, clear as day. The answer to our problems. Just as I suspected, the blade would take down Amram. The only question was: Who was the Slayer? The original Slayer must be dead at this point.

I stood. Elio and I needed to figure out who the Dragon Slayer was and locate the blade. I held my hand out to him. As much as I hated saying it, I needed him. "Do you want to form an alliance with me?"

He nodded slowly and took my hand. "You bet I do."

I helped him to his feet. "We need to figure out who the Slayer is and the location of their blade." I looked back and forth between the wreckage of text and the books still on the shelves. If the prophecy was found in the library, surely the Slayer's identity would be here, too. Or! Maybe that was the reason we needed to find my mother. Maybe Nimerah knew.

"The blade is here," Elio said, interrupting my thoughts.

I spun on my heels. "Where?"

"In the sanctuary. You probably saw it when you came in."

The statue. Of course! That's why the blade looked so real. "Does Amram know?" I held my breath, hoping the answer was no.

"Yes."

My father always told me to never get my hopes up.

"But he doesn't know who it is, which makes me think that when the Slayer killed Amram the first time, he was hooded, cloaked, or wore a helmet."

"That's what Valda told me. Hmm…I bet my mother knows how to get the blade."

"Then we need to find her."

"I know the area where she's at, but I won't lie to you. I don't completely trust you."

"That's fair." He reached out his hand, his palm facing

upward. It took me a second, but it finally registered what he wanted: the blade. I handed it to him slowly. He cut a small line in his palm then offered me the blade.

"What are you doing?"

"Initiating a blood oath. A blood oath ensures that I don't go back on my word. Should I do that, my magic will consume me."

The hilt of the blade was still suspended between us. "That seems excessive."

"If it's how I can get you to trust me so that we can end this war, then I'll do it."

I hesitated, not sure of what to think. I sent a quick prayer to Nimerah. *Mother, please forgive me if I'm making a mistake by doing this*. But I didn't see any other choice. Before I could change my mind, I grabbed the blade from Elio and drew it across my palm. I held out my hand and he took it.

We shook as he said, "I vow to be your ally. Should I find Nimerah, I vow not to take her life or tell others where she is."

I had no clue what to say. "I agree to your vow, and I make this vow of my own. I vow to be your ally. I vow to share whatever vital information I have so that we can work together to stop Amram."

A shining light formed between our palms and radiated throughout the library. It grew brighter and brighter before it slowly started to fade. We withdrew our hands, and I opened my palm. The cut was healed. "We have a slight problem."

"What's that?"

"Amram can enter my mind at will. Once he finds out what we're up to, he'll enter yours as well."

Elio shook his head. "He can't. Queen Hestia fortified my mind. It's how I've been able to spy on everyone here."

I sighed, appreciating the one thing we had going for us. "Then you'll go find Nimerah."

Elio nodded. "And you stay back to get the blade. Any leads on where Nimerah is?"

"Medora. Maybe the Kaimana Sea." It didn't matter if I shared that with Elio since I'd known Nimerah's whereabouts before Amram trespassed into my thoughts. I was certain the god already knew what I did.

Elio stepped past me. "I'll leave tonight. Valda doesn't keep her sights on me as much. I can shape-shift into a hawk, so it won't take me long to get there. Regardless if I'm successful or not, I'll be back in four days." He kept going, heading toward the staircase. He took a few steps upward.

"Where do the stairs lead?"

"To my chambers. There's a hidden door beneath my rug.

If you find your way blocked, you can enter there." He continued upward until I couldn't see him. Then I heard the closing of the hidden entrance to his chambers.

Four days is all I had to figure out how to get the blade dislocated from the statue without Valda noticing. How was I going to do that?

I was still contemplating the blade a few hours after Elio left. Despite my bed being the equivalent of a cloud, I couldn't sleep. My newfound alliance with Elio made my head spin. It was the opposite of what happened with Valda. With her, my friend was my enemy, but with Elio, my enemy was my friend. Well, I wasn't sure *friend* was the right word. But I was warming up to him. Again, my rationale told me that I couldn't hate him for his deception. He wanted to save his people. So, did I. And he hadn't been the one to kill Rehema—that was Valda. And if what he said was true, then he was the reason Calian was still alive.

Beads of sweat formed on my creased brow, and suddenly the room seemed to close in around me. I threw the sheets off my body and swung my legs over the side of the bed. The floor was cool to the touch, which was a relief from the heat of the blankets. The nightgown I wore was a luxurious black silk that hugged my every curve…and it made me feel uncomfortable.

I stood in front of the dimly lit fire and hugged myself. What I wanted—needed—was Calian's arms wrapped around me, not my own. Him not being near me was like I was missing a part of myself. Nothing eased my soul better than the tender touch of his hand in mine or the safety of his embrace. But he wasn't here. Instead, I was trapped in the presence of a malevolent god and a slimy ex-Dragonmaster. Sure, I had chosen this fate, but it was only to prevent more deaths. It was time to drop the warrior facade, channel my inner Fin, and be a spy.

In a tall wardrobe located in a corner of the room, I located a silk robe, and threw it over the nightgown. I slide my feet into slippers I'd discovered at the bottom of the wardrobe, and snuck quietly toward the door. The door creaked sightly at first, but it fell silent the further it opened. With one last glance behind me to ensure the tapestry covered the hidden doorway, I slipped out of the room in the darkened hallway.

The sconces were still lit, but just barely. Thankfully, my robe was just as black as my nightgown, so I blended into the shadows that lurked along the walls. With one foot placed carefully and silently in front of the other, I retraced the path Anwir had taken me. I wanted to see the blade while alone so that I could see if my strength alone would dislocate it from the statue.

The door to the sanctuary was ajar, and the glow from the purple crystals peeped through it.

"That's strange," I mumbled. I pressed my back against the wall containing the darkest shadows and crept alongside it until I could see into the sanctuary through the crack of the door. Valda sat on the throne. So much for my attempt at getting the blade. Kneeling at her feet was Anwir. His face was cast downward, but the flexing of his jaws indicated he spoke fervently to the goddess before him.

"I've done all that you've asked of me. Surely, it is time that I am rewarded for my loyalty."

Valda contemplated the Dragonborn's words. Her hands were pressed together with the tips of her fingers resting against her closed lips. "You have kept up your part of the bargain thus far," she replied lazily.

Anwir cautiously raised his head. "I serve only you and your father."

Valda snorted. "You serve yourself."

Anwir's eyes flashed with anger, but Valda made no indication that she cared. And why would she? She could decimate Anwir in a second.

She drummed her fingernails on the armrest of the throne. "Emera's presence with us is not just for your benefit."

Anwir's benefit?

"She was promised to me," Anwir spat, and he rushed to his feet.

Promised? To Anwir? Absolutely not! My stomach turned. I wasn't going to be surprised if I threw up.

Valda's fingers stopped. "Know your place," she warned. And like a trained dog, Anwir returned to a kneeling position.

With a careful tone, Anwir replied, "Of course, your highness. I apologize for my outburst. But the deal was that I would help resurrect your father, and in return, Emera would be stripped of her mate, stripped of her powers, and bound to me. That was the deal you made on your soul."

Valda leaned toward his Anwir, her weight on his shoulders. "Emera was bound to you the moment my father took his first breath. And as long as I am alive, she is yours. No force of magic will break that bond." She leaned back on the throne again. "As for her powers, my father cannot take those completely until her mother is dead. As long as Nimerah lives, her magic lives within her daughter. That's why it's imperative that we locate Nimerah before they do. Father has squashed her powers, but her Dragonsoul carries the final spark."

So, they still hadn't found her just yet. That was good.

And deep down, I still had my magic. That was good, too. That meant I could get it back.

"So, what happens to her while we wait for your father to find Nimerah?" Anwir asked.

"We keep our eyes on her. She can't get out and interfere with Father's mission. Once father kills Nimerah, Emera will be yours, and no magic will run through her Dragonblood. Quite a pity, though. It truly is fascinating how powerful she is becoming. I could say I'm impressed."

Anwir just nodded, although I could tell he didn't care. He only saw me as a prize to be won.

"Anwir, I suggest you be patient. You also might want to lay off the vulgar thoughts and incessant maneuvering to be closer to her. You won't have to worry about her being in your possession if she cuts off your head. I won't lie, though. I think I'd enjoy it."

Anwir remained silent.

Valda waved her hand. "I will be coming and going for a few days. Father and I have meetings with the Kingdom of Light."

"Where is his highness?"

"That is none of your concern," Valda snapped. "Keep watch of Emera, but know that Gawen is watching you. I'm growing weary of looking at you. Go." She waved Anwir off. He got up, and if looks could kill, Valda would have keeled over.

I turned from the door and bolted down the hall. I raced through the door to my chamber and locked it behind me. I placed my ear against the door and waited. Anwir's footsteps were faint at first, but the closer they approached the door, the louder they became. Instead of going straight to his bed chamber, he paused at my door. I withdrew from its surface and watched as he attempted to turn the handle. The pace of my heart exploded into a frantic cadence controlled by fear.

When the handle halted abruptly, it quietly receded back to its original position. I let out a small breath of relief but immediately sucked it back in. Scratching came from inside the keyhole.

He unlocked it slowly.

I rushed to my bed, hopped in, and brought the covers up to my shoulders just as Anwir pushed open the door. His light footsteps may have been quiet in the room, but they pounded in my ears. They came closer and closer until he was standing at the side of my bed. My heart beat faster and faster, yet I maintained control of my breathing.

Don't move. Don't move. Don't move.

The caress of Anwir's hand on my cheek sent a shock of alarm through my body. My magic was ready to attack, and had it been any other time, I may have given in. But he wasn't going to kill me, that much was clear. So, I just needed to bide my time until I could get the blade and escape.

Don't move. Don't move. Don't move.

He withdrew his hand, and then leaned down and kissed my forehead. "One day, you'll be mine," he whispered. Then he backed away from the bed and left my room.

When the door closed, I threw myself over the bed, and threw up.

CHAPTER TWENTY-ONE
CALIAN

"This doesn't do anything for my figure," Fin joked. "But again, Cal, you look breathtaking."

I glared at him.

"Don't look at me like that. It makes me blush."

Kedron snorted, and Nyx rolled her eyes.

"Okay, let's go over this plan one more time," I told them. "Kedron and Nyx will go meet their informant. Fin and I will enter the throne room with the other priestesses who should be gathering outside of it as we speak. Once Fin and I have the information we need, Fin will pretend to faint, and I'll volunteer to escort him out. We will meet at the Arden Inn.

I have a friend there who I know will accommodate us. We'll change, and Kedron can teleport us out. Am I missing anything?"

Fin addressed Nyx, "What are you going to do?"

"Go home."

"And where's that?"

Kedron and Nyx looked at each other. For a split second, they remained quiet, but then erupted in laughter. Fin looked from them to me and then back to them. "What did I say?"

"The Kingdom of Darkness. They're brother and sister. Can't you tell?" I answered. "Look at their hair, their eyes, their skin."

"Huh. You might be onto something."

"Keddie and I are twins," Nyx managed to get out between her fits of laughter. "I'm going back to Tamasvi to see our father."

Kedron stopped laughing, and his cheeks reddened. It took me a second to register what she'd said.

"Keddie?!" Fin shrieked. He must not have heard her call Kedron that in the kithen.

"Thanks, Nyx," Kedron mumbled.

"Anyway, our father is an advisor for King Orpheus. I stop in from time to time to see how he and the kingdom are doing."

"Who is your father? I have met with King Orpheus and his advisors."

"Perran Black."

I searched my memory for the name, but I didn't recall it being mentioned. "Sorry, it doesn't ring a bell. Besides, we need to move."

Fin nodded, and opened the door, holding it open for all of us to exit.

When we were back to the entrance of the kitchens, we parted ways. Nyx and Kedron exited down an empty corridor while Fin and I made our way down the hall and to the throne room.

The palace was one with nature, with ornate, ivy-covered stones that seamlessly blended with the surrounding Arden Forest. There were exotic plants, including luminescent flowers and trees that created archways at every corner. Every ten feet or so, magical artifacts and relics, which I was certain King Tellus took great pride in, were displayed in elaborate glass cases.

King Tellus ruled with an iron fist and maintained ruthless authority. His court was a place of fear and treachery. His advisors were not chosen for being kind and fair. No, they were just as ruthless as he was. They were chosen based on how cunning they were and their ability to carry out Tellus's every order without question.

The Kingdom of Earth was beautiful. The Arden Forest saw to that. And the City of Dhara was awe-inspiring to say the least. But that's where it ended. The people feared the king, and in turn, wouldn't dare speak out against him. He was a prime target for Amram to ally with.

We'd turned a final corner and knew we'd reached our destination. A small group of Dragonpriestesses, all donned in emerald robes, huddled outside of the great hall's double doors. I was surprised by their appearances. Their faces were serene and radiated peace and tranquility despite their youthful vitality. They spoke softly to one another, their voices as soothing as the autumn wind when it rustles through leaves. Fin and I made a pact not to talk unless it was absolutely necessary. Not only would it give away the fact that Fin was male, but it would reveal our ages. These priestesses were probably all young for a reason. I shuddered at the thought.

The doors opened wide, and a servant in impeccable emerald clothes and his hair tied at the nape of his neck motioned for us to follow. We just smiled and nodded as the other priestesses stepped into a line and fell into synchronous steps behind him. All of them clasped their hands together in front of their bodies, so Fin and I did the same. We took the two spots at the end of the line, hoping that left us closest to the door.

When we finally entered the throne room, the stench of wine and ale stung my nostrils. At the center of the throne room sat a plump Dragonborn King with a crown made of intertwining vines adorned with precious gemstones, leaves, and metal atop his balding head. His throne was designed to represent the Arden Forest. It was fashioned from a colossal tree stump the color of a rich dark oak. Twisted, gnarled roots extended from the bottom of the throne and traveled up, forming armrests for the king. Vines and leaves wrapped around the legs of the throne. The back was covered in carved forest creatures along with the Dragongoddess Dhara. It was lined with plush, moss-colored velvet.

The walls were covered in paintings. But instead of depicting the history of Dhara or the past monarchs, all the paintings were of King Tellus. So, he was arrogant, conceited, and a drunk. Standing to his left and right were several advisors. On their knees with their head bowed low, was a human in chains. The king remained slouched backward with a tankard of ale in his hand. His speech was slurred as he berated a human.

King Tellus was an unassuming man at first glance. His small, beady eyes were pale green and matched the colors of his scales. He had a round figure with a belly that protruded prominently over his belt like a sack of coins. No doubt he had a penchant for indulging in lavish banquets and feasts. It would explain his ample stature.

His face was also round, and its complexion was constantly red. Especially his cheeks which resembled apples. His bulbous nose sat atop a thick mustache that hid his pursed lips. His eyes were almost hidden underneath bushy eyebrows which were situated below a furrowed brow with deep creases in his forehead.

The robe he wore was adorned with emeralds and gold stitching. The robe was so tight, it barely covered his round frame. Even now, as he laughed and waved around his tankard, his stomach was exposed. Fin and I both exchanged unpleasant looks.

A priestess whispered to another. "By Dhara, he's inebriated again."

I leaned toward Fin. "I wonder if he's always like this."

The king carried on a few more minutes about how humans were good-for-nothing leeches.

"He's quite the leech himself by the looks of it," Fin quipped. A tiny chuckle burst from my mouth. The King stopped mid-sentence and turned his attention toward me.

"Are you questioning my decision to kill this thief?

Come. Enlighten us all on why I shouldn't kill him and feed him to the forest animals."

The priestess beside me gasped, and Fin snorted. I could hear the smirk on his face as he tried so desperately to hold in his laughter. He lived for moments like this. I however, liked carefully planned situations. This wasn't one of them.

"Go get 'em, tiger," Fin whispered followed by a slight wheezing. Oh yeah, he was enjoying this immensely. When the time came, I'd get back at him. And he wouldn't see it coming.

I inhaled deeply and took a few steps out of line. But I didn't go any further.

"I said to come here!" he barked. So not only was he self-conscious about himself, he didn't like to repeat himself. He was unnecessarily aggressive. I walk slowly, as slowly as I could, and took my place next to an advisor.

One of the king's advisors snickered as I approached. "Tread carefully, priestess," he said sharply. He didn't warn me out of the kindness of his heart. He just didn't want the king to throw a temper-tantrum.

"What is your name?" the king commanded. His voice ricocheted off the walls.

I hesitated, debating whether or not to answer. The king's face grew redder with each second that passed.

"My name is Fin," I replied sweetly.

The king balked. "A woman named Fin? That sounds preposterous."

"I tell no lies, your majesty. My mother longed for a boy. She was utterly disappointed when I was born. So, she kept the name as a reminder of her failure." I glanced out of the corner of my eye. Fin's eyes narrowed. He'd seek retribution for my slight against him. Inside, I was smiling like a fool, but on the outside, I showed no emotion.

"It seems her disappointment is justified. You think I should save this human. What say you?"

"I say nothing. It is the decision of the king."

"You laughed."

"I had a cough, your majesty."

"You call me a liar?"

"No, your majesty. I had a cough caught in my throat. I tried to hold it so as not to interrupt the proceedings, but I couldn't."

The look on his face was priceless. If steam was capable of bursting out of his ears, it would have. He was on his feet in an instant, his arms out wide. The floor beneath me started to rumble, and a small crack formed beneath my feet. I'd seen this trick before, and I had no air magic like Erjon to get me out should a hole open up and consume me. "I do not take kindly to Dragonpriestesses laughing and then lying about it. Especially ones that sympathize with humans."

So, this was the type of king that, no matter what anyone said, only believed what he wanted to. That was good information to have.

"I hear you've made a deal with a Dragongod, your majesty," I blurted. "If so, you are wise to do so. You will bring prosperity to the kingdom."

The compliment seemed to suffice for the moment. The shaking stopped, and the crack didn't spread.

King Tellus lowered his arms and angled his head, trying to figure me out. "How did you hear about that?"

"It is being whispered throughout the kingdom. Your praises are being sung as we speak."

"Good save," muttered the advisor next to me. I winked in response which he didn't seem to like. It was also subtle enough that the king didn't notice. To be more exact, he was too drunk to notice.

"Really?" the king asked. He lowered himself back down on the throne.

I lowered my head as a sign of respect. "I'm sure we'd all be delighted to hear how the king managed such a difficult feat. I'm sure it took wit and cunning to convince a god."

King Tellus took another swig of his ale and tossed it

behind him. A servant—the same that led us into the throne room—scrambled to pick it off the floor.

"He came to me while out hunting. Can you believe that he was a man? He was a scrawny, ugly man no taller than a child."

Thinking back to Emera's description of Amram, King Tellus hadn't met with the god. It was probably one of his shapeshifting lackeys.

"In exchange for allying my kingdom with him, he would provide protection. He also offered to clean up this great city and rebuild it into a true forest oasis! I jumped at the opportunity, of course. My ancestors fought alongside him in the great war. I will carry on that legacy."

"A true king of the people," I replied and bowed my head once more. With my eyes on the floor, I took in my face's reflection on the polished stone. My skin rippled. My shape-shifting started without me knowing it. My lips trembled, and my eyes grew wider, but it wasn't because of shock or fear. I whipped my head to the side and locked eyes with Fin just as my body began shifting back into itself. I fell to my knees, and my body convulsed from my limbs taking on a new formation. I hadn't shifted in so long that my body couldn't hold it. My legs and arms extended. The muscles thickened, filling out the clothes I'd kept on.

"Are you all right, priestess?" the king asked, his tone void of concern.

I had no way of telling if my voice was back to normal or not, so I raised my hand instead of answering. That was the wrong thing to do.

"Do not silence me!" he roared. "Guards, take her away!"

Well, there was no getting around it. I stood and faced the king. The man had so many expressions. First, he was shocked, then he was confused, and finally, he was angry. I'd made a spectacle of his court. He wouldn't have that.

"A shape shifter! Guard, seize him immediately!"

Thank the gods I'd decided to remain in my normal clothes under the robe. I tore off my cowl and mask then shrugged off the robe. With my Dragonscales on full display, and my eyes blazing red, I called flames to my hands. "I don't think so," I growled. The king's face went back to shock. With everyone's eyes on me, the human crawled away. Good.

"Cal!" Fin yelled from across the room. His robe was off, and he already launched an arrow through the air, knocking a sword out the hand of a guard.

I backed away from the king slowly, shaking my head at the guards who tried to advance. My hands were at my sides with red magic swirling in them. When one lunged for me, I threw a fireball at his head. I missed, of course, because I wasn't aiming at him. I just wanted to scare them. But King Tellus was unbothered by my magic. He ordered his men to attack at will. Their eyes darted back and forth between each other, waiting to see who would be brave enough to go first.

Tellus pounded his fists on the throne. "NOW!" he roared, but his men still hesitated. If they used their Dragonmagic, they were at risk of destroying the palace. If they didn't, they'd die quickly and not at my hands. Fin had enough arrows to take them all down.

"Fin, let's get out of here."

"Yes, sir," he replied.

We turned and ran out of the throne room at lightning speeds. When we cleared the doors, I closed them and melted the handles to buy us time. We sped down the hall and back toward the kitchens. The guards banged on the doors, trying to get out. Our hurried steps carried us to the spot where we'd separated from Nyx and Kedron. We turned the corner and took off down the twisting passageway. The clank of armor resounded through the cold, stale air that surrounded us. The guards had managed to break through the great hall's double-doors.

"Sound the alarm," cried a distant voice, and the ominous tolling of iron bells filled the city.

We reached the entrance to a narrow, spiraling staircase. Fin gestured for me to follow him upward. Our steps, now rushed and desperate, set echoes of our escape into motion. As we ascended the twisting staircase that made me dizzy, torchlight painted the outlines of our bodies onto the stone walls. How long had we been gone? It was already nightfall?

"We need to get back to the others," I told Fin through pants of heavy breathing.

In a moment of heart-pounding respite, we found ourselves in a moonlit tower, overlooking the castle courtyard. Fin looked over the edge of the tower we were now in. "How the hell do we get down without Kedron?" That's a long drop.

"I guess we climb down the wall?"

"And hold onto what?"

A dozen or so guards, now emboldened and frustrated, charged up the staircase.

"Looks like I have no choice," I muttered sadly.

The bells stopped, and the only sound was the ghostly whistle of the nighttime breeze. Ragnar, the Dragongod of Death, would be waiting for these souls. I stood atop the staircase and pointed my hands below me. I unleashed a torrent of scorching fire. Anguished screams echoed below, making me wince and turn my head away from the tortured souls I reaped.

As the fire blazed, Kedron appeared out of thin air.

"Aren't you a sight for sore eyes," Fin cried. He hugged Kedron tightly, lifting him into the air and twirling him.

"I heard the bells and saw the fire. I figured you two needed help."

"Let's get out here," Fin said.

Kedron took our hands, and we jumped. When we landed, we were back in the forest. Kedron reached into the pocket of his pants and pulled out an amulet. It took me a moment to realize he now wore gloves.

"Fin!" Morwen cried. She ran into his arms, almost tackling him to the ground. His hands entangled in her hair, and they kissed passionately.

Zeph took a step toward me. "Cal. Are you okay? What happened?" He placed a hand on my shoulder and leaned over to search my face. I was too stunned to speak or even look at him. I just stood frozen in place. I'd ordered lives to be taken. I'd taken lives myself…But not like this. Tonight, I was the slayer of Dragonborns.

CHAPTER TWENTY-TWO
EMERA

My stomach grumbled from the lack of proper nutrition I'd failed to give it. The grumbling I could put up with. It was the foul smell of vomit that I needed to take care of immediately. I found a washcloth and a bucket of fresh water waiting for me outside of the door. At first, I was pleasantly surprised. It meant I didn't need to go looking for them. But it also meant that Anwir was responsible for bringing them. He was the only person close enough to my room to hear my retching. I was going to stay as far away from him as possible.

I cleaned the floor and placed the water bucket and towel

back into the hall. I would find a proper location for them later. At the moment, I wanted nothing more than to change. The large wardrobe held numerous gowns; all an exquisite shade of violet. I chose what seemed to be the lightest dress because I needed the ability to run should the situation call for it. The dress was stunning. It was meant for a goddess to wear. It was fancier than what Queen Eteri had provided. But that made sense because we were essentially in the palace of a god.

I shimmied out of my nightgown and discarded it into the fireplace. It reminded me of last night, which reminded me of Anwir's cold lips on my forehead. Gross.

The violet dress fit like a dream. Its rich purple fabric was an elegant satin with a subtle iridescent shimmer when in the light. The fabric flowed gracefully, draping like liquid to the floor. The bodice featured a beautifully crafted corset that cinched at my waist, accentuating my figure. It was adorned with embroidery and beading, mimicking the enchanting night sky. Delicate lacing at the back added a touch of charm.

The gown had long sleeves that were sheer, made of a fine gossamer material. The sleeves billowed as they extended down to my wrists. Each sleeve had lace cuffs to match the lace on the corset. It added a sophisticated yet whimsical look to it. The neckline was subtle, covering my collarbone.

Good. The less skin Anwir could see, the better.

Before fastening the buttons behind my neck, I took a moment to lower the dress, exposing the bare skin above my heart. In the aftermath of last night's discovery, I hadn't had time to acknowledge that Calian and I were mates. I took a deep breath and exhaled slowly.

Calian Westbow was my Dragonmate.

Until now, I'd thought it was impossible. I thought that it had been Valda. It's what made sense. He had purple wings, and I didn't. She was the only other Chaos Dragon around at the time. But it was me.

It still is me.

I closed my eyes. A melodic tune played in my mind, and the lighting of the room lowered. I stood by the crystal lake in the Dragonsoul Plane of Existence. My eyes were fixed on Calian as he strolled up to me. My flowing, deep violet dress swayed in the cool breeze that rolled off the ripples of the lake. Loose waves cascaded over my left shoulder, but my right shoulder was bare. My purple Dragonwings were on display, and they shimmered in the pale moonlight.

Calian extended his hand, and a shy smile spread on my lips, concealing my excitement for this moment.

Would you like to dance, my Dragonmate?

"Why of course, Calian. I would love to dance with you,

my Dragonmate."

I draped my arms over Calian's shoulders and clasped my hands behind his neck. His hands slid around my waist, and he pulled me closer, creating an intimate space between us. Our bodies swayed in perfect harmony to the music. I was completely absorbed in the moment. My every movement was a hushed invitation of longing and carnal need; two emotions I was not familiar with. In my heart, I knew that Calian would one night guide me gently down that path of womanhood. Until then, we remained connected in heart, body, and soul.

The tap at the door brought me back to the foreign bed chamber. The daydream had been bittersweet. I so desperately wanted to escape and run into Calian's arms, declaring him as my Dragonmate. But that would be irresponsible. I had a duty to fulfill. I needed to identify the Dragon Slayer and to obtain their blade. It was the only way we'd defeat Amram.

"Emera?"

I froze. I was so lost in my thoughts, that I didn't hear the voice clearly enough. Was that Anwir at the door? No. Please, gods, no. I didn't want to deal with him.

"Emera?"

I slowly opened the door a crack, and peered out, coming

face-to-face with Gawen. He still wore the same clothes from the previous day, revealing his lack of sleep. He eyed me suspiciously before I closed the door completely, let out air I'd held captive in my chest, and smoothed out my dress. I opened the door all the way and stepped into the hall. Gawen looked at me, then at the vomit-filled bucket, and then back to me.

"Dare I ask?"

His words surprised me. It was the most he'd ever said to me. "The soup didn't agree with me, that's all."

He contemplated my words before turning away from me. "I guess I'll just have to kill the cook," he said nonchalantly, like killing people wasn't a big deal to him.

"No!" I grabbed his arm, and he stilled. His chin dropped, and he angled his head to inspect the hand that clutched his arm.

"I was kidding."

I let go of his arm. "Oh. Of course." But how would I know that? I didn't know him at all.

He didn't smile, but a slight tug at the corner of his lips told me he wanted to. He started walking back down the hallway while I patted my cheeks. They were warm from embarrassment.

Pull yourself together, Em. Time to make Fin proud. It's

spy time.

Gawen threw open the door to the sanctuary and passed by the vacant throne. He continued walking out of the sanctuary, down the dimly lit hallway, and out the front door into the courtyard. I followed closely behind him, my eyes scanning every area for Anwir.

When we finished descending the stairs to Gawen's landing spot, Anwir was in plain view, sitting atop a large green Dragon. It was the same Dragon we'd encountered at the bottom of the Mystral Mountains.

Anwir puffed out his chest. "Meet Bud." He patted the Dragon's hide.

Surely, he was joking. A Dragon named Bud? There was no way I heard that correctly.

Gawen pressed his lips together, closed his eyes, and nodded twice.

An awkward minute passed before I realized that Valda wasn't with us. The sun shone brightly in the sky, so it was well past morning. Maybe she went hunting for lunch. Did Dragons do that? I was a Dragon, and I had no inclination to hunt for my meal. But Valda was a killer, so...

"Emera will ride with me on Bud," Anwir announced as if his word was law. Deep down, I didn't think Valda would approve of it.

"Valda will not allow it," Gawen said, confirming my suspicion.

Anwir's eyes narrowed, and his jaw tightened. Gawen ignored him which only angered Anwir more.

Valda's large dark violet Dragon form sailed overhead and landed next to us. Her Dragon form was magnificent, and I could finally make out all the intricacies of her. I'd seen her form before, but it was in such a rush of chaos that I hadn't taken in the finer details of her form. She seemed larger than when I first encountered her. Did her father do this? I wouldn't put it past Amram to make his daughter larger and more lethal.

Her scales were the deepest shade of violet I'd ever seen. They were akin to twilight on the brink of night. Each was as large as saucers and glimmered with an iridescent shine. They weren't just a protective armor for her, but a canvas of bold patterns.

Valda's amethyst eyes looked me up and down, radiating an intense luminescence. They possessed an unsettling intelligence, as if they could pierce the very soul of anyone who looked into them.

She shook her colossal head, waving around a series of curved horns that created an illusion of a crown. They served as both ornaments and weapons. Along her spine were sharp, pointed ridges that ran down her back like a jagged mountain range. The ridges continued down along her tail which was muscular with a bony spire. It reminded me of a deadly mace that some sailors carried with them. I had no uncertainties that Valda's tail could shatter buildings and send men into the afterlife with one blow.

And if the tail didn't kill a man, her claws would. They looked sharp. I bet they could cleave through stone and metal with ease. I shuddered at the thought.

She stalked toward us and leaned down to make it easier to climb atop her. So, I wasn't even going to ride Gawen to wherever it was we were going. I was going to be riding atop Valda. I frowned, unsure of the situation. Valda didn't seem like the type of Dragon who would let anyone ride her. She was above that. I guessed it was a direct order from her father.

Climbing on her felt weird. My foot slipped, but her tail caught me before I hit the ground. She lifted me to her back, and I slid into a riding position. Valda chuckled at my expense. Hatred vibrated beneath my skin.

With three monstrous flaps of her wings, Valda was in the air. Gawen was not, so we were leaving him behind. Well, I guess someone had to watch the palace.

Still not used to riding the back of a Dragon, my body

jumbled back and forth while she ascended further into the sky.

"You might want to hang onto me," she crooned in my mind. For being my enemy, she was being awful friendly today. Well, maybe not friendly, but cordial. I wrapped my arms around her as best as I could and held on tight. After a few minutes of flying, I started to get the hang of it and loosened my grip. I glanced to the side and caught a flash of white.

We soared south over the mountains, out of the Realm of the Dragondead, and into the Kingdom of Water. A subtle ache started in my stomach and crept into my chest when I recognized the trees near the camp. Memories flooded my head of my time spent there. From the time I created a torrential downpour, to the time I was poisoned. Behind my closed eyes I saw the inside of Rehema's tent and the happiness on her face when I arrived. My nose smelled the aromas of Cook's stew mixed with the fire. Music from the soldiers filled my ears, making me sway slightly.

My eyes opened and the memories of the camp fluttered away. I chose to remain silent. I refused to engage in conversation. The day dragged on, and my legs grew sore and tired from the flight. Just when I thought I'd slide off from exhaustion, Valda began her descent. Thankfully, we'd passed right over Medora and into the Kingdom of Darkness. Valda landed just below its northern border into a barren field.

In the kingdom, a perpetual nighttime reigned over the land. The sky was shrouded in thick, impenetrable darkness with no trace of daylight. A traveler might fear the darkness, but I knew better. Tamasvi was a goddess of deep thought and contemplation, believing that darkness provided refuge for a lost soul.

Still, her choice of landscape was questionable. It was eerie and foreboding, characterized by a desolate and twisted terrain. Gnarled trees and rocky, treacherous hills dominated the land which was completely barren with no signs.

The air was silent, broken only by a distant, unsettling sound of a howling wind, creaking branches, or noises by unseen animals. The atmosphere elicited a sense of fear and doom.

I slid off Valda's back. Once I stood on solid ground, I took a few wobbly steps forward and surveyed the area. We'd landed at what looked to be another Dragon burial site. We were here to resurrect a Dragon.

After Bud landed, Anwir dismounted and strolled to my side. "Emera, you will help us give the breath of life to a fallen comrade."

"I think not," I spat.

Anwir pulled a gleaming purple dagger from the inside of his cloak. He sliced my palm without warning and did the same to himself. "You have no choice."

"What are you doing?" I closed my fist, but Anwir grabbed my arm and forced my hand into his. With our hands clasped together, our Dragonblood mixed. Heavy drips fell onto the ground. After several drops pooled onto the earth, Anwir let go of my hand and stepped back, leaving me standing there like a fool next to the burial site.

Valda hovered over us and her chanting began.

"Arthar, mir'seklor. Arthar et lenz."

"Awaken, my sister. Awaken and live," Anwir repeated. The Dragonborn really liked to hear himself talk.

Valda repeated the incantation over and over. All I could do was stand and watch. The ground beneath us trembled, and a low rumble echoed through the air. The earth opened up a crevice at the center of the burial site, and from the earth, a massive skeletal form emerged.

Valda switched her chant. "Mer flahk tosor flahk."

My flesh to your flesh. I remembered that one.

Again, she repeated the incantation several times.

Bone by bone, the dragon's remains materialized. Its colossal ribs arched upward like a vaulted ceiling, and its skull, adorned with sharp, spiraling horns, took shape. As it rose, Valda's chanting grew louder and more fervent. An energy buzzed through the air and enveloped the Dragon's form.

Valda's voice reached a crescendo when she finally called out, "Rovar, Risna. Mir'seklor. Mir'hlodar. Mir'shanar!"

"Rise, Risna. My sister. My watcher. My spy," Anwir all but sang. I rolled my eyes.

A shockwave of magic rippled outward, casting a bright blinding light. I covered my eyes with my arm as a shield. When the light faded, the Dragon's frame had morphed from a skeleton into a body made of flesh, muscle, and sparkling black scales. The Dragon's empty eye sockets now glowed a piercing onyx like the darkest night that glittered with a thousand stars. When her eyes fell upon me briefly, my body jolted. Could she see into my very soul? Surely, not.

When she moved, the little bit of light from the sky shimmered off her obsidian scales, creating an ever-changing palette of colors. Deep purple, midnight blue, and even a hint of emerald green flashed into my eyes with the smallest movement of her body.

This Dragon left me confounded. She was the living manifestation of night itself, a true daughter of Tamasvi. I just hoped she was as friendly as her mother.

Risna stretched her wings, sending a gust of wind that knocked me off my feet. I propped myself up on my elbows and witnessed the Dragon roar a thunderous roar that certainly shook the heavens. This resurrected Dragon was strong.

With the ritual complete, Valda glided down to the ground. Bud greeted the black Dragon—Risna. Bud nudged Risna's head, showing a friendly affection for one another. Valda lowered her head in respect, but that was all. Risna's eyes met mine, and I inhaled sharply. I searched for any sign of animosity toward me. There wasn't any. I didn't have my empathic abilities, but I knew there was no sense of hatred or mistrust. Instead, I found hope.

"I will ride Risna back to the sanctuary," I announced as I got back onto my feet.

Valda shook her head and gave me a look that said I was out of line. Well, that was a quick dismissal.

"I wasn't asking for permission, Cousin."

We stared at each other with glaring intensity. No one— not even Anwir—tried to intervene with this momentous stare-down. Valda might be a goddess, but what she didn't know was that I was an expert at staring contests. I beat everyone who tried me.

Finally, the Dragongoddess broke off her gaze and

blinked in rapid succession. I took that as a win.

Anwir stepped up beside me. "It doesn't matter, Valda," he called to the Dragon. "It's not like Risna can speak to Emera."

Did he know that I had no magic? "And why's that?"

"Risna has no trace of magic in her blood. That's what happens when you disobey Amram."

"I didn't know Amram could do that," I lied. I gazed at the beautiful black Dragon. "And wasn't she Amram's spy? It makes no sense that he'd take her magic." I waited patiently for Anwir to give up the information. Sure enough, he didn't disappoint.

"During the war, Risna withheld information from Amram about the location of his amulet. When he found out, she tried to deny it. He didn't believe her, so he punished Risna in the only way he thought fit the misdeed. The amulet takes away a human's vulnerability, so they can survive any magical attack. His idea of taking away any human-like vulnerability from her was by stripping her magic. She was demoted to a pet."

I gasped. "How did he know that she withheld information?"

Anwir stalked over to Bud. "He didn't. He just wanted to see how loyal she was to him."

Anger spiked in my chest, making my blood boil. "Did he do that to any other Dragons?"

"Most of his army consisted of Dragons from Endrit and Dhara's lines," Anwir continued as he hoisted himself up on the green Dragon. "They allied with Amram during the war, so he trusted them. Vukan, Ilmari, and Anahita allied with Nimerah. Tamasvi, being the fool that she is, did not want any part in the war. Although she didn't stand with Amram, she didn't stand against him. So, to prove Risna's loyalty, Amram tasked her with finding his amulet. She claimed she never did. Amram demanded that she tell him where it was, but Risna insisted that she didn't know. So, he punished her.

"With no proof!" I seethed.

"He didn't need any," Anwir said airily. "Let's go. Valda is growing impatient."

"Wait. One last question. If Amram didn't kill Risna, then how did she die?" My eyes met the Dragon and a profound anger rested within them. She couldn't speak to us, but she understood us.

"She flew into her mother's kingdom and was hit with a poisonous arrow to the chest. We don't know who shot it, but the aim was impeccable. Went straight into her heart. Because she couldn't change into a human, she had no way of taking out the arrow. So, she died." He let out a loud whistle, signaling Bud to take off. The green Dragon lifted and hovered beside Valda.

Risna studied my every move, never taking her large onyx eyes off of me. I reached out to touch her but hesitated. What if I was wrong? What if she had fooled me into thinking she was friendly.

When my fingers grazed her scales, she didn't ease her suspicions of me. But she didn't burn me to a crisp either, so that was good. She swung her tail around, leaving it at my feet to use as a step. When I climbed up on it, she lifted it slowly and I swung my leg over her back. Her scales were tough, but they were soft. How that was possible, I didn't know.

Her massive wings spread wide, and she ascended into the sky. Valda and Bud took off toward the Dragonrealm of the Dead. Risna hesitated, but then she followed them. When we finally reached the Obsidian Mountains, Valda veered off, but the rest of us continued our flight back to Ragnar's palace and landed by the large tree. Gawen stood, waiting for us. I didn't question Valda leaving us. In fact, I welcomed the idea of her not being in the palace.

For some unexplainable reason, I felt connected to Risna. The way she was treated by Amram. And then her death. I swallowed the knot in my throat while swinging my leg over her back to dismount. "I'm sorry about your death, Risna," I whispered.

Gawen, now standing next to Risna, held out his hand to help me off the Dragon. "That's war. If you are going to fight, you must be prepared to die."

I didn't know if his intention was to fill my head with doubt, but he did. Was I prepared to die?

CHAPTER TWENTY-THREE
CALIAN

"Where have you been?"

Hestia strolled out from the forest; her eyes slightly glazed over. Her meditation must not have been as invigorating as she'd hoped. The woman looked exhausted.

"I was unable to sleep, so I took a walk to clear my thoughts," she said.

I let out a hefty exhale. "Well, now that you've decided to join us, the rest of us can move on." I hopped up on Dhruv and steered him east. Fin was already up the path, scouting ahead for enemies or random Dragon resurrections.

Hestia looked around her. "The rest of us?" She'd finally

noticed that a few members of our group had already departed.

"Like we'd presumed, the Kingdom of Earth has allied with Amram. Kedron and Morwen left for the City of Anahita with the amulet that we found. Zeph is going to fly you back to the Kingdom of Fire. Erjon has already left for the Kingdom of Air. The kingdoms need to build their forces now."

"I am not going back to my kingdom. I am staying with you."

"Excuse me?"

"Zepherin can notify my general of what is happening. I trust her to fortify my kingdom. I will stay and help you." She was right in that she could help. She had the ability to tell me if our future held success or failure. But her kingdom needed her.

"I don't think that's a good idea. The Kingdom of Fire needs their queen."

"The Kingdom of Fire needs someone to prepare for battle. I am no expert in that, but my general is. She'll know what to do."

Zeph raised his hand.

I rolled my eyes. "You don't have to raise your hand like a schoolboy."

"How do I explain your absence to your general?" Zeph asked.

"You won't have to. My general is my daughter. Her name is Shula. We've planned for this moment, so she knows I will not return just yet."

Zeph's eyes met mine. "So, I'll be on my way then?" He phrased it more like a question than a statement.

"It would appear that way," I huffed and turned to Hestia. "You'll ride Zari. Zeph, take care of that kingdom."

"Be careful," he said and shook my hand. He then jettisoned himself into the air and flew south.

Dhruv took off in the direction Fin had taken, leaving Hestia scrambling to mount Zari. The horse wasted no time, and Hestia was at my side quickly. Both horses slowed down when we saw Fin in the distance. He sat there, quiet and still.

"Please tell me there isn't another ritual happening," I hissed.

Fin shook his head and pointed, commanding my eyes to follow his downward gaze. They did, and they landed on a small village nestled down in a valley. The village looked rough. The buildings looked like ransacked huts. The land was void of vegetation. I'd seen many maps in my days, and this place wasn't on it.

"We need to keep moving."

Fin scrunched his nose. "You're not going to like this, but I think we should stock up on food. When we packed, we weren't planning on two other mouths to feed. We're running low, and we still have a few more days to travel before we reach Medora."

I couldn't believe it. After Senna's death, Fin was adamant that we kept moving. Now that we were actually on our way without distractions, he wanted to stop. There had to be more to it than food rations. Which we had plenty of. I saw to it myself before we left Ilmari.

"I ensured we had additional rations. What happened to those?" The look on Fin's face said it all. Zepherin Coro, you Dragonass.

"Do we even have coins to spare?"

Fin held out a small coin purse and jiggled it. "I may or may not have stolen it from the palace."

He was lying. "When did you have time for that?"

"I have my ways," he said with an arrogant smirk.

I still didn't believe him. "Morwen gave that to you, didn't she?"

Fin looked down, accepting defeat. "Yeah…She did. But stealing it from the palace sounded so much better."

I shook my head and strained my eyes. "Does it even look like it's inhabited?"

"Only one way to find out." Fin nudged Shadow forward. So, we were going.

As the horses drew closer, a sign on the edge of a dirt path leading into the village said *Khaosar*. An interesting choice for a name, but what did I care? I didn't live here.

"*Khaosar* means Chaos in the old tongue," said Hestia.

Fin angled his body toward her. "You know the old Dragon language?"

"From an early age."

Fin put a finger to his lips. "How do you say Dragonass?"

"Did you really just ask a queen that?"

Without hesitation, Hestia said, "Drakonfren."

"I like it," Fin replied.

Dhruv snorted. It seemed that he and I shared the same thoughts about Fin. He snorted again once we neared a bridge. It was wide enough for a horse-drawn cart for merchants, but it looked like it hadn't been traveled over in years. I wanted to protest again. If people did live in Khaosar, they didn't care enough about it. We probably wouldn't be welcomed. We had to keep our guard up. Get in. Get food. Get out.

The horses stepped onto the bridge and cautiously walked over it. When they planted their feet on the other side, everything around us changed. We'd stepped across a magical barrier of some sort because the village no longer looked shoddy and unkempt. The village, which was actually a town, was booming with life. It was situated next to a crystal-clear lake that glittered beneath the glow of the sun. And rich, fertile farmland boasted numerous crops that swayed in the breeze.

We passed under a gated archway into the town. Each building was constructed from white polished stone and decorated with intricate carvings, telling stories of the town's history. The roofs were made from overlapping shingles of a deep forest green.

But those were the buildings for businesses. The homes in Khaosar were charming, characterized by their pristine conditions. They were constructed with windows that allowed ample natural light to flood their interiors. Ivy-covered walls included stones laid in swirling patterns. Colorful flowers hung in baskets, and sculpted bushes lined the streets. It all added to the vibrancy of the town.

We passed by many people who all stopped their duties and studied us as we went along. Some smiled, some frowned, and some raised their brows with concern. But all of them looked shocked at one point or the other. I didn't take offense to any of it because we were strangers in their home. And it appeared we were the first set of strangers to come through in a long time.

"From the looks on their faces, they probably don't get many visitors," I said.

"Makes sense," Fin responded, "because of the outward appearance. No normal person would cross that bridge into a shoddy village."

"Except us," Hestia pointed out.

Fin turned and grinned at her. "That's because we're not normal."

"No, we are not," I mumbled. "Fin, if anything happens, get the queen to safety." Fin and Hestia exchanged looks and then words, but I was too distracted after that to engage in conversation. A flash of movement caught my eye. I swore I'd seen a familiar face. But it was too quick to register within my memory. I'd have to keep an eye out during our visit.

We finally reached the central square, which was the heart of Khaosar which was its central square. It was unlike any other town I'd seen. The roads were laden with black stone. At the center of the square was a sparkling fountain with water spouting from the mouths of Nimerah and Ragnar. So, the village was dedicated to them? I wanted to know more.

A tall inn sat on the northern side of the square. Next to the inn was a small set of empty stables. We took the opportunity and tied up the horses. Each got their own stall, allowing them to have privacy. Dhruv wouldn't care if he was by himself. Zari would love it, I'm sure. I didn't know anything about Shadow, but being Fin's horse, the steed probably longed for quiet.

The door to the inn was tall and heavy. I had to put some muscle into opening it. Once inside, we were greeted by several townspeople seated at tables, drinking and laughing. Music played from a bard in the corner of the open hall. The owner stood behind a counter, talking friendly to a couple patrons. I led the way, and as soon as we were a few steps in, everyone took notice. The music halted and everything went quiet. All eyes were on us as we made our way to the man behind the counter.

"Hello, there. We were hoping you could point us in the direction of a few places to restock our supplies."

The man stood gawking. I wasn't sure if it was because we were outsiders or because there was a queen in his presence. I guessed the former because he made no move to bow to Hestia.

A middle-aged woman with flowing blue hair entered from an adjacent room. Her eyes were a startling shade of blue and they matched her scales. She wore tight dark blue pants with black riding boots and a black belt across her waist. Her silk long-sleeved shirt was a lighter blue covered with a black leather vest.

"The detailing of her vest is amazing," Hestia said. As a man more concerned with functionality than looks, I didn't really take notice of fashion. But she wasn't wrong. At a distance, the leather looked smooth and glittery, but up close, it was the fine detailing that made it sparkle. It looked like her vest was made of tiny Dragonscales. I was impressed by the craftsmanship. And upon further inspection, her boots and black leather gloves were crafted the same way. I even liked the dark blue cape around her neck.

Truth be told, her clothes weren't the most jaw-dropping thing about her. It was her hair. Vibrant wasn't even the best word for it. It was the color of the bluest oceans, and when the light hit her curls, they resembled the falling sea waves with the light creating white foam.

"Calian Westbow," the woman said with a friendly smile.

I didn't know how I knew...but I knew. "Anahita," I answered with a nod.

Hestia remained silent. Fin on the other hand…

"No way. There's absolutely no way. Oh, man. If Mor were here…" his voice trailed off, and he turned his head away. The continuous absence of Morwen was getting to him.

Anahita held out her hand, gesturing for us to sit at an open table. "Please sit."

We did as she asked because none of us were going to refuse a goddess. Four open chairs meant there was enough room for all of us.

"Mr. Brand, would you please be kind enough to bring us some drinks. My companions look thirsty."

The Dragonborn with red scales who stood behind the counter gathered four tankards and filled them all with water. As good as a swig of ale sounded, I needed water.

"I'm sure you have questions," Anahita, the Dragongoddess of Water, said.

Hestia wasted no time and sat at the table. "What is this place?"

Anahita's eyes brightened a little, like she recognized Hestia. I scolded myself silently for my skepticism. Of course, Anahita would know of Hestia. Hestia was the queen of a kingdom.

"This is the forgotten city. Well, it was a city. As the years have passed, it's diminished in size. But that was to be expected. The inhabitants are all the descendants of those that lived here before them. This hidden gem has withstood the test of time."

"And you've been here since…"

"Since Nimerah created it."

"Are you the only god here?"

Anahita didn't answer. She sat there, contemplating how much information she wished to divulge. It seemed that she didn't trust us. I wanted to know why.

Anahita stood from her chair, her eyes on me. "Would you like to see more?"

Hestia stood. "Yes, please."

But the goddess didn't so much as glance at Hestia. Her question had a deeper meaning. And judging by the way she stared straight into my soul; it was only meant for me.

The townspeople—Dragonborns and humans—were more welcoming than I thought they'd be. Even though they were surprised to see us, they still managed to smile and exchange pleasantries. It probably helped that Anahita was our guide. It was clear they all loved her. And Anahita loved them back. She shook their hands, asked them how their day went, and engaged in quick banter with the children. They treated her as if she were one of their own. Her status as a powerful Dragongoddess didn't have any influence on their demeanor toward her.

We passed an apothecary, a bakery, and a school. Children played outside, laughing and skipping around. Some adults carried fresh goods while others stood outside their homes chatting about their daily business. Daily business probably meant the new town gossip. And they were all mixed. Dragonborns and humans were talking and living equally together.

It was refreshing to see.

"It seems that you are truly one of the people," Hestia said warmly after Anahita greeted a group of children.

"I try to be," Anahita replied. "Over there is the church. It's dedicated mainly to Nimerah and Ragnar, but the rest of us have altars in our name."

"Do you find it weird that people pray to you in there?" Fin asked. It's not a question I would have thought to ask, but I found myself wanting to know the answer.

The goddess looked over her shoulder, her blue hair framing her face. "Very much. I've told them that praying to my father and aunt would suffice. Those that do pray to me, I think they do it out of habit." Anahita turned on her heels, and her eyes glowed when she locked onto my face. I stopped, and we just stared at each other. The air around us stilled, and for a moment, I thought she was going to launch a tidal wave or something at my face.

"Mr. Westbow, I need to speak with you privately." The way she glanced at Hestia didn't go unnoticed.

Fin raised an eyebrow, but I couldn't say anything, so I

just shrugged.

"Your highness," Fin said, offering his hand to Hestia. "Let's go see about that food we need." They walked off toward a merchant's cart filled with fresh meat and vegetables. Hestia glanced back over her shoulder. Anahita's expression remained neutral. "Come. We need privacy."

I followed the Dragongoddess closely, matching her speed as she weaved in and out of a few alleys. Every few minutes, she'd stop, see if anyone followed us, and then start walking in a different direction. How anyone could keep up with us was beyond me. We turned around so many corners that even I lost track of where we were. The only person who I guarantee could have kept up was Fin. I wouldn't be surprised if he'd somehow ditched Hestia and was shadowing us. Then again, Hestia might have been able to foresee where we were going. The precaution wasn't necessary in my mind.

Anahita finally stopped in front of a large wooden door. It was marked with ancient runes and symbols that were beyond my knowledge. But I recognized the area we were in. We'd passed through a few times prior, but I'd never noticed the door until now. Either we had to wait for it to show itself, or Anahita detected the presence of someone earlier. Hopefully, I'd get answers soon. Going around and around was giving me a headache.

Anahita placed her palm on a sigil at the center of the door. The sigil lit up, and the blue light pulsed a few times before the door opened. The Dragongoddess pushed it lightly, and it swung open. She stepped into a dark hallway, but I paused before following. Something was unusual about the entire situation. Sensing my struggle, my magic flared to life, ready and willing to release itself at any moment. Heat radiated from my palms and the cackling sound of sparks shot from my fingertips.

"You will not be harmed, Mr. Westbow," Anahita assured me.

"Then what's with all the secrecy? We passed by that door several times before it appeared."

"I am very particular about who is allowed to know of this place."

Fin was probably already aware.

"Your friend is no threat. It's Amram that concerns me."

"Amram? We've never even seen him."

"Amram has a way of turning up when you least expect him. Tread carefully."

I bit my tongue. I wasn't going to argue with her because I'd heard that the gods were skeptical creatures that didn't trust anyone. But then again, she trusted me. What did that mean?

The hallway opened into a small room. Numerous candles of varying sizes illuminated the space, casting an array of shadows on the walls. The eastern and western walls were adorned with two large tapestries: one dedicated to Nimerah and the other to Ragnar. Below each tapestry was a small bench sitting alongside one wall.

At the center of the room was a circular rug with a knee-high altar. Two blue velvet pillows were placed in front of it.

Sitting on the altar was a sapphire glass basin. It reminded me of the ones used for Partitions. But instead of it being empty with a dagger beside it, it was filled with water. When I leaned over and peered into the basin, my reflection greeted me. Then the water started to bubble until it was completely boiling. I withdrew hastily.

"What did I do?" I asked.

Anahita knelt in front of the altar. "Nothing. The water connects with your mind and shows you the past. It's called a Memorisar Dravir."

"Fancy."

She chuckled. "Nah. It just means Memory Basin in the old tongue."

We both laughed together for a minute before composing ourselves.

"What about Well of Memories? What would that be?"

"Vylar ol Memorisar."

"Yeah, I don't think that's any better."

Her voice lowered to an almost trance-like whisper, "When you stare into it, the water will connect to your mind telepathically and show you the memories you have long forgotten."

Ever since Elio was revealed to me as the true Dragonheir of Vukan, I'd questioned everything about my life. My uncertainties haunted my dreams, turning them into nightmares. Each nightmare was the same: a black void of nothingness. They represented my identity. A void of nothingness. Who was I? Would my memories tell me?

I fell to my knees, desperate for the water to tell me something valuable. Something that would give me meaning.

"Lean over as you did before and stay there. In the water, your suppressed memories will surface."

"Lean over. Stay put." My voice shook with every word. Was I…nervous? Yes. Yes, I was.

I lifted and leaned over the bowl. Just like before, the water started to bubble and then boil. At first, the hot steam shocked my skin, but the boiling stopped, and the heat cooled. The image that glimmered in the water morphed from my face to two people in a palace throne room. One person sat on an obsidian throne in the shape of a Dragon while the other person stood before it. When the image became still, the features of the person standing became clear.

It was me. I was the person that stood before the man on the obsidian throne. At least, it looked like it was me. I strained my eyes so that I could, hopefully, see the face clearer. It had to be. Anahita said that I would see my memories. Memories that were locked away.

I blinked my eyes. When they opened, I was no longer sitting next to Anahita, leaning over the water basin. I was looking out of the eyes of my memory self.

"You wished to see me, Father," I said. The words were automatic. I had no control of them.

"Vasuman, my son. You have made me proud in every way imaginable. You've fought bravely throughout this entire war. You even defeated Hadeon the Destroyer. But you are not finished. I hate to say that I have been keeping this final task from you. I tried to fight it. But it was prophesied by my father...and...well, we can't ignore a Chaos Dragongod, can we?"

"Of course, not, Father. I am ready and willing to do whatever it is that you ask of me."

"I knew you would. That is why you're my favorite son."

I laughed. It sounded different than usual. It was warm and airy. "I am your only son, Father."

A thunderous laugh followed, and a large grin spread across his face. "That you are." His voice lowered. "And that you will always be." The pride in the man's voice was evident.

The air stilled, and the room grew eerily silent. "What is it that you need me to do?"

The man shifted uncomfortably on the throne. "It has been prophesied that you will end this war. You will strike the final blow to kill Amram. It is up to you, my Dragon Slayer."

I nodded, understanding the dangerous path before me. But I wasn't scared. No, I was confident. I knew I'd be successful. I was going to kill the Dragongod Amram and end the war. "It shall be done," I said with utter certainty.

"Good. Nimerah will be pleased. She's taken refuge in a cavern on the Kaimana Sea, just east of a port town called Medora. I am heading there today. If you need me, go to the Medora docks, fly east until you see a small island. I will be there."

I nodded again.

The man stood from the throne and approached me, the bottom of his scarlet red robe swaying with each step. When he stopped, the light from the crystals suddenly hit his face, and I instantly knew him. Memories flooded through my mind of our life together. Memories that included him holding me in a too-tight embrace after I'd made my first kill. Memories of him angry with me after I accidentally burned a tree down. Memories of him congratulating me after my first shift. The memories harbored feelings of joy, sadness, and love.

My father stood before me and offered his hand. I took it, and he pulled me to my feet. Then a woman entered the room. She strolled past me and kissed my father's cheek.

"My love," my father said. His eyes sparkled with admiration.

"My love," she responded, her voice soft and tender.

She turned, and I gazed into the eyes of my parents. Vukan, the Dragongod of Fire, and Hestia, the Queen of the Kingdom of Fire.

CHAPTER TWENTY-FOUR
EMERA

Two emotions were at war within me. The first was disgust because Valda being gone meant that I was alone with Anwir. The second was elation. If Valda was gone, that meant I didn't have her watching my every move. Granted, Gawen was probably tasked with spying on me, but I was more powerful than him. Plus, I had Risna. I trusted her. I was going to get the blade and get the hell out of the Realm of the Dragondead.

Just after nightfall, once I heard Anwir snoring in his room, I escaped to the library. Gawen and Bud occupied rooms in a different part of Ragnar's palace, so unless something catastrophic happened, they wouldn't be near the library.

The candle I held, shined brightly in the hallway into the library. With the snap of my fingers, light filled the space, illuminating the shelves of books as well as the mess from my encounter with Elio. The mess was my doing, so it made sense for me to clean it. I scoured the library for a broom, a mop, or anything that would help me clean up the mess. Thankfully, I located a small alcove that had a broom. I half expected it to turn to dust because of how it looked. Clearly, no one had used it in years.

I didn't have a clue what to look for, so I meandered between the shelves, skimming the titles of the dusty books. Where in the gods' names would I find anything about the Dragon Slayer? Did anyone else know his identity? I knew it was a risk even looking since Amram could enter my mind at will, but with Valda gone, I had a window to escape.

"Please guide me, Nimerah. Please keep my mind safe from Amram for just a short period of time." Begging my mother wasn't beneath me. I needed all the help I could get.

A name in gold script caught my attention. It was a name that Dragonpriest Benigno mentioned during my studies. Orson Rafferty. A Dragonborn that descended from both

Anahita and Dhara. If my memory served me well, the priest gushed over the historian's expertise in The War of Three, particularly the downfall of Amram and his army. Apparently, the historian made significant contributions to the understanding of what exactly happened to Amram.

The book was nestled between Orson's Anthology of War Tactics and How to Live Free of Magic by Poppy Tree-Leaf. What an odd choice of placement. I shrugged and pulled it hastily.

"Please, please, please, have the answers I'm looking for."

My fingers flipped through the pages of the heavy manuscript, and I scanned the text for any mention of a Dragon Slayer. I was about to give up hope, but I glimpsed the words about two-thirds of the way through.

I looked to my left and then to my right, reassuring myself that no one else was in the present. Satisfied that I was alone, I read the words by the great historian. "Vasuman, the Dragon Slayer, and his blade, Vultarokar Eshvarin, which means unrelenting force, were responsible for the deaths of Hadeon the Destroyer and Gawen the Archer. Both Dragons held high positions in Amram's army and led the massacre at Pyrrhus in the Kingdom of Fire. The city, now reduced to nothing more than rubble and ash, was the location of the climax of the War. In the following days, Vasuman slayed the Destroyer and the Archer. Following their deaths, Dragongod Vukan, Vasuman's father, led a small legion of troops to the Blayr Plains in the Kingdom of Light. It was there, on the hilltop of Latona that Vasuman slayed Amram, the Dragongod."

So, the Slayer's true name was Vasuman. To be honest, it was a weird name. But Vultaroka Eshvarin? That sounded amazing. And it meant unrelenting force? Even better.

What really stood out to me was the third to last sentence. I reread it over and over. Vukan, the Dragongod of Fire, was Vasuman's father.

Suddenly, a door shut, and footsteps echoed from the staircase. I held the book tightly to my chest and backed away until my back was pressed into a bookcase. I had to get out. If Anwir found me, it would be bad. If Valda found me, it would be worse.

Thoughts raced through my head as the footsteps grew louder. Whoever was in the library was getting closer. At any moment, they could turn the corner, and I'd be exposed. I searched my surroundings, hoping to find something to conceal myself. My eyes shifted until it landed on my salvation: the staircase.

I crouched down. Going one soft step at a time, I

managed to turn a corner and walk down the next aisle of books undetected. The staircase was several feet in front of me. My foot bumped into the corner of a bookcase, and a small yelp burst from my mouth. The book dropped from my hand when I opened it to cover my mouth.

The footsteps suddenly stopped, and I scolded myself internally. But whoever walked through the library wasn't close to me yet because no one appeared in front of me.

Focus, Em, I thought to myself. *Seriously. Make Fin proud.*

I walked quickly but quietly until I finally reached the staircase. I slowly ascended the steps, keeping low so as not to draw attention. Miraculously, the stairs were quiet enough for me to make it to the second level of the library. Once I reached it, I dashed behind a large reading chair. I peeked out from behind it, hoping to catch the identity of the stranger. Gawen was crouching at the spot where I'd dropped the book. Gods! Why hadn't I grabbed it?

He thumbed through the pages, searching for any clue as to what I'd been reading. He slammed it shut, tucked it beneath his arm, and all but ran out the way he'd come in— an exit I hadn't yet discovered. I breathed a sigh of relief, knowing that he hadn't seen me.

The blazing flames in the fireplace of my room greeted

me once I exited the secret door. They whipped and crackled, casting glows on the opposite wall. My room didn't have a window, but the air still swept through the palace like a forest breeze. I wrapped myself tighter, and I contemplated sinking back into bed, but my stomach wasn't having it. It growled again.

"All right, all right. I'm up," I told it.

I slid my feet into the slippers by my bed and threw a robe around me. The door opened with a slight creak, so I left it slightly ajar and poked my head out. Sure enough, Anwir's snores echoed through the hallway. That was one less person to worry about. I pushed the door closed, and crept through the hallway, trying not to make any noise. The door leading into the sanctuary was closed tight, so there was no way of seeing if Gawen sat on the throne. It wasn't that I thought Gawen would be upset that I was out of my room. Yes, I was a prisoner, but I wasn't that kind of prisoner.

My stomach demanded attention, forcing me to decide how I wanted to proceed. Shapeshifting was out of the question. I'd have to open the door first and then change. I hesitated to teleport because I'd been to the kitchen only once. If I missed, who knows where I'd end up.

A door opened behind me. I listened intently for the sound of snoring, but there was only silence. Anwir was awake. I sent a quick prayer to Tamasvi and tiptoed through the sanctuary and through another door. A short hallway led to a staircase that led downward. I descended, hoping to find the kitchen. When I reached the bottom of the staircase, I faced an empty hallway. At the end of the hall was a metal door. It took some effort because it was extremely heavy, but I was able to open it.

I stepped into air that was cool and damp; a lower temperature than the sanctuary. Wherever I was, it smelled musty. I guessed that not too many people traveled down here. Numerous torches were spaced out on the walls, illuminating the outlines of straight metal bars. I was in a dungeon. I crept to the floor and out of the light as much as possible. A hidden library and now a hidden dungeon? What other secrets did this palace hold?

I crept past the cells, taking my time to peer inside each one before moving forward. I ignored the moan from my stomach. Food would have to wait. I would be a fool not to investigate. What if I found another hidden passageway to more ancient texts?

My stomach moaned again. No. That wasn't my stomach. Someone else was down in the dungeon with me. Was Amram down here? I'd yet to see him in person. Was this where he escaped to? If it was him, maybe I could finally figure out what his plan was exactly.

Another guttural moan filled the air, having come from the last cell. A small voice inside my head begged me to turn back. Whoever it was could be a powerful Dragon that Amram kept hidden for a surprise attack. But the other voice urged me to move forward. Maybe it was someone Amram needed out of the way? Someone who could help? Besides, the moan was thick and gravelly. Whoever it was, they sounded wounded. If I helped them, maybe they'd help me.

My feet treaded so lightly, that I almost floated past each cell. When I came to the last one on the left, I stopped, waited, and listened. From what I could see, it was a man slumped forward in the darkest part of the cell with his back facing me. He was emaciated and feeble, an indication that he had been tortured. His back straightened suddenly, and the prisoner glanced over his shoulder.

"Who's there?" His voice was gruff. It reminded me of Calian's voice in a way. "I may be a weakened version of myself, but I know when someone is lurking about. Make your presence known." Interesting that he was a prisoner, yet his voice demanded attention. He may not be now, but at one point, this man was powerful.

He stood and shuffled forward, deeper into the cell. Each step was slow and unsteady. When he turned, I strained my eyes to see his gaunt face. He looked utterly exhausted, yet there was a sudden spark of resilience in him. He rushed forward, startling me. His large hands gripped the bars, revealing the shackles he wore around his wrists. Our eyes met. "I will not ask again," he threatened and banged his shackles against the bars. But what could he do? Those shackles were around his wrists for a reason. My guess was they were used to prevent the use of magic.

"I think the better question is who are you?" I asked, trying to keep my voice from shaking. I took a step forward. "And what have you done to deserve such a fate?"

He lowered his arm, and his eyes glowed a vivid shade of crimson. "I am Vukan, the Dragongod of Fire and son of the Chaos Dragongod Ragnar." Despite living a destitute life in the cell of his father's palace, there was strength in his voice.

I cautiously stepped forward, taking in the severity of Vukan's situation. He stood on his feet; his frail, skeletal body on full display. Sunken cheeks exposed the stark outlines of his cheekbones, and his eyes were dark hollow sockets. What were probably once vibrant red scales were now faded, almost pink. His paper-thin skin clung to his bones, revealing protruding ribs, and his arms were like sticks. Even his hair was affected by his punishment. It was long, tangled, and greasy. Bruises and scars were everywhere. Just like what I experienced with Risna, deep down I knew this was Vukan.

"My name is Emera Edevane. I am the daughter of the Dragongoddess Nimerah."

The rough expression of the god's face vanished, replaced by one of hope. The glow of his eyes retreated, and his eyes remained a subdued red. He hung his head and wept. When he looked up, thick tears stained his shrunken cheeks. "I knew you would come," he choked out.

"How long have you been down here?" I asked, my voice barely a whisper. I knew I wasn't going to like the answer.

"Shortly after the war, General Valda, whom I thought had been killed, sent two Dragons to infiltrate the palace. To this day, I am ashamed because we had let our guard down. I was wounded during the attack, and Vasuman was killed. I watched in agony as the light faded from his eyes. At that moment, I gave up. I had no will to live. A green Dragon shackled me and brought me down here to spend the rest of my days which, as a god, are plentiful. Valda took over the palace and tortured me in a failed attempt to get me to give up Vasuman's name. I told her the Dragon Slayer died. She didn't believe me, but there was no way I'd give that up to her. After Amram was resurrected, he began siphoning my magic to make himself stronger."

"Mine as well."

He looked at me curiously.

"Magic no longer runs in my Dragonblood. He's taken it all."

"That is not good." He paused, and let his head fall back, letting the silence cleanse his soul. "But it can be returned, and he can be stopped."

"Let me get you out."

"You cannot."

"And why is that?"

"The bars are warded against magic, just like these shackles."

"I've got an idea. It's silly, but it's worked everywhere else." I rubbed my hands together before grabbing hold of the bars. I closed my eyes and repeated the familiar words. "Vylar, mir'draconar." I repeated the words over and over.

The magic within the bars surrendered, and the door to the cell opened. That seemed too easy, but I wasn't about to question it.

"There. You are free."

Vukan lifted his hands and jiggled the shackles. "Not just yet."

I grabbed the shackles and repeated the phrase. The

shackles broke free. They hit the floor with a resounding clank. It was the sound of Vukan's freedom.

Vukan stepped back and breathed deeply. Red smoke formed around his body, and for a split second I panicked. Was he going to shift into a Dragon? Surely, not.

The smoke cleared and Vukan stepped out, and boy, he looked different. He was no longer weak and frail. The angle of his facial features and dazzling crimson scales reminded me of Calian. Aside from his hair, Vukan was just a slightly older version of my Dragonmate. It was a little unnerving.

He threw open his hands and flames bust to life. They grew higher and higher until the god laughed, clearly satisfied with the return of his magic. His laughter quieted down, and he threw his arms around me. The god lifted me into the sky and twirled me around. When my feet hit the ground, I stumbled back into the wall.

"Oh! I'm so sorry. I got carried away."

"No!" I laughed. "Get as carried away as you need!"

The smile he gave me was warm and joyous. We both exited the cell and took off toward the entrance to the dungeon. "I think in order to figure out how to defeat Amram, we'll need to ask my mother."

"Is she still alive?" He took a step out, and we were back in the hallway.

"Yes," I answered. I followed quickly on his heels. "I don't know exactly where, but I think she's somewhere in the Kaimana Sea. But I need Vasuman's blade. I can't leave without it."

"Only the blood of the Dragon Slayer can release the blade from the statue."

"And his blood is your blood."

"Precisely." He motioned for me to stop. We were at the bottom of the stairs. He peered up them.

"The statue will be guarded."

"Then we fight first. We get the blade and fly out of here."

"Just one other problem: I don't know who the current Dragon Slayer is.

"What do you mean?"

"If Vasuman died so long ago, then he can't be who the prophecy is talking about."

"Let's focus on getting out of here first. One problem at a time."

Clapping, slow and steady, echoed throughout the hallway we'd just entered. When we rounded the next corner, we stood at the bottom of a stone staircase. At the top of it, applauding at us, was Anwir.

"Thank you, Emera," he drawled. "Now I have what I

need. I know Nimerah's location, and I know how to prevent Amram from dying. Valda will be pleased. I see a reward in my future."

"Lucky you," I snarled.

"Yes. Lucky me. Now, if you'll excuse me, there is a Dragongoddess with a soul that needs reaping. But first, the blade." He turned around and vanished.

We looked at each other, both confused about the situation. Anwir was just going to let us live? We bounded up the stone steps when Gawen appeared at the top of the stairs, his bow up and an arrow ready to be launched.

"I've got him," Vukan said confidently.

Three things happened simultaneously: Gawen released his arrow, I jumped out of Vukan's path, and Vukan released a current of blazing fire at Gawen. When the fire stopped, three more things happened simultaneously: Vukan shouted at me, Gawen smiled in triumph, and I dropped to my knees with an arrow protruding from my chest.

Vukan almost flew up the stairs. He threw a scorching fireball at Gawen, but the ball hit the wall where Gawen once stood. The archer was gone. Instead of following Gawen like he should have, Vukan knelt beside me.

I took a deep breath and pulled out the arrow during my exhale.

"It hurts," I croaked.

Vukan took the arrow from me and inspected it. "The arrow is laced with poison." The god dragged me onto his lap. I looked up into his fiery red eyes, his face etched with worry.

The beating of my heart intensified. "Poison?" I squeaked.

"This isn't just any poison. It's Khaosar Drakoyul. Chaos Poison. It can only be crafted by a Chaos Dragon. You won't die from it. It poisons your Dragonblood and, eventually, you will become a human. And you'll stay human."

Panic took control. My breathing quickened, and beads of sweat formed on the scales of my temples. The beads trickled past my cheekbones to my jaw. "Is there any cure?"

"Powerful healing magic. From a Dragon or Dragonheir."

Senna. I needed Senna. And Anwir had killed her. What looked like a randomized attack, was actually a well-calculated strike. Senna wasn't here to heal me, so I was going to become a human. Tears streamed down my cheeks, mixing with the sweat that formed along my jawline. The tears weren't for my demise. They were for Calian. Gods, I wished he was with me.

"Nimerah."

"Huh?"

"Nimerah is the only Dragon alive with the power to heal you. We must find her."

I winced from the pain in my chest. The poison moved at an agonizingly slow speed. I was meant to suffer.

Vukan scooped me up in his arms and ran. He finally reached the sanctuary only to find Anwir tugging on the hilt of the obsidian blade. He turned around, and his eyes narrowed.

"I will deal with you first. Then I'll get the blade and her. She belongs to me," Anwir said. I wondered where Valda was. Gawen had retreated, leaving just Anwir.

Vukan laid me down on the floor, delicately cradling my head and resting it carefully on the floor. "She belongs to no one."

Anwir's laughter followed, but Vukan wasn't having it. He spread his arms out wide and called to his fire magic. Anwir's eyes widened, and he gulped loudly. Vukan smirked and finished his threat. "You'll feel the wrath of a Dragongod. Choose your next move wisely." The fire in his hands grew taller and louder.

Anwir glanced from Vukan to me and back to Vukan. He was at war with himself. Should he stay and fight to claim what he thought was his? Or should he try to escape and save himself. Unsurprisingly, he chose the latter. He bolted for the door. Vukan just watched him run out, and to be honest, I was happy with his choice. Anwir would meet his fate…at Calian's hands.

Vukan rushed to an altar at the far end of the room. Sitting atop it was an ornate obsidian blade. In one swift movement, he sliced his skin and clenched his hand, holding captive the blood that gushed from his palm. He opened his fist over the foot of the statue, and the blood dripped onto the smooth obsidian stone. He backed away as the blade began to pulse a bright violet. It pulsed several times before it disconnected from the Dragon Slayer's grip. Vukan caught it before it fell to the floor.

"Let's get out of here," Vukan said and rushed to my side.

"Wait. Just one more thing."

Vukan sighed. "What's that?"

"I really think you should put on a shirt."

CHAPTER TWENTY-FIVE
CALIAN

Against my better judgment, we stayed in Khaosar for the night. I hadn't gotten much sleep the previous nights, and despite being a Dragongod or demi-Dragongod, I needed it. Sleeping on a bed sounded much better than sleeping on the cold ground. Anahita set us up with three rooms at Khaosar's inn. She had no trouble securing us our own rooms since the town didn't have visitors. I welcomed the privacy.

The break of dawn brought with it an array of smells and noises. Baked bread and freshly squeezed juice awaited us when Fin and I strolled downstairs. We also found a sack of bread, meat, and cheese for our journey to Medora along with a note from Anahita. She would not be seeing us off due to a prior engagement. I wasn't bothered. She was a busy goddess.

But what bothered me was the lack of Hestia's presence. I wanted to speak with her. I needed to speak with her. But she had retired to her room early. I wondered if she knew that I knew.

Fin and I finished our breakfast and returned to Hestia's room. After a few rapid taps of my knuckles against the door, we waited…and waited…and waited.

"Hestia. We need to leave. Come down and eat."

Fin leaned against the wall. "Maybe she's meditating."

"I don't care if she's dancing for Nimerah herself, she needs to get out here." I knocked on the door three more times. We waited…and waited…and waited. Still no answer.

"Maybe she's a heavy sleeper."

I glared at Fin who pressed his lips together and pretended to lock them shut. He'd have them open in ten seconds. "I'm going in."

"Well, that seems inappropriate," Hestia commented casually from behind, causing Fin and me to jump.

I held my hand up to keep Fin from commenting.

"Where were you?" If she didn't watch it, I was going to

explode. My entire world was turned upside down yesterday. Who cared if she was a queen? She was my mother, and she never told me. It was as good as lying. I leaned in, towering over her small stature. "I'm also in charge in case you've forgotten."

Fin whistled loudly, "Watch your tone, man. She's a queen."

Hestia's eyes widened. She knew that I knew.

I huffed loudly, walked past Fin, and descended the stairs. We needed to leave.

The morning was bleak and gray. It wasn't a good sign. We mounted the horses, bid farewell to the hospitable townspeople, and took off toward Medora. Dhruv and I took the lead with Shadow and Fin taking the rear. Zari and Hestia kept an easy pace between us. If the horses stayed strong, we'd reach it by the following morning. I had no plans of stopping to sleep if we could help it. Fin would survive, but I didn't know about Hestia.

Tread carefully.

The words Anahita—my aunt— said echoed in my mind. Amram had a way of turning up unexpectedly, so I needed all the help I could get in case that happened.

"Hestia," I called over my shoulder.

"Yes, my son."

I stopped Dhruv. The silence was suffocating me. I twisted in my seat. Fin looked confused, but Hestia looked unbothered. "Have you seen anything? Any…*visions*…or whatever you call them?"

"No. I need to know the plan in order to see a potential outcome."

"You know we ride to Medora to find Nimerah. Is that not enough?"

"No."

"We ride to Medora to find Nimerah. When we get there, we will rest the horses at the Edevane Apothecary."

"I'll see what I can do."

*   *   *

At nightfall, we reached the camp.

"It seems smaller than I remember," Fin whispered.

He was right. In retrospect, we hadn't been gone that long, but it still seemed like forever ago, and in a much simpler time. A time when there weren't Dragons flying around rampant.

As we walked through the ruins of the camp, the somber atmosphere weighed heavily on our emotions. I felt it. Fin felt it.

I buried my feelings and pushed through, stepping cautiously over fallen debris where the soldiers' tents had stood. We passed the blackened pit where the kitchen campfire once blazed with life. There were echoes of stories and songs being shared everywhere. It's also where Emera had unknowingly taken Stormshade. That night changed me. I'd never been so afraid for someone else. The memory ate away at my chest. I missed her.

Charred remains of our tent lay scattered on the ground. Wooden beams jutted from the earth, reminiscent of a graveyard. Memories flooded back, bringing to the surface a plethora of names and faces. One name in particular caused me to pause and gain composure. Rehema.

I moved in silence through the scorched wood and tattered fabric of her tent. It was a reminder of our failed attempt at keeping her alive. A faded banner with Nimerah's Dragonhead, tattered and torn, fluttered in the breeze. The sight of it just added to the weight of what transpired here.

Hestia remained silent as Fin and I continued our journey through the camp. We took the path toward the tree and where our friend slept for eternity. The torches that once lined the path were scattered on the ground. The candles that marked her resting spot were burnt out. Wildflowers had pushed their way up through the earth. Through my tears, a smile spread across my face. The wildflowers brought with them a sense of peace and a reminder that Rehema dedicated her life to a beautiful world. I'd do my best to ensure that the world she envisioned flourished.

The crack of a twig drew my attention. Hestia knelt at the mound of dirt that had gradually lowered to the ground. She put her palms together and prayed silently. I didn't know how to express my gratitude at that moment. We hadn't been able to give Rehema a proper Dragonpriestess burial. But in that moment, with Hestia praying over Rehema's eternal resting place, everything felt right.

My heart warmed at the sight of my mother, so I placed my hand on her shoulder. She ended her prayer, stood slowly, looked me deep in the eyes. A knowingness settled between us. Deep down, I knew that she hadn't meant to lie to me. She had a reason for keeping her identity a secret, and I would hear that reason when the time was right. She backed away and headed back toward the horses. I lingered a moment longer, wishing Emera could have witnessed the moment. She'd carried the blame for Rehema's death. Hopefully, Hestia's gesture would bring Emera comfort.

When I caught back up to Fin, he was already atop Shadow. Hestia sat on Zari. When our eyes met, I just nodded, and she nodded back. Then I mounted Dhruv, and we continued our journey to Medora.

CHAPTER TWENTY-SIX
EMERA

The night sky, complete with a blanket of stars, greeted us when we exited the palace. Vukan was now dressed appropriately in refined clothes fit for a god. His black pants were tucked into knee-high black riding boots. His red coat with a high collar was decorated with swirling appliqués that mimicked the tangling of flames. The black vest underneath was adorned with shining red buttons and red appliqués that matched the ones on the coat. He carried me out the doors, through the courtyard, and down the steps. He hurried across the bridge but stopped when a large figure sitting beneath the pale moonlight blocked his path. It was Risna.

"Risna, we need to get to Medora. Will you fly us there?"

She lowered her head to the ground, indicating she understood. Vukan climbed up, trying his best not to wobble. I cried out in pain when she lifted from the ground, flapped her magnificent wings, and flew into the sky.

The poison was doing its job quickly and efficiently. My body ached, and my breathing was labored. Knowing I would live, I did my best to ignore it. A clear image of father's face emerged in my mind. He was smiling, his teeth white as pearls. I would hold onto that image as we flew. I would hold onto it as we sailed over the Obsidian Mountains and down to Medora. Down to my home.

"You will want to land outside of the city," I told Risna. "I need to do something else before we go to Nimerah."

"There's a clearing just west of the town. Land there." It was the same clearing where I last saw my father. I kept his image alive in my head. I needed to hold onto him to keep the pain at bay.

"We cannot land there. We must get to Nimerah. Not only is your magic gone, but soon your Dragonblood will be human blood."

I forced myself to speak between my heavy breathing. "I will not have magic to help you should we encounter Amram on the island. However, I am skilled with a bow. My own bow is still strapped to my horse, but I can get one from home. We just need to stop quick enough to grab it."

Vukan nodded silently. "It's not a terrible idea. But we need to make it fast and hope that Nimerah has enough strength left to defend herself in case Amram or Valda gets to her first."

The wind caressed my face as we soared through the dazzling night sky. The moon offered to guide us through the wispy clouds. Vukan held me tightly in a cocoon of his body heat. That coupled with Risna's body swaying through the air, caused my eyelids to droop. They struggled against the weight of exhaustion and from the poison that ravaged my insides. I didn't know if sleep would drag me to Death's door, so I compelled myself to stay awake. I focused on Calian's face. His wavy hair curled slightly over his forehead. His dark eyes and how they sparkled when he smiled.

I'd lost track of time. One minute we soared over the border of the kingdom, and the next, Risna descended to the landscape below. Once Risna landed, which was smooth for a Dragon, Vukan slid off. I tried to keep my face neutral, but I winced when his feet hit the ground. I wished Calian was with me.

"Where to?" he asked.

"Head for the docks. My family's apothecary is just a little way north of them. There are more direct routes, but I'd have to guide you there. I don't think I have the energy." I couldn't help but groan from the poison that almost electrified my body. I tried to reach deep within my well of magic, but I couldn't grab hold of any, so I had no way of numbing the pain. But I bet my parents did.

Risna agreed to keep an eye on the skies for any sight of Amram or his Dragons. Amram didn't know exactly where my Dragonmother was, so that along with it being dark out, helped.

The lullaby from the rolling waves and the smell of saltwater drifting in on the cool sea breeze eased my heart. I was still in pain, but the tension in my shoulders eased a little. It was good to be home even if it was due to these circumstances.

Vukan located the docks in no time since he'd been to them before, but getting him to the apothecary could be tricky. I'd told him to go north of the docks, but it wasn't straight north. There were a couple turns he'd need to take. My doubts vanished after hearing the words of a low voice from the shadows.

"Emera? Is that you?"

"Elio?" I breathed.

"Yeah. What are you doing here? I was just about to fly back. I've located Nimerah…"

Vukan cut him off. "I'm taking her to her family's apothecary. Do you know the way?"

If I said Elio was in shock, I would have been lying. He was completely immobilized by Vukan's presence – telling me he hadn't known of Vukan's imprisonment. And here he was, face to face with his ancestor.

"I…Uh…Yes, sir…I do."

"Then take me."

Elio took off hastily toward my family home. Vukan followed closely behind him, occasionally glancing around to ensure no one followed us.

When we stepped in front of the apothecary, I finally recalled that the town had been on fire when I left. My gaze lifted, and I glimpsed the top of the building. Most of it looked the same with the exception of the roof. Father had wasted no time in rebuilding it.

Vukan knocked on the door repeatedly until my father's voice boomed from behind the door.

"All right, all right. I'm coming." The door opened slowly. "In the middle of night, no less," he mumbled. He stepped outside holding a lit candle. His eyes widened and his mouth parted when he laid eyes on us.

"May we enter?" Vukan asked.

My father nodded and held the door open for us.

"Where can I set her down?"

"Follow me."

Vukan bolted up the stairs, taking two at a time, and rounded the corner, heading to my old room. When we neared it, my mother stood in its doorway. Had she been sleeping in there?

"What's going…" She stopped speaking and gasped. She covered her mouth with her hand.

Vukan rushed past her and laid me down on my old bed. It was still warm from my mother's body. So, she was sleeping in here. Was she and my father all right? I so desperately wanted to ask, but the poison continued to drain me. Stupid poison.

"Emera was wounded with a poisoned arrow. The poison won't kill her, but she cannot use magic to heal herself. The only being that can save her magic is Nimerah. She insisted that we take her to you before we fly over the Kaimana Sea."

My father was at my side and placed his palm to my head. "What can we do to help?"

"My magic is all but gone. If Amram is there when we arrive, I will need to find another way to fight."

My father stood and backed toward the door, shaking his finger. "Ah. I know what you need." He left the room, and my mother immediately took his place. She took my hand and held it. Nobody said a word while we waited.

Father was back in just a few minutes, but he didn't have my bow. The bow he carried was constructed of Waterion Ironwood. Waterion Ironwood was the strongest wood known throughout the Kingdom of Water. Its unique design was amplified by swirls carved into the blue-stained wood. There was no way I was taking it.

"Absolutely not."

My father placed the bow on the blanket that covered my legs. "Yes, you will."

I worked my way to a sitting position, ignoring the pain from the poison. I "If…anything… happened to it…" I stammered.

Elio propped himself up in the doorway. "It sounds like you need it." He was right. I was defenseless without it.

I held the bow in my hands, admiring the feel of the smooth wood in my skin. I never imagined I'd use it.

"Thank you," I whispered. I swung my legs over the side of the bed and stood. Before I could take a step, pain shot up through my legs, and I lost my balance. Mother grabbed ahold of me and guided me down on the bed. "No, no, no.

You need to rest." She grabbed my hand and squeezed it. I didn't dare shake her off. She'd scold me for it.

"We need to leave." I looked to Vukan, my eyes pleading for back-up. But it was Elio who spoke first.

"I'll shift and fly out over the waters. I can keep an eye out for Amram. Since I know Nimerah's location, I can wait there. If I see anything at all, I'll head back immediately."

I didn't have the energy to argue. A yawn pushed through my lips, and my eyelids fluttered. Sleep tempted me, singing its lullaby.

"Sounds like a yes to me," Elio said. He bowed and retreated out of the room before I could thank him.

CHAPTER TWENTY-SEVEN
CALIAN

Medora was a glorious sight to see. We'd traveled through the night and were ready for a break. It would be a quick break, though, and I knew just the place.

Even though riding through a town on horseback was frowned upon, I just didn't care. Emera's family's apothecary wasn't close to the stables, so leaving the horses there wasn't an option. I needed Dhruv close.

It was still early enough that the apothecary was closed for business. But I figured being in love with the owner's daughter gave me special privileges. Or, at least I hoped it did. I knocked on the door a few times, but there was no answer. I heard the shuffling of feet and murmuring of hushed voices behind the door, so her parents were awake. I knocked a few more times, but there was still no answer.

"Maybe you should knock louder?" Fin suggested. "Use your whole fist."

"I don't need to. I can hear movement from inside."

Hestia yawned. "They probably aren't used to people interrupting their sleep."

"No. I don't think that's it." I raised my fist to knock again but stopped when the door opened slightly, exposing a sliver of light. A man revealed himself in the open space, but it wasn't Emera's father. It was mine.

My breath caught in my throat. "You're…"

"And you're…" The Dragongod of Fire stepped out from the door with his hands outstretched. I remained still as he gently cupped my face in his hands. Tears leaked from his eyes, and he pulled me into a tight embrace. His arms were wrapped around me so tight, my chest hurt. "I thought you were dead."

"I am not."

Vukan, my father, finally released me and backed up a few steps. He wiped his face, but the tears kept rolling.

"Hestia?" He threw his arms around my mother, kissed her, and then pushed her back. He gazed into her watered eyes. Tears fell down both of their cheeks. "How?"

"Valda did not kill our son, my love. Instead, she tortured him to give up his own name as the Dragon Slayer. He was at the brink of death when my spies located him. He was being held captive beneath Ragnar's palace." She dropped her head. "I am so sorry. I would have gotten you out, but I was told by my informant that you were dead."

"Do not concern yourself with what happened to me. I am just elated to see that you and Vasuman are still alive."

My parents—an unusual thought—looked at me fondly. I caught a glimpse of Fin from the corner of my eye. This must have been a confusing sight for him.

He leaned over and whispered to me, his eyes locked on Vukan and Hestia. "I'm missing valuable information. Care to share?"

Vukan wrapped his arm around Hestia's shoulder. "Vasuman—"

"Calian," Hestia corrected him.

The Dragongod's brows furrowed.

"My name is Calian. The Vasuman you knew doesn't exist. I've only just discovered my identity."

Vukan contemplated his next words. Then he waved us toward the apothecary. "Please, come inside. There is much to discuss."

The inside of the apothecary was warm and inviting. There was no question in my mind as to why Emera loved it so much. Everything about it, from the view of the herbs on the counter, to the smell of the spices on the shelves, was comforting. A fire still blazed in the fireplace, keeping the place bright and warm while the sun took its time rising from the east.

My heart raced, and my mind fought to find the right words to say. How did I tell Vukan, the Dragongod of Fire and my father, that I didn't remember who I used to be? I wasn't the Vasuman he once knew. I was Calian Westbow now. Would he be disappointed in me? Would he dismiss me? Knots formed in my stomach.

Vukan held his smile in place. "As much as I would love to catch up and explain, we don't have the luxury of time. Follow me."

A frown tugged at my lips while we followed Vukan up a set of stairs. He stopped in front of a door that stood slightly ajar. Before I'd entered the apothecary, something felt off. And now, the same unsettling feeling was back. I pushed open the door and took a heavy step forward.

The room was occupied by a man and a woman. The woman didn't look familiar, but the man...I knew him. He was Emera's father. He leaned against the wall, looking out a window and searching the skies. A woman, whom I assumed was her mother, sat on a bed.

"Queen Hestia," they said simultaneously after we entered the room. Both of them dropped to their knees.

"Please. Do not kneel on my account. We are here on such irregular circumstances."

"Regardless, I am Cordelia Edevane, and this is my husband, Struan."

With Emera's mother kneeling on the floor, I got a glimpse of what was on the bed. Emera. My heart stopped, and my lungs expelled any air I had swirling inside my chest. Was she? No. She couldn't. I rushed forward and fell to my knees at her side. Her eyes opened, and the rush of air returned to my lungs. "You're alive."

She turned her head, and our eyes met. "I'm alive."

"But you are not well?"

"I am better. I was resting." She sat up, closed her eyes, and took a heavy breath.

Vukan appeared at my side. "An arrow with Khaosar Drakoyul—chaos poison—was shot into her chest. Its purpose is not to kill her but to take her magic from her permanently. We stopped briefly to get a bow, but then the pain worsened, so we stayed a bit longer to let her rest."

"I'm feeling so much better. Truly."

"Take your magic?" I asked, heat blazing beneath my skin.

"Nimerah is the only one who can heal that kind of poison." Hestia said. Her eyes clouded over.

"What's going on?" Emera whispered.

"A vision," I whispered back.

Hestia's eyes cleared. Her usual cool demeanor was replaced with concern. "It's imperative that you leave at once. If you don't…" her voice trailed on his last words.

"She'll be human," I mumbled. Anger flared in my chest.

Emera lifted her palm and rested it against my cheek. "Please, don't make it sound like being a human is a bad thing. I'm still me."

"My reaction has nothing to do with you being a human and everything to do with that godsdamn maniac who stole your magic." I looked up into her beautiful violet eyes. "I'll love you whatever you are."

"Love?" she asked somewhat sheepishly.

Without hesitation I said, "Love."

Fin appeared at the foot of Emera's bed. "Can't you heal her? You healed her when she took Stormshade and when she flew into a mountain."

"Fin," Emera groaned.

"You did what?" Hestia asked.

"I wasn't used to my Dragon form and flew into a mountain," Emera muttered.

Fin chuckled, Struan went wide-eyed, and Cordelia gasped.

"I was talking to Calian," Hestia said. My cheeks warmed from embarrassment upon hearing her say my name.

"I didn't heal her completely. I'm pretty sure she siphoned some of my magic and helped heal herself." I looked at Vukan. "Don't you have healing magic, too?"

"No."

"Then how do I?"

"Me," Hestia said matter-of-factly.

"How? You know what? We can discuss family matters later because that's not important right now. Emera is." I stretched out my hands over Emera's chest and channeled my magic. A faint glow pulsed from my hands and grew brighter and brighter with each of my nervous heartbeats. It grew until it covered Emera's whole body, pouring energy into her weakened soul. The glowing slowly dissipated.

"Did it work?" I asked. The room went still; the only sound was my beating heart.

"I can still feel the poison inside me, but it's not as painful. I certainly feel relief in my joints." She threw her arms around my neck and rested her head on my shoulder. I breathed in her calming scent. She released me, which I didn't like. I could have stayed in her arms for eternity.

"We need a plan on how to get all of us to the island," she said. She took hold of the bow and got off the bed. Her father crossed to her and handed her a quiver of arrows. "But can we please first get out of this room. There are so many people in here that I can barely breathe."

Vukan and Struan both chuckled. We all followed Emera out of the room and down the stairs into the main area of the apothecary.

"I can shift and take you there. There is another Dragon—an ally—hidden in the trees just outside Medora. She will help. We will find Nimerah and cure this poison," Vukan replied. He sat on a stool at the shop's counter.

"And get the magic back that you've lost," I growled.

Hestia cocked her head to the side. "You've lost all your magic? How?"

Emera looked into my mother's face from the chair she'd taken by the fireplace. Mother. The term of endearment repeated over and over in my mind. Surprisingly, I felt comfortable thinking it. It felt…right.

"Amram keeps invading my thoughts. Apparently, he's been siphoning my magic."

My mother scoffed. "Well, that we can fix."

"We can?"

Mother winked. "May I?" she bent over beside Emera and raised her hands to Emera's head. Closing her eyes, she started to speak softly, "Ol shadarthor skarn, yulnol vyth. Ol trakanar'kyn mir'el, naak ol craskar pryth. Vel magikar weylunzor Drakonar'set, Klornar tolun'kyn mir'ol vyth ol sholar'kyn naak."

"Huh?" Fin barked.

"In the shadows of thoughts, where secrets lie; In the realm of the mind, let no trespasser pry. By magical weave and Dragon decree, lock this mind from the eyes that seek to see," my mother translated. A bright light emanated from her hands. They glowed until finally, she closed her fists. "It is done."

"Just like that?" Emera asked.

Mother smiled. "Just like that."

"You must be a powerful Dragonborn," Cordelia said.

The smile on my mother's face reached her eyes. "Not exactly."

"Well, thank you. That's one problem down," Emera said. "Now for the next: the blade."

"What blade?"

My father stood and walked behind the counter. He reached beneath it and pulled out an obsidian blade. My heart flipped at the realization that referring to Vukan as my father felt right. Just like calling Hestia my mother. The void of my past had been partially filled. I started to feel somewhat whole again.

"You're smiling," Emera whispered.

I cleared my throat and admired the obsidian blade. My obsidian blade. "Vultarokar Eshvarin," my father said proudly. "Or, as you referred to it years and years ago, Vultesh."

"Because it was easier to say," I replied. Wait. How had I remembered that so easily? Hopefully, I would come to recall many more memories of my past, including when I used the blade. My father handed it over, and it was heavier than I expected. It took some strength to hold it steady. Backing away a few steps from everyone, I rotated it left and then right. It was just as immaculate as it had been when it was new. A sense of determination and purpose washed through me. Although I'd fought with Vultesh before, I felt like I was holding it for the first time. Vultesh wasn't just a weapon, it was a…friend. Did that even make sense?

"It's you. You're the Dragon Slayer," Emera said.

"I am. And when we're done. I'm going to kill Amram all over again."

Emera's smile grew, brightening her face. "There he is.

My General…My mate."

I snorted. "I don't think this is the time to make jokes, Em."

She stood from her chair and took my other hand. "I'm not joking. We are mates, Calian Westbow."

I almost dropped the blade. "Come again?"

She laughed, and it was music to my ears. It was probably music to all our ears. "I wish you could see your face right now." She kissed me hard on the mouth and jolt of electric energy shot down my spine. After a minute, I pulled back and saw that she was smiling. It was the most gorgeous smile I'd ever seen.

"So…You're not joking?"

"Not at all," she murmured.

I pressed my lips to hers.

"Do you want us to leave? Because we can," Fin teased.

Emera pulled back; her face serious. "But you're not going to like why I don't have wings to match yours."

"Why?"

"Valda used her power to bind me to Anwir."

Cordelia gasped, Struan cursed, and I saw red. Blazing red. "I will kill them all."

Emera nodded slowly. "I have no doubt. But in order to kill Amram, the magic of the blade must be reactivated."

"How do we do that?"

"It needs chaos magic."

I ran my hands through my hair in frustration. "The magic you don't have."

"Correct."

"Anything else?" There was probably something else.

"That's pretty much it," Emera said.

Fin leaned against the wall and crossed his arms. "So, we get to the island. Wake Nimerah. Get your magic back. Magicify the blade."

Struan's brow raised. "Magicify?"

"Sounded like a legitimate word."

"It's not," I mumbled.

Fin shrugged. "We'll let Zari take…" he said and addressed my father, "Wait. I don't even know who you are."

My father straightened his jacket and straightened his back. "Vukan. Dragongod of Fire." Cordelia and Struan both fell to their knees to honor the god that stood in their home. Fin on the other hand just stood there, blinking. No words. Just blinking. I snapped my fingers in front of his face, and he shook his head. "And you're Calian's father?"

"Yes," I answered.

Fin turned to my mother. "And you're his mother?"

Hestia smiled. "Yes."

Fin turned to me. "How old are you?"

I wasn't sure what to say because I didn't know. "Old, I guess."

Emera tapped both of her parents on the shoulders and motioned for them to stand. "We are all equal in this house."

"We are mere humans. We cannot call ourselves equal," Cordelia said.

"Fine. As the highest ranking Dragongoddess here, I say we are."

Father and Mother didn't argue.

Emera sighed. "As much as I'd love to hear about this family reunion, we need to focus." She started for the door.

But before she got there, it opened, and someone I hadn't expected entered the shop. "I'd like to help," said Elio, the lying snake of a man.

"Absolutely not," I snarled. I moved swiftly to the door between Emera and Elio, grabbed Elio by the neck, and raised him in the air. "How very bold of you to just show up here."

Elio tried to respond, but my grip was cutting off his air.

Emera placed her hand on my arm. "Elio has been helping me."

I held Elio in the air and squeezed his neck tighter. "He's

been playing you."

"No, he hasn't." She gently pushed down on my arm. Right. She was the focus. Find Nimerah and save my mate. Elio wasn't worth it.

I released Elio from my grasp, and he dropped to the wooden floor. If he'd hurt his knees upon impact, no one would have been able to tell. He didn't make a sound. Instead, he massaged his throat where I'd left a mark.

I dragged my hand through my hair, taking a minute to keep a lock on my emotions. A quick tapping came from the door. Everyone in the room tensed, and an electric charge of magic buzzed around us. I raised my finger to my lips, motioning for them to stay quiet. My father and I exchanged looks and nodded. He crossed to the door and turned the handle. Slowly, but surely, the door inched open.

"And who might you be?" he asked the stranger.

"My name is Kedron Black, sir."

I pushed myself in between my father and the door. Kedron stood on the opposite side. I pulled the door open and relief flooded through my veins. "I sure am glad to see you!" We needed all the help we could get at this point.

Fin bounded over to me. "Keddie!" he cried out.

"I'm glad to see you, too?" Kedron's statement sounded more like a question.

When Fin realized Kedron wasn't alone, he visibly stopped breathing. Morwen rushed into his arms.

"More of your friends, I take it," said my father.

"This is Kedron Black, Dragonheir of Tamasvi. And this is Princess Morwen Elderbrook, Dragonheir of Anahita. They're more than friends. They're family."

CHAPTER TWENTY-EIGHT
EMERA

Kedron teleported me to Risna after I said my good-byes to my parents. I may or may not have also hugged them to almost the brink of death before Kedron pulled me away.

Risna stepped out from the woods and into the clearing. She angled her head one way and then another, trying to figure out what was going on. After a few minutes, Dhruv and Zari arrived carrying Calian, Vukan, and Hestia. Fin and Morwen were not with them.

He dismounted Dhruv faster than I'd ever seen and was immediately by my side.

"Father will fly us to the island. The other three will ride on…Whoever the other Dragon is."

"Risna." I elevated on my toes and kissed Calian on the cheek. "I love that you called him Father. And Queen Hestia is your mother? You're finally getting the answers you needed."

A black and red hawk dove out of the sky and glided right past Calian's ear.

"What the…" Calian spat.

The hawk landed on Dhruv, cocked its head to the side, and started to make the weirdest noise. Like a high-pitched shriek. Was it…? Yes…it was laughing.

"Elio?" I asked.

The hawk stopped screeching and nodded. Never in my life did I think I'd see a bird nod at me. I stifled a giggle and looked Calian. He was fuming.

"Why don't you go on ahead and scout for us?"

Elio nodded again and took off. I shook my head in disbelief.

"I am staying behind," Kedron said, appearing at my side. "Should Amram arrive in Medora, I'll teleport to you."

I shook my head. "No. That is too dangerous."

"I'll be the judge of that." The corners of his mouth turned slightly upward.

Red smoke rose around us, grabbing our attention. When

it dissipated, a monstrous scarlet Dragon stood in its place. Vukan towered over all of us, including Risna. Being Vukan's son, I wondered if Calian had a Dragon form as well? As curious as I was, it wasn't the time to ask. Nor did I want Calian to concern himself with anything else.

Shadow finally arrived, galloping up beside Vukan with Fin and Morwen atop him. Fin and Morwen dismounted and crossed toward us. Morwen's buttoned up blue coat and her dark brown knee-high leather boots over black skin-tight pants made me jealous. I glanced down at the dark trousers and blue tunic. I didn't have my own pants in the apothecary, so my mother had helped me dress in my father's clothes. I also didn't have a metal breastplate like Morwen did. It was fastened over her jacket to protect her from blades and other weapons.

I have my bow, I reminded myself. *It's all I need.*

Vukan lowered his wing and Calian climbed on. His father raised his wing backward slightly so that Calian could get onto his back. Vukan did the same for Queen Hestia and me.

"That's Risna," I yelled to Morwen. "She's an ally." Morwen would be able to communicate with Risna telepathically. I could tell that they spoke from the way Risna's eyes lit up. She gladly lowered herself so that

Morwen and Fin could ride her.

We flew over the Kaimana Sea. With the wind blowing in my face, I relaxed and let my mind drift into a make-believe world. Everything was as it should be. Dragonborns and humans were treated as equals, and the Dragongods ensured peace and tranquility amongst the kingdoms. Kings and queens still ruled, but they were fair and just. And it didn't matter if they were a Dragonborn or a human. The Dragoncouncil remained, but it was made of an equal number of Dragonborns and humans. There were two Dragonmasters: one human and one Dragonborn.

My thoughts blurred then solidified into a picturesque vision of Calian and me.

We held hands as we swung on a porch swing, watching our children play in the golden rays of a summer sun. The wedding ring on my finger, complete with a band of pure obsidian stone and a violet gem with swirling chaos trapped inside, fit perfectly. My summer dress exposed the pair of purple Dragonwings that matched his. We lived in the country, just outside the City of Anahita. The wildflowers were in bloom, their bright colors decorating the green grass that swayed in the summer breeze.

The vision faded, bringing me back to the real world. I angled my chin toward the sky and let the cool wind caress my face. I was free and relaxed up in the air, the pressure of saving the unnamed world blew off my shoulders with each forceful gust. I was safe in Calian's arms.

Vukan flew gracefully through the sky, keeping us from rocking back and forth. Elio's hawk form kept pace with us. Calian occasionally called upon his healing magic. It radiated off of his skin and into mine. Although I was ecstatic that Calian had healing magic to keep the poison from completely turning me human, I couldn't figure out why. Hestia had said it was because of her. Was she a descendant of Endrit? She was a sorceress, so she had Dragonblood, but no magic to accompany it.

In the distance, a small island with trees and white sand grabbed my attention. I searched the sky for any signs of Amram or Valda, but I saw nothing. Would we be lucky for once?

Vukan landed on a small deserted island. I hopped off his back and cautiously stepped forward a few paces. The atmosphere almost seemed to pulse with electric energy. There was powerful magic here. Ancient and powerful. The atmosphere was vastly different from the mainland.

"Vukan and Risna will remain on the beach in case we need a quick getaway," Morwen said. It was a terrible idea. Vukan was a powerful god. It made more sense for him to find Nimerah with us. Just in case we ran into trouble.

"You don't like the idea," Calian murmured. "I can tell because you get this look on your face."

"What look?"

"This look." He dramatically scrunched his brows and narrowed his eyes. His lips pressed together in a fine line. The look was atrocious.

"I don't look like that." Did I look like that? I hoped I didn't look like that.

He laughed. "Yes, you do."

Morwen joined in on Calian's laughter. "Vukan doesn't have any clothes," she said. "So, he'd be naked. Not appropriate when meeting Nimerah."

"Makes sense."

Calian held out his hand. "Ladies first."

I elbowed him in the ribs. "I do not look like that." I left Calian and joined Morwen on the path. My mate bid his father good-bye and followed after us. The further we walked, the more the island seemed to grow. It became a labyrinth of foliage, expanding around us. The scent of sea salt lessened, replaced by the potent aroma of the exotic flowers. Honestly, I almost gagged. And that was saying something since I grew up in an apothecary.

Despite my overwhelmed sense of smell, the island was

beautiful. Vibrant birds soared overhead and perched in the trees, watching our every move. Moss-covered stones, tall trees, and plants with leaves the size of a Lightenion Wolf blocked our passage, so Fin took out a dagger and did his best to chop them down. Calian's blade would have done a better job, but it remained strapped to his back.

Fin continued to hack away at the plants, but the island didn't like it. The wind shifted and the ground trembled beneath our feet.

I whipped my head from side to side, scanning the area.

"The island is angry," Morwen said. "Fin, you must stop."

Fin scoffed. "What's the island going to do?"

The largest snake I'd ever laid eyes on dropped suddenly from a tree. It coiled around Fin's body and tightened, suffocating our friend. Fin clawed at it, but the snake's body was so thick, nothing happened. Morwen rushed to Fin. She placed her hand on the serpent and closed her eyes. In just a few seconds, the snake loosened and slithered down Fin's body, retreating into the bushes. Fin choked as he tried to catch his breath.

"The island is Nimerah's protector. The snake mentioned a trespasser came through earlier."

"Amram?" Calian asked, his senses now on high alert.

Morwen shook her head. "A woman."

Valda.

Calian took off running, and I followed as fast I could. He stopped when we finally arrived at the mouth of a cave. The energy I'd felt when we landed was even more intense once we stepped inside. We ventured in until there was no light, and I cursed under my breath. If I had my magic, I could light the way.

Calian strode ahead and whipped his wrists. Fire blazed from his palms. The flickering flames cast shadows on the cavern walls from the rock formations that protruded from the floor and ceiling. Moisture dripped into pools at our feet, echoing throughout the eerie chamber. We wound our way through passages, and at times, had to crouch low or squeeze through narrow tunnels. Despite not feeling any pain, my legs were still weak. Once we were finally greeted by a violet glow, I sighed from relief. I was tired, but I refused to rest.

Calian extinguished his flames but remained silent. He cocked his head to the side and studied the chamber we'd just entered. It was illuminated by six torches that were spaced equally apart on the walls. At its center was a small wooden table with a vial containing a glowing, bubbling black liquid. Calian turned to Fin. He lifted a finger in the air and moved it in a circular motion. Fin nodded, unsheathed a dagger at his thigh, and backed into the darkness. Calian,

Morwen, and I waited silently while Fin crept around the room, checking for any hidden enemy in the dark corners.

"All clear," Fin called from across the room.

Calian huffed a quick breath. "Careful. You never know what type of trap has been set." Traps were inevitable. If Nimerah knew she would be sleeping for hundreds of years, she'd need protection.

Fin grabbed the handle of the wooden door and tugged. No luck. The door didn't budge. He inspected the door frame while Morwen and I decided to check out the vial on the table. Calian joined Fin at the door.

The vial sat alone on the table with nothing else surrounding it. "Is a list of instructions too much to ask for?" I mumbled.

Morwen picked up the vial and turned it over in her hand, inspecting the glass that imprisoned the liquid. After a minute, the bubbling increased into a boil. "Ouch!" She cried out and hastily put the vial back on the table.

I immediately picked up the glass vial. Probably not the smartest thing to do since Morwen's fingers were just burned, but I was too curious. The tiny bottle was cool to the touch when I picked it up, but just as it did with Morwen, it warmed my hand quickly to a burning temperature. I placed it back on the table without hesitating. This would have been a great time to have my healing magic. But I didn't, so I resorted to the only option I had to cool my fingers. I stuck them in my mouth. Classy, I know. But they burned!

"Are you ladies okay?" Calian asked over his shoulder.

Morwen's brows furrowed together. "It's cool to the touch at first. But the longer you hold it, the warmer it gets until it's scalding hot."

"So, we have a vial of some kind of hot magical liquid and a locked door."

"And no key." Calian pounded his fist on the door.

Fin piped up. "Wait a minute. Isn't this the old Dragonlanguage?"

We all looked to where Fin pointed. Sure enough, atop the door were words written in the ancient Dragontongue. I left Morwen still standing at the table and headed toward the door.

"What does it say?" Calian asked.

I scrunched my face in frustration. Where was Erjon when you needed him?

"Something about a black potion? Um…It hides the secret to unlock this door? Do we pour it on the door?"

Fin grabbed the handle of the door but immediately brought back his hand, yelling out a colorful curse.

"Hot?" I asked.

"Mmm-hmm. Little bit. It wasn't before, though." He held out his hand to Cal who healed the bright red skin of Fin's hand.

"That's odd." Calian then attempted to open the door, but the same thing happened. There was no way I was going to try. The handle turned scalding hot like the vial.

Fin walked back over to the table, lowered himself, and peered into the vial, examining its contents. "What if we are supposed to drink it? That sounds fun, right? Drinking a scalding hot, glowing black liquid?"

"I'm sorry," I said after searching my memory for the information needed to translate the other words. "I don't know what the rest says. I wasn't able to learn all the words of the language."

Calian marched to the table and picked up the vial. "Only one way to find out. I'll drink it. I'm the son of the Dragongod of Fire. Surely, it being hot won't affect me too much. Plus, I have healing magic."

"Conceited much?" Fin quipped. His joke was answered by a foul gesture from Calian.

"No. I'll do it." I tried to snatch the bottle from Calian's hands. He raised his arm above my head. I swiped at it a few more times, but it was no use. He was too tall. I placed my hands on my hips. He needed to know I was serious. "You're the most powerful of us all. If you take it, and it renders you useless—no offense—then we're in big trouble should Valda find us. I have no magic, so it wouldn't do anything."

"That burning liquid could do some damage," Morwen said. "I'll take it. I can use my water magic to extinguish the heat."

"What about me?" Fin asked. We all turned to look at him. He'd pulled back the collar of his shirt to reveal the amulet hanging around his neck. "If this thing really does stifle all Dragonmagic from hurting me, then I won't feel a thing, right?"

Calian shook his head. "But if you need the magic within it open the door, you couldn't. The amulet would stifle that as well. If anyone should take it, it should be me. I also have the healing magic, remember." He lowered his arm, and I took the opportunity to grab the vial. I swiped my arm, but in doing so, stumbled over a rock. I hit the vial from Calian's grasp, and it went flying. The little glass bottle fell on the table's surface and rolled off. Fin, whose sudden closeness startled me, dove and caught the bottle before it crashed on the floor. He climbed to his knees and then stood.

"C'mon, Cal. You have to be more careful." He took in our gaping faces. "What?"

"It doesn't burn," Morwen stated.

Only then did Fin remember he still held the bottle in his enclosed fist. When he opened his palm, I gasped. The liquid was no longer bubbling. It was still.

In the quickest motion I'd ever seen from him, Cal grabbed the vial out of Fin's hand, uncorked it, and drained the black liquid in one gulp.

"Cal!" Fin yelled angrily.

I rushed to my mate's side. "You idiot! What were you thinking?"

Calian wrapped his arms around his waist and doubled over. He groaned loudly and fell to his knees. A scream ripped through my throat, and my knees buckled. I dropped beside him and wrapped him in my arms. Calian suddenly stopped groaning. A second passed. Then another. And another. The silence was deafening. *Please be okay. Please be okay.*

"Cal?" I asked, my voice unsteady.

Cal lifted his head up and smiled. I pushed him off of me, and he rolled a few feet. "Calian Westbow, you are the worst!" I stomped off toward the door at the back of the room.

"Can't I joke? Fin jokes around all the time?" Calian argued from the ground.

I whipped around and faced him. "No! You can't." The

tears were coming, but I refused to let them fall. I was mad as Dragonhell at his stupid joke. "What if the liquid was poison? Why would you risk that? After finding out that we're mates!" Okay, so I may have overreacted.

Fin leaned on the table. "If you tell her your former last name, I'm sure she'll forgive you."

Calian's eyes became lethal. Fin had my curiosity. I shifted my gaze from Calian to Fin. "Former name? Do tell." Morwen nodded furiously in agreement.

Calian pressed his lips together and shook his head. He wasn't going to spill. But Fin would. I looked at him, widening my eyes in a pleading fashion.

"Poots," he whispered with a toothy grin.

My anger dissolved, and I cackled. "Cal…Calian…Poots," I managed to get out between laughs. I laughed so much that I started to wheeze. Morwen giggled beside me which caused Fin to start chuckling.

"It was my name on the streets. I don't remember how I got it." Was it just me? Or was his voice a little high-pitched?

"I have my suspicions," Fin howled.

"All right. All right. Give it a good laugh."

We did give it a good laugh. And my gods, it felt good to laugh again with friends. With family. Calian rolled his eyes and headed toward the door. He grabbed hold of the handle and pulled it open. So, Fin was right. Someone had to drink the liquid in order to open the door. The three of us took deep breaths to gather our composure before following Calian through the open door.

CHAPTER TWENTY-NINE
EMERA

The chamber we entered was larger than the previous one. There were even more torches on the walls and some were atop wooden stakes, lining the path to the next door we needed to go through. There were two levels to this chamber: the level we stood on, and a level that looked like a long balcony that stretched from one side of the chamber to the other. Seriously, a banquet table would have fit up there. It made me wonder if the cave had been a palace at one point. Ragnar had his palace. Was this Nimerah's? I planned on asking her when we found her.

Again, Calian motioned for Fin to check out the room.

Fin moved stealthily around the chamber, making sure no one lurked in the shadows besides him. I turned my attention on the three rocks before me. Their shapes were odd, mimicking tombstones. A head of a Dragongod was carved into each stone. The left stone was Ilmari, the middle was Anahita, and the right was Vukan.

Their heads were also carved into three tablets that were embedded into the chamber wall of the second level. The level spread out above the wooden door that Calian now tried to open. Just like before, this door was also locked. There was no vial of black liquid, so we needed to figure out how to get through.

"Look," Morwen said and pointed above the door. There were more words in the ancient tongue.

I followed the path until I stood next to Calian. He was inspecting the hinges of the door while I inspected the words.

"Each stone stands with a Dragon's face. Intricately carved, they fortify this space. The door to the path beyond will not yield. Until the Dragons' matches are revealed," Morwen said. We all looked at her. "What? I did some light reading."

Fin kicked the stone with Vukan's face. "Another stupid task."

"The door opens when we match the faces," Morwen said.

"I'm assuming the stones on the floor must match the tablets on the walls up there."

Fin said, looking up. "So, how do we do that?"

"Arrows?" I suggested.

"Hmm. Arrows, you say." He whipped out an arrow and shot it at the middle tablet containing the head of Vukan. The tablet rotated, revealing Anahita's head."

Calian glanced at the tablet and back to the stone on the floor. "Shoot the one on the left until it matches Ilmari. Fin did as Calian suggested. "Now the right until it matches Vukan."

"Let me do it," I said before Fin could shoot again. "You've already shot three arrows." I took an arrow out of my quiver and readied it in my bow. With a quick breath, I unleashed the string and watched the arrow fly. My aim was true. The third tablet rotated to match Vukan's head.

"Look!" Morwen was pointing at the door that now glowed purple.

Calian ran to it, grabbed ahold of the handle, and opened the door. We followed him through, hoping we made it to Nimerah. But our hopes were squashed. We'd entered another chamber.

"Maybe this is the last task?" Morwen offered.

"I hope so," Calian spat. I didn't blame his aggravation. I was getting frustrated with the situation myself.

The third chamber didn't have any torches. Instead, the bottom of the cavern floor was replaced with large stone tiles. The Dragonheads of the three Chaos Dragons were etched into the stone. To get to the door, we'd have to walk on the tiles, and I wasn't the only one suspicious of them. Calian threw his arm out, signaling us to remain where we stood. He lifted his foot and took a step on the first tile. The tile broke and Calian fell forward. Thank the gods that Fin was close behind him. Fin reached out and grabbed Calian's arm just in time before Calian fell through the floor.

"Thanks," Calian huffed. He took a moment to catch his breath. "Obviously, we can't just stroll over there."

"Obviously," Fin repeated.

I peered over the hole in the floor. Nothing but darkness stared back up at me. There was no telling how far down one would fall. I stood back from the hole. "Do you remember which god was on the tile?"

"Amram, I think."

"So, we stay away from his head," Morwen said.

Fin studied the tiles. "Why don't you just shift into some kind of animal and fly us over there. Or throw us. I don't care."

"I can try," Calian said. He closed his eyes and scrunched up his face.

"Are you going to shift soon?" Fin pressed.

"I'm trying!"

Morwen placed her hand on Calian's shoulder. "Don't strain yourself. You won't be able to shift in here. I've tried to use my magic, but I can't. This place is warded."

"Great," Calian grumbled.

I lifted my foot and placed the toe of my boot on a tile with Nimerah's head. The tile glowed purple. More importantly, it didn't break. I took a deep breath. "Here goes nothing," I whispered. With one foot firmly on the stone, I brought my other foot down beside it, putting all my body weight on the tile.

Calian was immediately at my side. He leaned into my ear. "Don't do that again."

I couldn't help but smile. "Did I scare you?"

"Immensely."

"Prepare yourself then. Because it looks like I'm the line leader." To my left was a tile with Ragnar's head. I tapped the tile with my toe. But this time, the tile didn't light up. Instead, it started to crack, so I withdrew my foot before the tile fell through. The tile immediately to my right was Amram's head, and something told me that no tile with his head would stay firm. The one straight in front was Ragnar. I had to try, so again, I placed the toe of my boot on the tile. It didn't light up either. A large crack formed down its center. I heaved a sigh and gave the tile with Amram's head a try. The same thing happened. Another crack. I looked past the tile with Ragnar's head. It was Nimerah.

"Don't even think about it," Calian warned.

"We don't have another choice."

"We'll find another way."

I twisted around slowly to face him. "What other way is there?"

He looked around the chamber, searching for an answer.

"What's going on?" Morwen asked.

"The tiles in front of me won't hold us. I put the toe of my boot down, and they cracked. The only tiles that will work are the ones with Nimerah's head." I twisted back around and located the tile again. I took a couple of deep breaths to calm myself—or try to.

I expected Calian to object again, but this time it was Fin. "Absolutely not," he said.

I closed my eyes and sighed. "There's no other way."

Before anyone could argue again, I jumped. When I landed on Nimerah's tile, my body swayed. I waved my hands to keep from falling over. Thankfully, I regained my balance. The tile below my feet glowed.

"We have to stay on the tiles with Nimerah's head. I'll lead." I scanned the tiles ahead of me. There were a total of four left to get to the door. I mapped out their zig-zag pattern and leaped forward. Wasting no time, I jumped from one tile to the other. Each tile lit up when I landed, creating a beautiful violet path behind me. When my feet reached the natural floor of the cave, my knees gave out, and I stumbled into the door. My hand grazed the handle and it lit up like the tiles. I twisted the handle, and the door creaked open, revealing a dark passageway. The others quickly followed me. Calian stepped past me and called flames to his palms.

We followed close behind him for what felt like hours, but it was only a few minutes. Finally, the passageway opened up into a large chamber that was illuminated by glowing crystals of deep violet that hung from the ceiling. They were the same crystals that hung in Ragnar's sanctuary.

But the crystals weren't the most mesmerizing thing in the chamber. Lying in the center was Nimerah, the most beautiful Dragon I'd ever seen. Her scales were a deep shade of violet and glistened from the light that poured through a hole above her. It was the reflection of the scales in the light that emitted a violet glow around her. Her wings were folded around her, and her eyes remained closed. She was in an eternal slumber. The problem was, I didn't have any magic to connect to her mind. How could I wake her up?

"Mother?" I murmured as I walked carefully toward her. I caressed her snout, but Nimerah didn't stir. "Mother? I am here. We are here now." She still didn't stir.

I turned to Calian, my eyes wide with fear. I didn't need magic to know that something was wrong. "Something's not…right," I breathed. I rested my head against Nimerah. "I need you," I whispered.

"She can't answer you."

Valda stepped out from behind my mother. Dangling from one hand was a dead hawk. Elio. My heart fell. Anger swelled within me, and it was at that moment that I noticed the dagger in her other hand. It was the same dagger that had cut my hand, thus starting my activation and throwing me into a new life. And from that dagger, dripped blood.

"And why's that?" Morwen asked.

A cruel smile spread across Valda's face as she tossed Elio's hawk form on the ground. "Because she's dead."

CHAPTER THIRTY
CALIAN

In an instant, my soul left my body. The voices around me faded until only a slight ringing filled my ears. I shook my head because there was no way I heard Valda correctly. Nimerah was dead? We were too late? I looked at Emera. Her face said it all. Angry wasn't a strong enough word to describe her. If fire was within her soul, it would have exploded with such force, she'd have brought the whole cave in.

Morwen ran to Emera's side and wrapped her arm around Em's shoulder to steady her. The look of pure hatred on my Dragonmate's face shook me to my core and made me realize that if Nimerah was dead, then Emera would be human forever. That might not bother Emera, but it for sure as hell bothered me.

"I will kill you," I said. I called to my fire magic and threw a large ball of flames at Valda's head. She leaned her shoulder away, and the fire missed her. She laughed, and it was the creepiest laugh I'd ever heard. Her voice sent a shiver down my spine. She lifted her hands out and began the familiar incantation.

"Arthar, mir'gadar. Arthar et lenz."

I looked to Emera. She was just as confused.

"Arthar, mir'gadar. Arthar et lenz."

"What does gadar mean?"

Emera dropped her eyes, concentrating on remembering what the word translated to. Her eyes widened in terror. "Father," she whispered.

Nimerah's limbs began to quiver, and her features twisted and contorted. Her massive body decreased in size as purple smoke billowed around her. Through the thinly veiled smoke, a transformation began. Nimerah's deep purple scales smoothed out and became lighter. Her tail shortened until it disappeared. Light skin stretched out over human-like muscles. Every essence of her Dragon form vanished, and in its place was a man. A god. The smoke cleared completely, and Amram stood where Nimerah had been slayed.

"You've got to be kidding me," Fin groaned.

Amram waved his arm around him and clothes appeared over his body.

Fin reached behind him and in the blink of an eye, sent an arrow soaring toward the Dragongod. It plunged into Amram's chest. It was no use. The god chuckled and pulled the arrow out. The wound healed instantly.

"Should have gone for the neck. That's what my daughter did." He lowered the collar of his shirt and revealed a long scar.

"Right across the throat," Valda purred. "Your mother never saw it coming."

"You monster," Emera hissed. She shot an arrow of her own, but Valda was quick and teleported next to her father. Amram remained silent.

Valda laughed. "I had to make sure the job was done. She had to die so that my father could possess her body. It was a little cramped in mine."

I was confused. "Cramped?"

"Where do you think I've been all this time?" Amram asked. Valda tapped the side of her head.

Emera's shoulders tensed. "You were never here, were you?"

Amram smiled. "Only in your head, siphoning your

magic. Thank you, by the way. Without it, I wouldn't have had enough power to materialize. Now, my daughter can replenish her own and not feed it to me."

"I'd give all my power to you Father, you know that." Amram held out his hand, and Valda took it, planting a light kiss on his knuckles.

"So, you only succeeded in killing Nimerah because she was sleeping? You're a powerless coward," I hissed at Valda.

"I still have power," Valda roared. She glanced at Amram. He nodded once and then he was gone. He'd teleported away. The god had every faith in his General to finish the job of killing us off.

"And I'm going to use it to kill you. Once and for all."

"Hardly." Emera unleashed arrows at Valda. Valda teleported all over the chamber. Each time, her arrows barely missed. Fin joined in, but Valda kept moving. Emera stopped and waited. She looked at the spot Valda had started from and retraced her jumps. When she reappeared, Emera was ready. An arrow lodged right in between Valda's eyes. The light in her eyes began to fade, but not before she threw out the last of her chaos magic into Emera's chest. Valda slumped to the ground, and her body stilled.

Emera collapsed to the ground. Whatever little energy she

had was gone, and she had no scales. Emera was human. I rushed to her side and let my healing magic take over. I thanked the gods that Valda's chaos magic wasn't strong. She must have given most of it to her father to raise him from the dead. After a few more seconds of healing, Emera coughed, and color returned to her face.

"Thank the gods. I thought I'd lost you." She smiled meekly in response.

Fin cursed from behind me. I glanced at him over my shoulder, but our eyes didn't meet. He was focused on Valda's corpse. Valda's living corpse.

The goddess's arm extended upward, gripped the arrow that was wedged between her eyes, and pulled it out. Her healing magic glowed, and the wound closed. "You can only kill chaos with chaos, Vasuman," she taunted.

"You knew?"

Her attention was solely on me. "That's your real name, isn't it? Vasuman, the Dragon Slayer? You killed my father with your fancy blade. Did you know that it's not just chaos that's needed to activate your blade? Your Dragonmate has to gift their magic to reignite it. Only then can it kill me or my father." She started to drum her fingers against her chin, pretending to think. "But you don't have a Dragonmate, do you? Turns out Anwir was good for something." She raised her arms, and they started to glow purple. I could tell from her clenched jaw that she was using whatever chaos magic she had left to bring down the cave. The ground below us quaked, rocks from the ceiling fell, and fire erupted around us.

A shriek echoed throughout the chamber. A sharp rock form had fallen from the ceiling into Morwen's foot. Fin was instantly at her side.

"Don't take it out. Wait until I'm there to heal it."

Valda chuckled. "How chivalrous?" What she didn't know was that while she was focused on me, Emera had crept up behind her without making a sound. Emera let out a warrior's cry and tackled the goddess from behind. Valda flipped herself over right as Emera pounded her fists into Valda's nose. Blood spilled out, and she kept hitting Valda over and over, trying to buy me time to get to them. I ran forward, but Valda managed to throw Emera off of her and thrust out her arm, sending a gust of chaos magic into my stomach. If it wasn't for her weakened state and the shield of healing magic that I conjured over myself, I would have been dead. I flew backward but was still able to hurl my dagger toward Emera. But it wasn't enough. The dagger landed just beyond her reach.

Right beside Valda.

"Oh, how the tables have turned. And in a cave, no less!" Valda ignored the blood oozing from her nose and grabbed the blade. Emera stood just as Valda thrust the blade into her stomach. My mate rocked back and forth, but before she fell, Valda took ahold of her hair and pulled, exposing her neck. Emera clenched her teeth to keep from screaming.

Good, gods. No.

"You once took my father's life. Now, I'm taking your mate's. What's even sweeter is that I don't need a magical blade to do it." And with her final words, Valda slid the blade across Emera's throat.

"Emera!" Morwen screamed while Fin cursed loudly behind her. They'd managed to free Morwen's foot.

Valda winked at me and pushed Emera to the ground. She looked down upon her. "Looks like you won't get that chance to watch your loved ones burn." She shot a burst of chaos magic into the air and it struck the ceiling of the chamber. I took off running toward them, but my pace was slowed as the chunks of rock that fell around me. I finally reached Emera and lowered to my knees. I scooped her up and placed her in my lap, searching for Valda. She was gone.

"Emera, please hold on," I begged. I held my hands to her throat, and my healing magic flared to life. Blood stained my hands, but I didn't care. "Please, don't leave me. Please."

But Emera didn't respond. I was too late.

A deafening roar of unadulterated rage rippled through the air. It took me a few seconds to realize that it wasn't from the cave tumbling in. It was from me. With all my strength, I picked Emera up and ran to the others. I shot healing magic from my hands while Fin supported Morwen's weight off her foot. None of us looked behind us as we exited the cave before it fell in completely. I didn't even slow down to tell my father what happened. I leaped onto him, and he took off, flying as fast as lightning. I couldn't breathe. Because in my heart, I knew it didn't matter how fast he flew.

Kedron was in the clearing when my father landed.

"I will teleport her to the apothecary," he offered.

"No," I barked.

Kedron didn't say a word, and I didn't apologize. I didn't care. I walked past Dhruv and Zari. She reared back on her hindlegs and whinnied loudly. The horse knew. The townspeople must have heard the Dragons because they all stood outside of their homes, looking up into the sky with bewildered expressions on their faces. They looked curiously at me as I carried Emera's body to her childhood home.

When we got there, the door to the apothecary was already open thanks to Kedron. Morwen—teleported by

Kedron—stood by the fire, her face flushed from crying. Emera's mother let out a high-pitched scream as she laid eyes on her daughter. No amount of tranquil water magic from Morwen could have prepared Cordelia.

I ascended the stairs, my feet making heavy thuds as I carried Emera to her room and placed her on the bed. She was a stark contrast to the bright and lively girl I loved. The bleeding had stopped since I healed the cut, but the scar was a reminder of my failure. The color of her face was an ashen hue, and her violet eyes that once sparkled when she laughed, were dull and void of all light. Her red hair was sprawled across the pillow, all tangled and limp. Instead of the warrior goddess she'd grown to be, she was now frail and lifeless. Her death drained my soul.

My heart broke into a thousand jagged pieces that pierced my chest. I laid my head on her stomach and stared at the wall of her room. Shock was a simple way of describing how I felt.

"I'm so sorry, Cal," Fin whispered from the doorway. So, he had made it back. Dhruv was faster than I thought. Everything was faster than I thought. Love. Life. Death.

My mind was blank, and my body numb. I needed to get out. I needed air. I cupped Emera's cheek with my hand and then leaned over and kissed her lips. Then I lowered my head to her chest and closed my eyes. After a few more seconds, I opened them once more, catching a glimpse of purple. With a heavy heart, I brushed back her shirt and saw them. Violet wings. Wings that matched my own. The pain in my chest increased, so I broke away from her, stood up, and walked out of the room, holding my hand to the wings that decorated my skin.

"Cal…"

I raised my hand to silence Fin. He was probably going to ask what our next plan of attack was, but I didn't care. I didn't have a plan. I didn't want a plan. I didn't need a plan. I needed to get out of the room.

My footsteps hit each wooden step with a resounding thud. They were even louder than Emera's parents' cries of pain upstairs. When I reached the bottom, the door opened, and my father stepped into the apothecary. At the sight of him, I crumpled. He threw his arms around me and guided me to the floor. I rested my head on his shoulder and cried.

*   *   *

The moon hung unusually low, and a gentle breeze blew across the abandoned camp. Thirteen candles held by thirteen people bobbled in the darkness. I didn't carry a candle, but instead, carried the body of my mate. Emera's body was wrapped in purple silk, the color of her once vibrant eyes.

In a silent, somber line, we walked to the marked grave of our fallen friend. The only sounds that echoed throughout the stillness of the night were from the rustling of leaves in the breeze. Burying Emera next to the Rehema is what she would have wanted.

When we reached the spot, I stopped and stifled the sob that clogged my throat. Avani held out her hands, and the ground beneath my feet trembled. An opening formed, just big enough for the body of my mate. With a heart full of grief, I lowered Emera's body to the hole. Avani closed it, and Emera's body disappeared into the unnamed world.

I backed away, letting Cordelia and Struan Edevane cover Emera's resting place with Twilight Orchids. Between the sniffles and sobs, Cordelia also dusted the ground with Waterion Lily Powder which was said to ward off evil spirits. Emera's parents placed their hands on the ground for several minutes before standing. Cordelia started to back away, but Struan just stood there. After a few seconds of silence, he fell to his knees. "My honeybee," he cried. "This wasn't supposed to be your fate. You were to make the world a better place." His shoulders shook while he cried. "My honeybee," he stammered.

Cordelia bent over and took Struan's elbow. She guided him back to his fee, and he held his wife as they walked away from their daughter's grave.

One by one, everyone placed a flower from their kingdom over Emera. When Erjon walked up to Emera's grave, my grief momentarily gave way to shock. Erjon rarely showed his emotions, and when he did, it was typically out of annoyance. But this time, the façade was cracked. His eyes were red and puffy, and his chest rose up and down quickly with every ragged breath he took. He took his time kneeling and placing an Airian Rose on Emera's grave. The red of the rose reminded me of Emera's vibrant red hair that would no longer blow in the breeze. I stifled a sob. Erjon's gesture spoke volumes. He then lowered his head in silent prayer before getting back up to his feet and walking off for a moment of solitude.

When my mother kneeled, she didn't have a flower, but a prayer. As if she were singing a lullaby, she placed both of her hands on the grave and blessed the eternal resting spot. She stood, and everyone looked at me. It was my turn.

Once more, I lowered to my knees. I sat back on my heels and closed my eyes. Behind my closed eyelids, I pictured Emera's face. Her warm cheeks and soft lips. The way her violet eyes sparkled when she smiled. The breeze carried the bittersweet scent of her: wildflowers mixed with the earth.

The pain in my heart was so heavy, I doubled over. "Emera. You have left me in agony." I wiped my nose with the sleeve of my shirt as a hiccup burst from my throat. Then I cried. And I cried. Everyone else was silent. The only evidence that my companions were still with me was the flickering light from the candles.

With a sharp exhale, I straightened my back. "I will carry you with me on my wings." I slid my hand under my shirt and let it rest over the purple wings on my heart. I stood and backed away.

A hand rested on my shoulder, and I turned to see the cloudy eyes of my mother. After a few seconds, her eyes cleared. Sadness was replaced with hope. "You will see her again, my son. You will see your mate again."

ABOUT THE AUTHOR

From an early age, Sarah Edgerton had an active imagination, creating stories, make-believe worlds, and songs. Now, she's using that creativity to share stories with others.

Sarah currently lives in Kansas with her husband, Michael, and their two children, Dexter and Penelope. The family has a dog named Hugo and a cat named Ari. When not pursuing her writing career, Sarah teaches at her local middle school.

Sarah considers herself to be a geek. She loves Star Trek, The Mandalorian, and Marvel. If she's not reading or writing, she's watching movies and television shows, traveling, training for half marathons, or shopping.

For more information, including new book announcements, please go to www.sarahedgerton.com.

COMING SUMMER 2024

THE FINAL BOOK OF THE DRAGONHEIR TRILOGY

BY

SARAH EDGERTON